The screen illuminated the cabin of their homemade spacecraft with an eerie blue glow.

"Field on," he announced, flipping a knob on the console.

Slowly, silently, the ship lifted off the ground. The three boys looked at each other in amazement. . . . It was working! They gazed out the windows at the changing perspective as they rose over familiar backyards.

With a jolt, the ship halted—hanging thirty feet above a lawn.

A dog, wakened by the hum of the machine, jumped off his porch and started to whine in confusion. Suddenly the entire block was full of barking, howling dogs . . . running circles and jumping crazily at the ship.

Then the boys saw house lights blink on.

"People are coming out!" Darren cried. "Get us out of here!"

"I'M TRYING!" shouted Wolfgang, typing frantic instructions into the computer. Sweat began to bead on his forehead as he punched the final button.

Then, smoothly, the ship began to float across the neighborhood. . . .

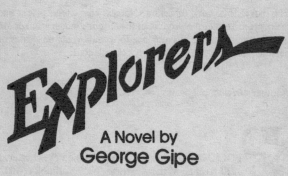

Explorers

A Novel by
George Gipe

Based on the Screenplay by
Eric Luke

PUBLISHED BY POCKET BOOKS NEW YORK

Another *Original* publication of POCKET BOOKS

POCKET BOOKS, a division of Simon & Schuster, Inc.
1230 Avenue of the Americas, New York, N.Y. 10020

ISBN: 9-671-60173-3

First Pocket Books printing July, 1985

10 9 8 7 6 5 4 3 2 1

Explorers

Chapter One

It began with a dream.

Fourteen-year old Ben Crandall's dream was part this world and part a world he had never seen before. As far as he could tell, it was uninhabited by living things, seeming to be a barren, sterile planet untouched even by microorganisms. Above the plain on which he stood rolled dark green clouds, whipped by a wind that felt curiously gentle against his cheeks. Clad in pajamas —an aspect that seemed neither strange nor embarrassing to him in his dream state—he looked toward the horizon and the jagged peaks rising from the featureless plain. Then he glanced downward at his bare feet. He appeared to be standing on a surface of large crystals, which yielded like sand as he moved his toes, causing a colorful rippling effect beneath him.

For a long moment, he simply stood in this strange environment, sniffing, watching, allowing his body to be manipulated by whatever was here. Curiously, he felt neither threatened nor awed by this world. If it contained a mystery, the solution would soon be revealed to him. All he had to do was be receptive, perhaps explore gently.

Suddenly he felt that he would be able to jump. Not hop a few inches into the air, but effortlessly rise to a height he had never attained in his earthly existence. He took a deep breath, but allowed the air to escape before doing anything. Fear had taken over his mind. Suppose, it said, you are able to jump so high that you kill yourself on the return trip?

He decided to chance it. Taking another deep breath, he leaned forward onto his toes and gently pushed himself upward. To his surprise, he rose about six feet into the air before floating slowly back to the crystalline surface. It was a decidedly pleasant sensation. With a little grunt of pleasure, he bent his legs deeply and pushed himself from the ground with all his might.

After the immediate shock of being hurled upwards some twenty or thirty feet, Ben relaxed and watched the ground recede beneath him. As it did so, the discolorations of the barren plain formed patterns, sharp angles and U-turns which resembled a gigantic drawing or schematic for a circuit board. The effect was dazzling, causing him to experience a sensation of lightheadedness.

Twisting his body in the air, he discovered he could hold himself suspended by kicking his feet like a swimmer, falling at a nearly imperceptible rate. Turned sideways in this manner, he studied the details of the colorful pattern, trying to discover its meaning or, failing that, to memorize it for future study. His body gradually lost its buoyancy during the long moment of intense concentration and soon he found himself swooping downward toward the surface at an uncomfortably rapid rate. He found that he could brake his speed, however, by throwing out his arms, and even change his direction by altering their positions. Fascinated, he watched as the schematic patterns blended together, becoming more and more diffuse as he neared the strange world's surface.

Closer and closer it came. He seemed to be gaining speed rather than losing it. No matter how much he flapped his arms or twisted his body, he continued falling, out of control now, a dead weight plunging toward the ground, the wind stinging his eyes, forcing his breath back into his throat.

A scream started to burst forth—and then, suddenly, he was awake.

He remained in a state of shock for less than five seconds. Then, reacting to his instincts, he blindly fumbled for a pencil and paper by his bedside, knocking over a glass of water in his haste. Forgetting the water and closing his eyes, he started to make notes even as he summoned the details of the dream back to his mind. For nearly a minute, the pencil flew across the page, writing a curious mixture of shorthand and numbers.

Then it stopped. Ben's eyes slowly opened, blinked, and closed again. His fingers pressed to his forehead, he frowned and gritted his teeth in an effort to extract more details of the dream which was now rapidly fading from his mind.

"That's it," he muttered finally. "The one section's still blank but it's better than nothing."

He looked at the page before him, changed a few symbols so that they were more legible, and leaned back against the pillow. Perhaps it would be possible to take up the dream where it had left off. It had happened before. He recalled that once, following an American history class, he had dreamed a plan of how to save Abraham Lincoln from being shot by John Wilkes Booth. He had awakened at least five times during the cliffhanger of a dream, each time taking up exactly where he had left off. He had saved the President, too, only to see him run over by a horsecart a few minutes afterward.

The dream dealing with the strange schematic pattern world did not return, however, no matter how hard he tried to force it into his mind.

"Darn," he said. "Now I'll probably never be able to get back to sleep."

He sat up, felt the drip of lukewarm water against his toe, and remembered the knocked-over glass. Setting it upright, he used a sweater hanging across the back of a chair to wipe up the mess.

War of the Worlds was on the television set next to Ben's bed. He had dropped off to sleep just after the American general had ordered an atom bomb dropped on the martian invaders. Now Ben watched disinterestedly as Gene Barry and the young woman huddled in the house, awaiting their doom. He had already memorized the movie and knew that soon the single eye of the martian would project itself into the room only to be destroyed and analyzed by the Americans. The first time he had seen the movie, Ben had actually hidden under the covers during the more frightening parts, but now he was totally blasé about the classic film.

Taking the paper on which he had scribbled the notes, he got up and turned on the lamp next to his bed. The dim illumination revealed that the walls were covered with a colorful assortment of science fiction posters; from the ceiling dangled a winged dinosaur and several flying dragon models; on Ben's desk was a large model of a robot.

Crossing the room, he stopped at a shelf and picked up a high-powered walkie-talkie. He flipped it on, turned the squelch button until the frequency was adjusted, pressed a homemade signal button, and then spoke into the mouthpiece with an authoritative voice.

"Hey, wake up," he said.

Wolfgang Muller's dream was less ethereal than that of his friend Ben, although Sigmund Freud might have had some fun analyzing it. In it, he was walking the familiar corridors of school when he suddenly noticed that his left shoe was missing. Stopping, he looked back down the hallway but could see no sign of the shoe. At about the same time, he discovered that his shirt was gone. Ducking behind a locker, he pondered his dilemma even as more items of clothing mysteriously disappeared from his body, leaving no clue as to their whereabouts.

"What's going on?" he muttered.

An inner urgency warned him that he had to continue moving down the hallway despite his situation. Bent over nearly double, he therefore resumed his walking, crab-style, past dozens of students who, strangely, seemed completely unaware of his rapidly approaching nakedness. Finally, near the end of the corridor, he possessed not a stitch of clothing. He ducked into the bathroom just as the bell rang.

Except that it was not the school bell. It was the buzzer of his walkie-talkie.

Wolfgang's eyes popped open. Thank God, he thought, when he realized he was safe in his own bed rather than stranded, stark naked, in the bathroom of Charles M. Jones Junior High. Small for his size, with delicate features, he lay in a tangle of sheets and blankets, his arms still forming a V down the front of his body as a holdover gesture from the dream. Realizing he was safe now, he exhaled loudly just as the walkie-talkie buzzed again.

"Hey," said Ben Crandall's familiar voice, "wake up."

Wolfgang found his glasses on the end table next to his bed and extricated himself slowly from the sheets and blankets. Putting his feet gently on the floor—prior experience had taught him that he was likely to step on a variety of sharp objects if he was not careful—he grabbed the walkie-talkie and replied.

"It's three o'clock," he said. "This better be good."

"It is," Ben continued. "At least I think so."

"Go ahead."

"I had this weird dream," Ben said.

"So did I."

"Really?" Ben asked, the thought crossing his mind that the dreams might be identical.

"Yeah," Wolfgang replied. "What was yours?"

Still clutching the piece of paper with strange markings on it, Ben stared at it as he spoke. "It was so real," he began. "I was flying in the air above the ground on this strange planet. Only the ground wasn't ground. It was a huge drawing, like a circuit board or something."

"Interesting," Wolfgang muttered.

"And I wasn't flying in a plane," Ben added. "I was doing it by myself, like the planet had next to zero gravity. I could jump hundreds of feet in the air."

Wolfgang scratched his neck, waiting for more. "Is that it?" he asked finally.

"Yeah, just about."

"I dreamed I was at school without any clothes on," Wolfgang said. "I was walking down the hallway when they just disappeared and I had to hide in the bathroom."

"Anyway," Ben continued, "I made a diagram of what the ground looked like, as much as I could remember, and I thought you'd take a look at it tomorrow."

"You mean, today."

"Yeah, that's right."

"Sure," Wolfgang yawned. "I can do that. Now can I go back to sleep?"

"My Mom's coming," Ben said hurriedly. "Over and out."

Wolfgang's walkie-talkie went silent. He looked at it a moment before switching it off, then sat on the edge of the bed and yawned again. His room, he admitted during this quiet moment, was, as his mother so often said, quite a mess. In every corner and available space was a clutter of old chemistry sets, gutted radios with their parts hanging out like disembowelled creatures, electronic games and dismantled home computers. A soldering gun sat in the middle of his desk, surrounded by piles of transistors, resistors, and coils of wire.

"I'll clean it up," he resolved. "Maybe tomorrow. Or the day after."

Leaning back against the pillow, he closed his eyes and tried not to think of his wandering the school halls with no clothes on.

Back at the Crandall home, Ben dropped the walkie-talkie to the floor next to his bed as he ducked beneath the covers and closed his eyes. The footsteps he thought he'd heard became more pronounced as his mother slowly opened the door of his room and peeked inside. Opening his left eye just a crack, Ben could see her familiar silhouette in the doorway just to the right of the television set, on which Los Angeles was being fire-bombed by marauding men from Mars. Gene Barry continued to run for his life as the city burned around him.

Shaking her head, Mrs. Crandall tiptoed into the room, looked at Ben for a moment, then turned off the television set without even glancing at it. The violent sounds had already convinced her it wasn't her kind of show.

Darren Woods's dream was rather more disjointed.

In it, he was wrestling with the problem of how to convert an ordinary bicycle to a mini-motorcycle with racing capabilities. He was working in the family's living room, which was strewn with oily parts, tools, and dirty rags. On the sofa lay the bicycle chain, its black grease marring the new beige upholstery. Darren wondered what had possessed him to tackle such a job in the family's best room.

He heard two voices in the next room. For an instant he thought one of them was his mother until he remembered with a sudden pang of despair that she was dead. The voices belonged to his father and his father's girlfriend, Mona, who were arguing about Darren. Paradoxically, it was Mona who was defending him against an onslaught of invective from his father.

"The kid's no good!" his father shouted. "Yesterday he got in my truck with his greasy hands and left prints all over the place. I coulda killed him."

"He's just a boy. Let him be."

"He's out in left field some place. Nothing but trouble. I'll bet he's in trouble now. Where the hell is he anyway?"

Darren looked around the room, which looked as if it had been struck by the Three Stooges. If his father came in and saw the mess, he would kill him on the spot. He reached for the greasy chain and tried to pull it off the sofa, but to his dismay it clung to the upholstery as if it were glued. Darren could feel perspiration stinging his eyes as the sound of footsteps grew louder.

A moment later, his father entered the room, cursed wildly and aimed a huge fist at his son's head. As the blow landed, Darren's eyes flew open and he suddenly realized he was no longer in the living room of his dream but in his own bed. Through the thin walls he could plainly hear his father and Mona engaged in their usual early morning squabble. It wasn't a happy household. Closing his eyes again, Darren thought about happier days before his mother died and wondered how long it would be before he could escape.

By the time Ben was awake and dressed, his older brother Bill was already ready to leave. Hopeful of bumming a ride with him, Ben raced into the kitchen, threw a pop-tart into the toaster and then withdrew it as he saw Bill heading for the front door.

"Hey, Bill," he said. "Wait up."

Bill continued out the door.

Mrs. Crandall, in the process of unloading the dishwasher, looked up as Ben started after his brother.

"Your lunch," she said.

Ben did a 180-degree turn to pick his lunch bag off the kitchen counter.

"So long, Mom," he said, tossing the pop-tart wrapper in the general direction of the trash can.

He darted onto the front porch just as Bill was getting into his car, a shiny ten-year-old model.

"Hey, Bill," he said. "Can I have a ride over to Wolfgang's house? It's on the way to school. Won't take you a second."

Bill shook his head. "Sorry, kid. I'm giving Andrea a ride. There's a student-principal committee meeting today."

"So what?"

"So there's no time to fool around."

"You probably just want to be alone with Andrea," Ben charged.

"Maybe," Bill smiled.

"Bet you're gonna ask to take her to the drive-in."

"Friday night." Bill smirked before turning away from his younger brother as though he didn't exist.

Having forgotten his dream diagram anyway, Ben trotted back into the house and got it. As he was leaving by the back door, which he'd left open, he heard his mother calling after him.

"Hey, Ben!"

He kept moving, pretending he didn't hear her, but she followed him onto the porch and intercepted him just as he was getting onto his bike.

"Please keep the screen door shut," his mother said. Her tone implied that she was weary of begging for this simple act.

"Sure, Mom," Ben replied.

"And another thing," she said. "Don't I get a good-morning anymore? Even your brother says goodbye."

Ben threw his leg over the bike and gave himself a strong push toward the corner of the house.

"Good morning, Mom!" he shouted over his shoulder as he moved off.

A minute later, he was on the main street in front of his house, the rattles of his old bike blending with the pervasive white noise of rush-hour traffic.

Despite his being a very intelligent young man, Wolfgang Muller hated school more than anything, ranking it ahead of brussel sprouts and turnips for sheer revulsion. He simply could not understand why students weren't assigned a year's work and allowed to return 365 days later with their completed projects for grading. He loved working by himself in the privacy of his own home. If the school system allowed him to do that, he wouldn't have to transport tons of books back and forth, losing papers and sometimes entire volumes in the process. Now, as he lugged no less than ten books, he thought of the time and energy expended just to get to and from school. If that time could be put to more useful work—

But what was the sense of even thinking about it? The system and Wolfgang simply did not see eye-to-eye. The morning sun was clear and bright, shining through the trees that lined the street in this pleasant part of town; the leaves were colorfully brown and orange, the air crisp and bracing, but Wolfgang felt like a prisoner, nonetheless. What sort of embarrassment or annoyance would he encounter today? Each and every morning, he trudged to school in the same state of quiet desperation, like an accident-prone person waiting for the next ladder, tree, or safe to fall. His unruly hair falling over his forehead, eyes staring dully ahead, his face resembled a clenched fist as he moved, trancelike, toward his temple of doom.

The other students—conscripts, Wolfgang called them—did not seem to mind school all that much. Now they ran past him or rode their bikes, roughly brushing him on their way to their classes. Yelling and even laughing, they seemed almost to enjoy their involuntary servitude.

With the school in sight, the first incident of the day happened, as Wolfgang knew it must. One of his prime tormentors, in and out of school, was Steve Jackson, a burly, flunked fifteen-year-old who was also very large for his age. The first humiliation at the hands of Steve had taken place so long ago Wolfgang could not even remember it. Since that dark day, Steve had usually managed to get in at least one physical or mental jab at him, despite Wolfgang's going out of his way to avoid the larger boy. Now he heard the footsteps approach from the rear, followed a moment later by the familiar grating voice of Steve.

"You can always tell a kid's weird when he wears his pants up to his elbow."

Wolfgang felt the muscles at the base of his neck tense up. This was it. But perhaps the uncomplimentary remark was all he would be subjected to on this occasion. He even had to admit that the hostile Jackson boy had a point; his pants *were* too short.

"Hey, Muller, you waiting for a flood?" Steve challenged, generating a titter of appreciation from two sycophants flanking him.

Wolfgang did not answer. What, after all, could he say?

"Now there's a guy who looks like he'd try to buy a tuxedo from an army surplus store," Steve continued. His companions howled with mirth.

Not funny, Wolfgang thought.

"He'd be voted the worst-dressed person at a nudists' colony, I bet," Steve added.

Weak, Wolfgang thought, noting with satisfaction that at least they were close to school now. As long as he was subjected to verbal abuse only, it wouldn't be so bad. Tucking the pile of books tighter beneath his arm, he quickened his pace just enough so that it wouldn't look as if he were running away.

The conversation behind him now was low and ominous, with an occasional suppressed laugh, leading Wolfgang to the pessimistic assumption that Steve and his cohorts were hatching some harassment plan. On the other hand—

Any thoughts of a more sanguine nature were dashed with the sound of rapidly approaching footsteps. Wolfgang had time only to turn his head before the rushing figures passed, their arms and hands reaching out to knock the books loose from his grasp. For a long moment, the pile hung in mid-air like a stack of pancakes. Wolfgang reached out, touched the topmost book and held it as the rest hit the ground and slid every which way onto the curb and street.

"Don't be so sloppy next time!" Steve Jackson called back as he trotted away. One of his pals held up a finger and grinned at Wolfgang.

"Creeps," Wolfgang muttered.

He was in the process of recovering the books when Ben Crandall rode up on his bicycle. Well aware of Wolfgang's continuing battle with Steve Jackson, he realized immediately what had happened.

"You okay?" Ben asked.

Wolfgang nodded soberly.

"I don't guess you just dropped them," Ben offered hopefully.

"No. It's that Cro-Magnon Steve Jackson and his friends again."

Ben located one of his companion's books beneath a rosebush and handed it to him. "Is that it?" he asked.

"Looks like we got 'em all."

"Yeah," Wolfgang muttered. As he started to resume the walk to school, he added, "Some days you're lucky if you just *get* to school."

Ben didn't answer. After taking a dozen paces and not hearing the sound of the squeaky bike, Wolfgang stopped and looked around. Ben was no longer with him, either physically or mentally, his gaze being firmly riveted on the big white corner house. More specifically, his line of sight went directly to a second-story bedroom window, where the head and shoulders of an attractive teenaged girl were visible. Oblivious to the soulful gaze of Ben on the street below, she was very deliberately brushing her long, golden hair. Wolfgang thought Ben's infatuation with the girl quite revolting and was embarrassed that his friend would make such a fool of himself as to stand and practically drool for her in public.

"Come on," he called back.

Ben didn't move. "If I could only see inside her room, just once," he said.

"Give me a break," Wolfgang sighed. "How would you get any kicks from that?"

"Don't you ever wonder what it's like in there?" Ben asked.

"I know what it's like," Wolfgang replied. "There's a floor, ceiling, and four walls. Probably a closet and a bed and a rug."

"But don't you want to know what she reads, what records she has—"

"No."

"What she does after school?"

"Definitely not that."

He walked back and grabbed Ben by the arm. "Come on," he urged. "You're drooling all over the sidewalk. It's disgusting."

Ben wasn't bothered in the least by the remark. In fact, he seemed almost to regard it as some sort of perverse compliment. "God, she's beautiful," he sighed. "If I could only—"

"—use her toothbrush," Wolfgang said. "Come on, it's getting late."

Still reluctant to withdraw his gaze while the girl was primping, Ben shook his head. "Don't you ever think about anything worthwhile?" he asked.

"If what you're thinking about is worthwhile, I guess the answer is no."

"I really feel sorry for you."

Wolfgang exhaled wearily.

The girl disappeared from view then and Ben re-mounted his bike and started to pedal. He had covered only a few yards when he suddenly stopped again, remembering his dream of the night before. Reaching into his jacket pocket, he withdrew the schematic diagram.

"Here's that diagram from last night," he said, handing it to his friend.

Wolfgang frowned. Annoyed at the prospect of having to endure another day of school, an annoyance which was compounded by Steve Jackson's raid on his books, he was not in the mood for constructive thinking.

"Please, Ben," he muttered. "Later, okay? I don't need this right now."

Ben shrugged. "Have it your way," he said, reaching out for the drawing.

As he started to return it, Wolfgang saw something intriguing. "Hmmm," he said, his grip tightening on the slip of paper. "Standard components. This hooks up to a computer here. I could use my Apple. That looks like some kind of antenna."

Ben smiled, realizing that his friend was now totally enmeshed in the puzzle. Pointing to one section of the diagram, he said, "There were three of these that were all the same. They connected up around the central gizmo. It looked like there might be room for a fourth connector but it wasn't there. At least I didn't see it."

A bell rang in the distance, the first warning at school, but neither boy moved.

"Interesting output stage," Wolfgang observed, pursing his lips thoughtfully. "I didn't know you knew anything about electronics."

"I've never studied," Ben replied.

"But this is so right."

Ben shrugged, impressed with himself and pleased that Wolfgang was interested. "Maybe I learned things without realizing it," he suggested.

"Well," Wolfgang said. "They say Einstein went into a dream state when he thought up his theories. Maybe that's what happened with you."

Ben had never been mentioned in the same breath with the great scientist before. He found it pleasant. "Yeah," he smiled. "That could be."

Having coupled his friend with the ultimate thinker of all time, Wolfgang immediately drew back. "I don't know, now that I think of it," he said. "This looks good and all that, but it reminds me of that time you told me the rock in your yard was a meteor."

Ben rolled his eyes wearily. "Give me a break," he pleaded. "That was when we were kids."

"Some people think we're still kids," Wolfgang observed sagely.

"Yeah, but we know better."

"Usually. But when you stand and gawk at some dumb girl combing her hair, it makes me wonder."

"Let's go," Ben said, giving his bike a push toward school.

The forbidding facade of Charles M. Jones Junior High soon rose before them. It was a three-story building with minimum ornamentation and even less personality. The usual things were there—a long concrete pathway with a flagpole set in the middle, triple doors across the front, a dedication block in the northwest corner, and a smidgen of decorative paneling across the center door. As to the identity of Charles M. Jones, most of the students assumed he was some long-deceased politician or community benefactor and few bothered to ask. Ben Crandall had a theory that

Charles M. Jones had never really existed but was a pleasant-sounding name selected by some committee.

As Ben and Wolfgang reached the entrance to the school, a couple of late kids raced up the walkway. One of them reached out to grab at the small strip of material on the back of Wolfgang's shirt.

"Fruit loop! Fruit loop!" one of them yelled. Reaching out as he raced past, the kid pulled the edge of the shirt, causing the material to rip down the back.

"That's it," Wolfgang muttered angrily, glaring at his new tormentors as they disappeared, laughing, into the building.

Ben looked at the damage. It seemed reparable, but not at the moment. "Can your mother sew?" he asked.

Wolfgang looked at the ground. He appeared to be mulling over his situation.

"Maybe somebody at the office can help," Ben offered weakly.

"You know," Wolfgang said, "for some strange reason I don't feel like going to school today."

"But you're already here," Ben murmured. "It seems a shame to waste the trip."

Wolfgang shook his head and coughed loudly. "I'm going to stay home and have a cold," he said.

Ben looked toward the office window. "Maybe somebody saw you already. Won't it look suspicious—?"

"I just discovered the cold now," Wolfgang replied. "It's not fair to take it into class and pass it along to all those nice kids."

Ben nodded. Suddenly he was excited. If Wolfgang stayed home, he would be able to pore over the diagram and perhaps decipher the key to its meaning. Better still, he might even be able to construct a rough, working model from his vast inventory of spare electronic parts so they could see what purpose it had.

Knowing Wolfgang was in his homemade laboratory working on the problem would add excitement to Ben's otherwise dreary day in school.

"You think you can make this?" he asked, thrusting the diagram at his friend.

Wolfgang took the paper but didn't answer. Ben suspected he was still seething inside, furious at the indignities he was forced to endure at the hands of Steve Jackson and his bully buddies. As if reading his mind, Wolfgang called back to him as he started homeward.

"Look out for Jackson," he said.

"Not me," Ben returned. "I'm not afraid of that idiot." Then, as a group of kids raced toward the school, Ben threw back his head and shouted as loudly as he could.

"Steve Jackson's got elephantitis of the ego!"

The sound reverberated through the courtyard and even drew glances from students in a first-floor class-room. Pausing as they moved up the walkway, the outside kids laughed and repeated the phrase.

Ben experienced a feeling of both exultation and fear. He knew that by mid-morning the phrase and its author would be all over school.

Chapter Two

IT WAS JUST BEFORE LUNCHTIME, THE SCHOOL WAS OVER-
heated, and Mrs. Seebo was speaking in a voice that
had all the animation of a metronome. Standing next to
a diagram of the solar system, she droned on, the only
movement in her lecture-demonstration being the slight
shift of her index finger from one planet to the next.

"The chances of other intelligent life existing in our
solar system have by now, of course, been proven
impossible," she said. "Venus is too hot . . . Mars
doesn't have enough moisture, Jupiter has too much
gravity and surface turbulence, and the planets beyond
that are just too cold . . ."

Unlike several in Mrs. Seebo's class who dozed
behind their notebooks or cupped hands, Ben seemed
reasonably interested in what the teacher said. His eyes
were wide open, his posture good, and his face was
turned in Mrs. Seebo's direction. Unfortunately for
her, he didn't hear a word she said. Instead, his mind
was once again wrestling with the dream he had had the
night before, trying to remember the missing pieces of
the mysterious schematic diagram.

"The fact that there may be life elsewhere in the

universe is rendered inconsequential by the distances involved," Mrs. Seebo continued. "We'll never be able to prove it exists because we just won't be able to reach it. So for all intents and purposes, we can consider ourselves alone in not only our solar system but the entire universe."

Those few students who had listened carefully from beginning to end and comprehended the crux of her statement had reason to feel a bit depressed. The vast majority merely stared ahead or dozed away with no visible display of emotion.

The lunch bell rang a minute later, bringing a merciful end to the soporific lecture. Ben got to his feet and pulled his lunch bag from his desk. He had decided to wander out to the farthest corner of the playground and eat while continuing to ponder his dream.

He never made it. No sooner was he out the door than he felt a rough hand on his shoulder.

"Hey, you," a familiar voice said.

Ben knew it was Steve Jackson even before he turned to look into the menacing eyes.

"Yeah?" Ben said as roughly as he could, determined to brazen it out.

"I hear you called me something funny," Steve said. "What's so funny?"

Ben had three choices. He could deny he had said anything about Steve Jackson, which probably wouldn't work or satisfy the bully; he could try to convince him that what he said wasn't that bad, or was actually a compliment; or he could own up to what he had said and take his punishment, if such was forthcoming. Although the last alternative was likely to involve pain and embarrassment, he much preferred it to the first two choices.

So he stood his ground. "I said you had elephantitis of the ego," he replied evenly.

For a moment, Steve Jackson's eyes clouded with puzzlement. "Why can't you talk like everyone else, Crandall?" he said.

"I do, pal," Ben returned.

"Well, I never heard a word like that. I don't like people calling me stuff when I don't know what it is."

"Then carry a dictionary." Ben smiled.

Steve's reaction was so quick Ben hardly knew what hit him. A moment later, he was lying on his back and Steve was sitting on his chest. A burning sensation near his eye let him know where the telling blow had struck. Soon other kids gathered to watch the fight—or human sacrifice, as the class genius later called it. Ben recognized a few familiar faces, including that of Lori Swenson, the girl of his other dreams who only a few hours ago had been entertaining and exciting him via the simple act of brushing her golden hair.

Seeing her had a beneficial effect on Ben, especially when she gave him a sympathetic smile. He was on the bottom, he knew, but he was definitely no loser. With Lori even nominally on his side, he was no more capable of showing fear or cowardice than a warrior about to die for a noble cause. Thus, when Steve Jackson issued his challenge, Ben could do nothing but hurl it back at him.

"I dare you to call me that again!" Steve grated.

"Certainly. I said you have elephantitis of the ego," Ben shot back. "And now I'll explain it since you're so dense. Elephantitis is when something gets bloated and ugly, like your butt!"

The onlookers broke into gales of laughter. Steve could hardly believe his ears. Drawing back his right fist, he struck Ben on the nose, a very hard punch that landed with a squishy thwack.

"Boy, you don't learn, do you?" Steve said.

"There's nothing to learn from you," Ben snarled, "except how to be dumb."

With a sound that was very close to a dog's growl, Steve lunged downward, aiming one blow after another at Ben's face. Then he stopped suddenly as the back of someone's hand struck him dead-center between the eyes.

"God . . ." Steve gasped.

He looked up. Standing directly above him, casting a long shadow over both himself and the fallen Ben, was the tall figure of Darren Woods. He was dressed in jeans, a torn jacket, and had a pair of Walkman headphones in his ears. His long hair fell over his eyes as he regarded Steve with an expression that was somewhere between a scowl and a smirk. Steve did not feel confident about taking this tough kid one-on-one. But his reputation was at stake, so he directed his most malevolent look at Darren.

"Beat it," he said.

"And you cut it out, Jackson," Darren ordered. "Get up off the guy."

"Who's gonna make me—you?"

"Sure," Darren replied. "Sure, elephantitis-butt."

Some in the crowd applauded, anticipating a come-uppance for the class bully or at least a closer fight. Darren reached out and shoved Steve roughly off Ben, then squared off in a very businesslike manner, ready to fight. But Steve Jackson had no stomach for the tough Darren. Taking a quick step backwards, he gestured toward his three burly cohorts standing near-by, one of whom carried a bicycle chain.

"Get him!" he ordered.

Darren hesitated. Two of the friends stepped forward and shoved him hard against the chest. The Walkman cassette player fell out of Darren's pocket, unnoticed by the other kids, who were by now quite caught up in the drama of the situation. A few yelled epithets at Steve for his cowardly conduct but none came to Darren's assistance. After another moment of hesitation during which he debated the pros and cons of fighting four guys, Darren suddenly broke and ran. The four took off after him, chasing the zigzagging figure toward the far end of the schoolyard.

Ben slowly got to his feet, quickly tilting his head back when he realized his nose was bleeding. Then, noticing the Walkman cassette player, he gingerly bent over to pick it up. The very least he could do by way of thanks was to rescue the guy's music.

Darren was a good runner, fast and shifty enough to play football running-back if he wanted, but outmaneuvering four potential tacklers was a tall order. Using short bursts of speed alternating with near-stops and clever turns, he extricated himself from being trapped in the corner of the schoolyard and headed back across the grass toward the school wings. His best bet for survival now seemed to be inside, with the protection of crowded hallways and teachers.

Rounding a corner, he tried a side door of the school. It was locked. Whirling out of the arms of two pursuers, he found another door that was open and darted into the school. The hallway was completely deserted and, even worse, it dead-ended into the locked gymnasium. Definitely cornered now, Darren watched as the four grinning hoods slowed their pace and instinctively spaced themselves so that any possible escape routes were cut off.

Darren took a deep breath and balled his hands into fists. All that remained was a last-ditch fight . . . Unless—

He spotted the fire alarm on the wall and lunged

toward it. Lashing backwards with his elbow, he felt the glass break and just had time to pull the handle before Steve Jackson and the hood with the bicycle chain fell on him. A moment later, the alarm bell started to ring and Darren was suddenly free. A fat, bald male teacher stuck his head out of a nearby classroom.

"I saw that, Mr. Smart Guy," he yelled. "You just bought yourself a trip to the vice-principal's office."

He glared at Darren, who smiled blandly back.

"You won't think it's so funny later," the teacher promised.

Oh, yes I will, Darren thought.

Grabbing Darren by the arm, the teacher led him away from the four pursuers and toward the office. As he moved down the hallway, Darren could not resist the urge to turn and smile back at Steve.

The rest of his day was uneventful by comparison. Surprisingly, Mr. Strauss, the vice-principal, believed his explanation as to why he had set off the fire alarm, so the worst thing that happened to Darren was having to listen to a lecture on how to avoid getting into fights. Even so, missing part of algebra class as a result was a distinct plus.

When school was over for the day, he headed for his motorbike, watching carefully to make sure he wasn't being followed. Predictably, the temperamental bike failed to start, so he was forced to perform maintenance that had become all too routine during the past few weeks. The bike was a paste-up vehicle, made from parts cannibalized from many other bikes, all put together by Darren himself into a custom, souped-up, mini-motorcycle. When it worked, it was a thing of beauty.

As he tightened several bolts with a crescent wrench, he kept one eye peeled for Steve Jackson's gang, but the only person who even came close to him was Ben Crandall. At first, Darren didn't even recognize him.

"Everything okay?" Ben asked, sliding forward off the seat of his bicycle.

"Yeah."

"I'd like to say thanks."

"For what?"

"Saving me from that elephantitis-butt."

Darren looked up from his work, nodding. "Oh, yeah," he muttered. "No charge."

"Well, it meant a lot to me," Ben continued. "He really had me in a bad spot. I'm sorry your helping me out got you in trouble."

"He tries it again and I'll kick his butt," Darren said through clenched teeth. "I'll kick all their butts. I'll make 'em eat that bicycle chain."

Ben looked at him silently a moment, admiring his strength and coolness.

Giving the last bolt a final turn, Darren got to his feet.

"What's the trouble?" Ben asked.

"It's this damn starter. I must have rebuilt the damn thing a hundred times."

"Maybe you should buy a new one."

"That's no fun. Anybody can do that."

Hopping on the motorbike, he gave the adjusted starter a shot. It worked.

"Well, see you, kid," Darren said.

"Hey, you want to come over to my house?" Ben offered. "I just got the cassette of *This Island Earth*. It's a pretty good movie. There's this great mutant with two brains that's kind of interesting . . ."

"Sounds great," Darren said sarcastically. He wasn't really into science fiction movies, or any kind of movie, for that matter.

"I got some other—" Ben continued.

"No, thanks."

With a little wave, Darren peeled out onto the school parking lot heading for the main drag. Ben watched him a moment before realizing he still had Darren's Walkman in his pocket. Leaping back on his bike, he pedaled furiously after the figure on the motorbike, remaining just far enough to his rear to not lose him, but too far to be heard when he yelled.

Separated by a quarter of a mile, the two moved along the river road that marked the east boundary of town. Fortunately, Darren was in no particular hurry to get home, there being little in the way of warmth or excitement to give him a sense of urgency. If anything, he usually tried to find an excuse to avoid going home until just before dinner hour, but today he was too lethargic to try finding something diverting.

He slowed the bike as he neared the familiar pale pink house, one of a long line of identically run-down tract houses with overgrown front yards and battered cars in the driveways or out front. Darren's house was slightly different in that a large dump truck was in the driveway and the hedge was marred by several large openings. He eased the motorbike through the largest of these and got off. A moment later, he heard the kid yelling his name from the end of the block. Hands on hips, he waited impatiently until Ben pedaled up to the Woods's house.

"Look," Darren said before Ben could even speak. "Why don't you just take off, okay? I did you a favor but I didn't know you were going to bug me about it and follow me around the rest of my life."

Shocked and offended, Ben shook his head, reached into his pocket and withdrew the Walkman. "Okay, forget it," he said. "Here."

He handed the cassette player to Darren.

As he turned away, the sound of yelling and breaking glass caused him to stop and look back at the house.

"I was on time!" a male voice shouted. "Don't tell me what time I got there! You weren't there!"

"You said yourself, five after!" a woman yelled back. "That was late!"

"Go to hell!" the man shot back.

Darren looked down at the grass, well worn and infested with weeds; he kicked a stone aside with the side of his foot.

"My dad's home," he said simply.

Ben didn't reply, reasoning that whatever he said would be inappropriate.

"I guess he didn't get the job," Darren murmured.

"What does he do?"

"Hauls away junk."

Ben turned over a few thoughts in his mind but could think of nothing that would make junk-hauling seem ennobling or even tolerable. He was relieved from having to comment by a sudden increase in the volume of the woman's voice.

"Your mom's got a strong voice," Ben observed.

'That's not my mom," Darren said.

"Oh."

"It's my Dad's girlfriend. Mona. She's okay when she's not yelling."

Now, however, she was definitely yelling, having launched an all-out verbal assault on the man inside, whose protests became weaker and less frequent.

"Maybe I will come over to your house," Darren suggested. "If it's still okay."

Ben nodded. "Sure. Let's take the creek."

"You within walking distance?"

"Yeah. If we go that way."

Darren leaned his motorbike against the side of the porch. He and Ben cut across the back yard and down into an enormous, overgrown creek bed that ran along the backs of many houses in town. The water of the creek was not more than ten feet wide and seldom as deep as a foot. Brownish gray in color, it was lined with battered beer cans, plastic bottles, and other assorted debris. Despite its unwholesome character, Ben regarded the stream as a pleasant thing in his life, a place to be alone, think, or just amuse himself by throwing rocks at bits of paper as they floated by.

For a while, they walked parallel to the creek, then crossed over at its narrowest point near Ben's house.

"Your folks fight a lot?" Ben asked finally. "I mean, does your dad and his girlfriend fight a lot?"

"Yeah. He's okay, though. He just isn't very lucky. He always breaks things or loses them. Anyway, he taught me how to run. Now he can't catch me anymore. And neither can anybody else."

"Yeah, I saw how quick you are," Ben smiled. "I wish I could run like that."

Darren laughed. "It's gotten me out of trouble more than once."

After another long moment of silence, Ben asked, "Are your folks divorced?"

"No," Darren replied. "My mom died when I was a kid. Cancer."

"Oh."

They were quiet until they reached Wolfgang's house, a neat, two-story building nestled in the trees lining the creek's bank.

"How about you?" Darren asked then.

"What?"

"Your mom and dad still together?"

"Yeah," Ben replied. "I guess they get along okay. They don't yell at each other. They just talk about the stupidest things all the time."

"This where you live?"

Ben shook his head. "This is my best friend's house. You want to stop here a second?"

"I don't know. What's his name?"

"Wolfgang Muller. I think he's a brilliant scientist."

"Wolfgang? Are you kidding me?"

"No."

"What kind of name is that? It sounds like a joke or something."

"I think it's German," Ben explained. "Anyway, Wolfgang's folks speak with kind of an accent."

"Well, I'd change that name pretty quick if I was him," Darren smiled.

"He can't. His parents won't let him. You'll probably think he's weird, anyway."

"Do you think he's weird?"

"Sometimes. But not that often."

"Okay." Darren shrugged. "Let's go."

They trudged up the steep incline to the Muller home and walked around to the front door. The door of the garage was open, revealing a variety of machines in different stages of repair. The inventory included washing machines, radios, television sets, oscilloscopes, vacuum tube testers, and even several ancient food blenders.

"What's all this junk?" Darren asked. "Maybe I should send my father around here with his truck."

"Wolfgang woldn't like that," Ben said. "He says he's got a use for every one of these things."

"It still looks like junk to me."

"Try not to make fun of him," Ben urged. "He's serious about his work. Matter of fact, he's working on something important now, pretending he's sick. I want to see how it's going."

"Now that you mention it, they got some pretty good spare parts here," Darren admitted. "Maybe I can use some of this stuff."

"Some of it's his dad's," Ben said. "Talk about strange parents. Wait till you meet his. They're both research scientists or something. From West Germany. They're polite and everything, but kind of weird."

"Anybody who would stick their kid with a name like Wolfgang has got to be a little strange."

"Yeah."

"If I had a name like Wolfgang I think I'd kill myself."

"Me, too, but don't say that around his parents, okay, Darren?"

Darren nodded as Ben rang the doorbell.

Mrs. Muller came to the door. She was a stocky woman with a pale complexion, plain features, thick glasses, and hair pulled back in a bun. Her expression was kind although somewhat unfocused or vacant, as if she were constantly thinking of something else.

She smiled at Ben. "Benjamin," she said. "Come in. And this is—"

"Darren," Darren said.

"Darren," Mrs. Muller repeated. "You only have to tell me once. I never forget anything."

"That's wonderful," Darren muttered politely.

As Mrs. Muller turned away, Ben rolled his eyes at Darren and walked into the living room. "Watch out for the boxes and things," he warned, keeping his voice low.

Although the Mullers had lived in the house for several years, it looked as if someone were either moving in or moving out. Boxes, bags, bundles of tied books were everywhere except for the very center of the floor. In one corner of the living room sat a packing crate large enough for a refrigerator. On top of it sat a large gray and white cat, nonchalantly licking its stomach. The noise level of the house was quite high as four children, ranging in age from two to six, ran screaming and laughing from room to room and back again. Mrs. Muller made a halfhearted attempt to maintain order, but it was obvious she was no disciplinarian.

"Ludwig!" she shouted once to one of the children who was tormenting another. "Stop that right now!"

Ludwig stopped pulling his sister's hair for about ten seconds, returning immediately to the task as soon as his mother's gaze went elsewhere.

"This place looks like a loony bin," Darren whispered to Ben.

"They're just not into neatness," Ben explained. "They're all thinking about something else."

Mrs. Muller led them through the jungle trail of boxes into the kitchen and to the basement door, which bore a sign that read: KEEP OUT: IMPORTANT RESEARCH.

"Wolfgang is down in his lab," she smiled. "Just a second. I'll ring him."

She pressed a button on the homemade intercom system put together from spare radio, TV, and telephone parts.

"Wolfgang," she said.

The voice that answered was small and tinny, like the sound produced by an old crystal set.

"Hello?" Wolfgang replied.

"Benjamin is here," Mrs. Muller continued, "with his friend Derek."

Darren looked at Ben, who shrugged.

"Great," Wolfgang replied from the lower depths. "Tell them I'm busy on something but I'll be up in a minute or two."

"Did you hear that?" Mrs. Muller asked.

"Yes, ma'am," Ben said.

"He says he's busy on something but he'll be up in a couple minutes." Mrs. Muller smiled.

Darren shook his head like a dog shedding water and looked out the kitchen window.

"Have a seat, boys," Mrs. Muller suggested. "Can I offer you anything while we're waiting for Wolfgang to finish? How about some nice baklava?"

She looked at Darren for a response.

"What?" he said.

"You've never had baklava?"

"No."

"It's a Greek pastry."

With that, Mrs. Muller produced a couple of plates and handed each of the boys a sizable portion of the delicacy. Darren looked at it suspiciously.

"Did she say this is Geek pastry?" he whispered to Ben when Wolfgang's mother looked the other way.

"No," Ben said, laughing. "Greek."

"Oh."

"What's it taste like? It looks awful. The last time I saw something like this I stepped over it."

"You'll like it," Ben promised.

Ben had taken a large bite and Darren a tentative one when Wolfgang burst into the kitchen, a maniacal gleam in his eyes. Then, remembering that his mother expected him to be under the weather, he brought his hands to his mouth and coughed loudly into them.

"How are you feeling?" his mother asked.

"A little better," Wolfgang replied, and then added, "but not much."

"You shouldn't be down in that cold basement."

"It's not that cold."

"Colder than in bed."

Wolfgang shrugged. Then, looking at Darren, he asked bluntly, "Who're you?"

"Derek," Darren said.

"Darren," corrected Ben.

"Damon," said Mrs. Muller.

Wolfgang, now thoroughly confused, looked to his friend Ben for help.

"He looks human," Ben said, straight-faced, reciting old science fiction dialogue for Wolfgang's benefit. "But remember, the aliens can assume any shape they wish."

"That means we can trust no one," Wolfgang added, continuing the charade.

"Exactly," Ben said, emulating as best he could the deep voice of the movie character who had rendered the lines. "Even you and I must be suspicious of each other."

"Surely you don't think—" Wolfgang emoted.

"What are you boys talking about?" Mrs. Muller asked.

"Nothing," Wolfgang replied brusquely. "So what's your real name?"

"Darren," said Darren.

"Hi. Come on downstairs."

As they closed the basement door behind them, Wolfgang's gleam returned. "I finished it," he said, slapping Ben on the shoulder. "But I don't know how it's gonna work. I waited until you got here to turn it on."

"What's 'it'?" Darren asked.

"You'll see." Ben smiled. He then launched into his version of the high-pitched eerie "theramin" sound used in science fiction movies of the forties and fifties. Wolfgang chimed in with his own rendition, pitched a third higher, producing a weird, dissonant effect.

Darren looked at both of them and frowned. He was beginning to wonder if he'd done a wise thing, associating with these two characters.

A moment later, when they descended into the

basement, he wondered even more. The room looked every bit like the typical mad scientist's laboratory depicted in books and movies. The only things missing were test tubes pouring smoke and electric sparks leaping from one connector to another. In fact, Darren would not have been surprised to see a huge, strapped-down monster lying on a table across the room. He deduced that the only reason the creature wasn't there was because there simply wasn't space for it. Nearly every inch of the sizable area was crowded with boxes of broken TV sets, old radio tubes, circuit boards, soldering guns, and every imaginable tool from wrench to scalpel. Adding to the confusion was a network of wires strung across the room, presumably leading out of the basement and connecting with the exterior power lines. Against the walls were shelves crammed with comic books and science fiction paperbacks. Darren wondered how a supposedly brilliant scientist would be able to find anything to work with here.

"Over here," Wolfgang said.

He led them toward a workbench, which was also crowded with electronic components and tools. Nearby was a small cage containing a white mouse.

Ben, obviously no stranger to Wolfgang's cluttered world, walked over to the cage and bent close to it. "That's Heinlein," he said to Darren. Then, to the mouse, he said, "Hello, Heinlein."

Heinlein, a veteran of Wolfgang's experimental wizardry, pressed a large key in his cage that was connected to a voice synthesizer. A split-second later, a mechanical-sounding, but quite intelligible male voice replied.

"Hello," it said.

Ben looked at Darren. "How about that?" he said, smiling. "Heinlein gets it right seventy percent of the time. If he keeps it up, he'll be perfect one day."

Heinlein, realizing he had someone's close attention, pressed another key.

"I would like . . ." the voice synthesizer said.

Heinlein lifted his body off the first key and pressed yet another.

". . . some cheese," the voice synthesizer continued.

"Good work." Ben laughed. He picked up a piece of cheese from a bowl nearby and passed it through the bars of the cage to the mouse.

"That's pretty weird," Darren muttered.

As the boys watched Heinlein attack the cheese, a large cat jumped onto the table by the cage and stared intently at the mouse. For a while Heinlein alternated his gaze between the cheese and the intense face of the cat; then he moved away from his meal to press another key.

The voice synthesizer went into action. "Help," it said with a precision and lack of emotion that belied the words' content, "the cat is drooling on me again."

Darren looked at Ben in surprise.

"I put a bunch of sentences into its voice synthesizer," Ben explained. "Sometimes it makes sense."

The cat continued to stare at Heinlein.

"Down, Erhart," Wolfgang ordered, moving toward the cage and cat.

Erhart the cat directed another long, malevolent glare at the cage before slinking away, foiled for the moment. Taking up a position at the far end of the work bench, he continued to watch Heinlein carefully for another couple of minutes, then closed his eyes and went to sleep.

"What else does it say?" Darren asked.

"I forget," Ben replied. "Some of them are pretty silly."

Wolfgang nodded darkly. He was at his Apple computer, punching in data.

Darren strolled around the basement, occasionally picking up a dusty object, looking at it a moment and then returning it. "It smells down here," he said.

"All the old comics and stuff are mine," Ben said. "My dad got sick of seeing them at our house and told me to throw them out. But Wolfgang said I could keep them here. Maybe Dad was right, though. It's an awful lot of stuff."

Darren picked up a comic book, the *Classics Illustrated* version of H.G. Wells's *War of the Worlds*. On the cover was an artist's brilliant rendition of the martian tripod. In the background, of course, was a city in flames, with people fleeing for their lives.

"That's one of my favorites." Ben smiled. "The movie was on last night. Did you see it?"

"No," Darren replied. He picked up another science fiction comic, this one about mutants from outer space, glanced briefly at the cover and tossed it back onto the pile.

"Weird," he said.

"I like it," Ben replied a bit defensively. He was used to people attacking science fiction. He realized that older people, with their rigid minds, could not be swayed by any arguments in favor of it, but was hopeful that his contemporaries could accept logic.

"I never could get into that stuff," Darren said, sniffing. "It's too far out."

"Hey, people thought we'd never get to the moon," Ben said.

"That's different," Darren replied.

"How's it different?"

"That's us doing something. This stuff in the comics is about other people or things doing something. It's too far out. What's it got to do with anything?"

"Don't you wonder what's up there?" Ben asked. "Out in the universe, on other planets?"

Darren laughed. "That's what I mean," he said. "There's nobody out there."

"Can you prove it?"

"I don't have to prove it," Darren retorted. "It's up to you to prove those other people or things *are* up there."

Ben frowned, realizing this time logic was on his opponent's side. "Well," he said finally, falling back on one of his favorite arguments, "it stands to reason that with billions of planets and stars out there, one of them contains life."

"And it stands to reason that with billions of grains of sand on the beach, one of them would be gold," Darren countered. "But I don't see people digging up the beach for gold."

"This is silly," Wolfgang grumbled from across the room. "Why don't you guys give it up?"

"It's okay with me," Darren said, sensing that he was the victor in the discussion. "I just don't think you should believe everything you read in the comics or see in the movies."

Ben shrugged.

"Anyway," Wolfgang said, brightening, "Here it is. We can go to work now."

Darren and Ben walked quickly to the computer. Amid the clutter and dust of the downstairs laboratory-junk room, the Apple special looked clean and compact, like something that had been dropped from another, more sophisticated world. The unit was basically gray, with controls on the front, including a small TV screen. The home computer portion was patched into the back, with two disk drives attached. Now the screen was blank except for a small blinking green square in the lower left portion of the area. A complicated schematic diagram was on the table next to the machine.

"Did you have a lot of trouble?" Ben asked.

"Yeah," he replied. "Until I tied it in to my father's computer on the modem."

Darren blinked. "Modem?" he said.

"Never mind," Ben replied shortly. He was anxious now to see what, if anything, his dream schematic meant.

Caught up in his own explanation, Wolfgang poured out a torrent of words.

"I had to fill in some details on your drawing," he said. "They may not be perfect but I guess they're close enough. Anyway, they're logical, which is most important. There's only so many ways a schematic can go and make sense, you know, and we have to assume it makes sense. If it doesn't, it's all useless and dumb anyway. So that box houses your circuit board, which called for a terminal here, so I used my computer, which only has 128 K, but that should be enough to find out what it does, if it does anything at all, which it probably doesn't. Got that?"

"Makes sense to me," Ben nodded.

"Not to me," Darren muttered. "What's this all about, anyway?"

"You'll see," Ben said.

Something in his tone irritated Darren. He wasn't used to being talked down to by a fourteen-year-old, or anyone else for that matter.

"Wait a minute," he said, a definite edge to his voice. "Maybe I don't want to 'see' after it's over. Maybe I'd like to know what's going on beforehand, right? Then I'll be able to appreciate it."

"It'll take too long to explain," Ben replied. "And it may not amount to anything, in which case I'll have gone through a long spiel for nothing."

"There's really no point in waiting," Wolfgang added, reaching for the power switch. "Ready?"

"No," Darren interrupted. "I want to know what this is all about. You might blow up the place with me in it."

Wolfgang rolled his eyes toward the top of his head and sighed.

But Darren was undeterred. "Look at these wires," he continued. "I'll bet there's enough juice in this cellar to fry us all ten times. I'm not kidding. Unless you tell me what you're doing, I'm walking. Just give me two minutes to get far enough away from this house."

Wolfgang was content to let Darren walk, but Ben felt a certain responsibility for having brought Darren into the laboratory, and did not want him to just stomp out. He also wanted his new friend and benefactor to be around if something really interesting developed.

"Hold it, Wolfgang," he said. "I'll give Darren a quick rundown and then he'll know, okay?"

Wolfgang shrugged. "If that's what you want," he replied. "But there's no danger. The worst that can happen is we'll burn out the computer."

"It'll only take a minute," Ben said.

He then proceeded to describe the dream he'd had and how Wolfgang was about to test the schematic to find out what it meant. Darren's eyes told Ben that he didn't really understand everything, but he lost some of his hard-nosed attitude as the explanation continued.

"Get it?" Ben asked.

Darren nodded.

Wolfgang smiled tightly. "Then we'll just flip the switch and see what happens."

He flipped the switch.

Nothing happened. The screen remained blank.

"Oh, well," Wolfgang said philosophically. "This kind of stuff usually takes years to develop and work out the bugs . . ."

Ben sighed and frowned. It was much more disappointing than he'd thought it would be. As Wolfgang had been setting up the machine, Ben had told himself that what they were doing did not involve an enormous expenditure of time and effort; if anything, this dream interpretation-via-computer was something of a lark. No advanced theory was going down the drain, no costly materials, or meticulous computations. That being the case, why did he feel such a sensation of utter loss?

"I guess I should have stayed in bed," he said aloud, forcing a smile.

Wolfgang continued to stare at the blank screen. Darren shrugged, put his hands in his pockets, and took a step toward the stairs.

"It's not over yet," Wolfgang whispered.

"What?" Ben said.

"I said, it's not over. Listen."

A strange sound was emanating from the computer, very faint at first, and then building into something quite beautiful and mysterious. It had a bell-like quality, a long, single note like the rim of a glass being traced by a finger. As its volume increased, the tone modulated up the scale in a gentle, haunting series of steps.

"Have you ever heard this before?" Ben asked.

Wolfgang shook his head.

Darren, puzzled by it all, walked back to the table and stared down at the computer.

Something was happening now. The screen was no longer blank. In fact, read-outs and displays were going by so fast it was impossible to keep track of them, much less interpret their meaning. In the dimness of the basement, the flickering from the TV screen illuminated the three boys' faces with a glowing, magical light.

"What's happening?" Ben whispered.

Wolfgang leaned closer to the TV screen, glancing at the disk drives as they hummed and clicked.

"It's . . . um . . . it's programming itself," Wolfgang murmured.

"Can it do that?"

"If it's doing it, I guess it can."

As they spoke, the displays continued to flash across the screen, huge blocks of figures and equations and formulas interspersed with footnoted material. Line after line, block after block, faster and faster they moved until, suddenly, everything stopped. A single line of figures remained on the screen, the cursor blinking beneath it as if it had finally located the key to something.

Wolfgang looked at the figures, his mouth open in disbelief.

"What is it?" Ben asked.

Wolfgang licked his lips. "I can't believe this," he said finally. "It's asking for the coordinates on X, Y, and Z axes, in order to locate a point in space relative to the terminal. How did you ever . . . ?

He looked at Ben strangely.

"It's not my doing," Ben said.

"Are you sure?"

Ben nodded.

"You not only had a pretty sophisticated dream but a darn good aftermath," Wolfgang said. "I think even Einstein would have been impressed."

"What are you guys talking about?" Darren demanded. His sense of amazement and wonder had worn off and now he was merely puzzled and annoyed.

"I don't understand how the schematic knows so much," Wolfgang explained. "It seems too well thought out to be part of a dream."

Ben stared at the machine. He was beginning to think that perhaps he was a latent genius after all. "I guess maybe I'm just the same kind of guy as Einstein," he said.

"Well, let's give it the material it wants and see what happens," Wolfgang suggested. Frowning, he typed in some figures on the terminal.

"What are you doing?" Darren asked.

"Giving it some points to chew on," Wolfgang replied. "Something on that shelf over there."

He pointed to a bookcase across the room.

A moment later, the three boys could see a small amount of movement in the books on one of the shelves, almost as if an unseen hand had touched them ever so gently. Spellbound, Wolfgang stared at the phenomenon for a moment and then returned to the keyboard. "I'll move it to the right," he said.

He typed in more instructions. Immediately, the books started moving toward one end of the shelf until they were squeezed tightly together.

"Now," Wolfgang said.

He tapped one more key.

A sharp, explosive sound followed—actually a double blast. One burst of violence came from the machine as it shorted out; the other came from the bookshelf as the books were thrown to the floor and the bookcase slammed sideways against the wall.

All three boys jumped and looked at each other, their eyes wide with terror and excitement.

"Look at that," Ben said.

He pointed to the computer, which was still buzzing as smoke rose from its innards. A half-minute later, the buzzing stopped and all was silent in the room.

"What happened?" Ben asked.

Wolfgang shrugged. "I have no idea," he replied, his face quite pale.

The boys walked to the bookcase and gingerly examined it. A hole the size of a quarter was punched through the side of it. Pulling the shelf away from the wall, Ben saw that the same smooth hole continued *into* the wall. He touched it.

"It's warm," he said.

Sliding his finger into the wall, he found that the hole apparently went all the way through.

"Look at this," Wolfgang said.

He held up a half dozen of the books. Each one had the same hole neatly punched through its center.

Ben had no idea what was going on, but he did know that the genesis of all this tremendously exciting action was his dream. Somehow everything was connected— the machine programming itself, asking for reference points, the movement of the books, and now this burst of violence.

"How'd you do that?" Darren asked bluntly, glaring first at Wolfgang and then Ben.

"We didn't do it," Wolfgang said.

"Then who did?"

"It was from my dream," Ben explained. "My dream caused it."

"No," Wolfgang said emphatically. "Your dream didn't do that. All your dream did was give us the basic information for something. We used it to build an electrically generated point of force."

"But the dream—" Ben interjected.

"Now, Ben, just calm down," Wolfgang urged. "There's got to be a logical explanation for this, a scientific reason, and that doesn't include dreams."

"What are you guys talking about, anyway?" Darren demanded. "This was a trick, right?"

"No," Ben replied.

Wolfgang shook his head emphatically. "Nothing like that," he said. "Listen, we have to swear to secrecy . . ."

Darren rolled his eyes to the top of his head. "Why

would I want to tell anybody about this?" he said with a laugh. "It's so stupid."

Wolfgang continued as if he had not heard Darren. "I don't know what this is," he announced solemnly, "but I don't want anybody to take it away from us, or tell us what to do with it." He looked at Ben, his eyes blazing intensely. "Because you dreamed it, I built it, and it's our secret."

Darren looked at Wolfgang as if he had gone mad. He picked up a copy of *War of the Worlds* and another comic book, both of which had identical holes in them.

"Listen, you guys," he said. "I know this is a trick. You pull this on every sucker who comes over here, right? It's a good joke, but I'm not buying."

"No," Ben protested. "That's not true, Darren. Honest. You've got to believe me."

"Let him think that if he wants," Wolfgang muttered. "I don't care."

"Wolfgang!"

A deep voice from the top of the stairs interrupted their discussion. It was Mr. Muller.

"Wolfgang," he said, coming down the steps. "Have you seen any signs of infestation down here?"

Wolfgang quickly threw a newspaper over the smoldering computer. "No, Father," he said.

"Well, I'm going to have a look around."

As he came down the last two steps, Darren gave Ben and Wolfgang a disgusted look and walked up the stairs, barely nodding at Mr. Muller. He had obviously had enough and just wanted to get out of the Muller madhouse. While his father was distracted by Darren, Wolfgang was able to throw a large tarp over the machine.

"Now that I think about it," he said, concerned that his father might still notice the computer, "I saw some insect waste products in that corner."

Mr. Muller nodded and went to the corner indicated by his son. As soon as he was out of earshot, Wolfgang whispered to Ben, "I have to get it running again, anyway. I'll call you later tonight."

"Okay," Ben whispered back. "What do you think we've done?"

"I think we've done something nobody else has ever done before," Wolfgang said. "I think we've somehow made contact wth a force outside our universe."

Ben felt a cold shiver run up his spine. Then he was running up the stairs after Darren.

Chapter Three

"WELL, IT'S OFFICIAL. I TALKED TO SOME PEOPLE TODAY and I think I've got a pretty good shot at being elected student body president."

For the better part of a half hour, Bill had been talking about himself at the dinner table, impressing his parents and infuriating Ben.

"That's great," Mrs. Crandall said enthusiastically, clapping her hands together.

"Congratulations," Mr. Crandall said, smiling.

Ben remained silent.

"I'll be the only candidate on the football team, and all that work on the student-principal committee can't do me any harm," Bill continued.

His parents smiled warmly. To Ben, they looked like a couple of trained seals. This was the way it usually went at dinner. Bill was the major achiever in the family and he did very little to stifle his immodesty. Every night Ben sat and tried to think of things to say that would top Bill's latest accomplishments, but he usually held his tongue because there was no chance of doing so. Tonight, however, there was one shocker he could hit them with.

"I got massacred today," he said when Bill finally stopped to take a breath.

He realized two things immediately after he delivered the line. First, he probably shouldn't have said it; second, he was glad he had said it. Bill's litany of his own accomplishments and aspirations promptly died in mid-thought and all family attention was directed at Ben. Mrs. Crandall's eyes widened as she looked in alarm and disapproval at her younger son. Ben's father, on the other hand, seemed almost pleased, as a slight smile crossed his face. Only Bill, no doubt retaliating against Ben's silent, emotional boycott of his own stories, remained impassive.

"You what?" Mrs. Crandall gasped.

"I got massacred," Ben said.

"Massacred means killed," Bill said didactically, unable to resist correcting his brother.

Ben was forced to partially recant. "Well, not massacred, then," he said. "But it wasn't far from that. It was more of an argument, really . . ."

"Oh," his mother said, somewhat relieved.

"An argument with fists," Ben continued.

The disapproval returned to her eyes.

"You got in a fight, huh?" Mr. Crandall said evenly, just as calmly as he might have reacted to Ben's getting a C-minus in gym. Mrs. Crandall switched her disapproving gaze from Ben to her husband. He didn't seem to be taking Ben's news with appropriate alarm or at least seriousness. Boys fighting made her nervous. When Bill had gone through a period of almost daily battles several years before, she had lost weight and sleep as a result. She didn't wish to repeat the process with Ben, who was more delicate than Bill and much more likely to be "massacred" on a regular basis.

Before she could castigate her husband, Bill leaped into the vacuum with a continuation of his student body presidential campaign story. "So, anyway," he said loudly, "the nominations are tomorrow—"

"How big was he?" Mrs. Crandall asked, ignoring Bill in favor of Ben.

"Big," Ben replied, enjoying being the center of attention for a change. "Very big. And he had three guys to help him. One of them had a bicycle chain—"

"Lord help us," Mrs. Crandall moaned.

Bill heaved a heavy sigh and looked out the dining room window. There was nothing to see except a few street lights, but he managed to feign intense interest in them.

"How did it start?" Mr. Crandall asked.

"Well, this one kid pushed the books out of Wolfgang's arms so I said he had elephantitis of the ego. He told me to take it back, but I wouldn't."

"That's the stuff!"

"I don't see any reason to encourage him," Mrs. Crandall interjected.

"I'm not encouraging him," Mr. Crandall retorted. "I just think it's time that Ben"—here he gestured to Ben as opposed to Bill—"starts getting a taste of the real world out there."

"By getting himself beat up?"

"No. By taking it and dishing it out. That's what life's about, honey. There are a lot of mean folks out there and sometimes you have to deal with them in the only way they understand—with a rap on the jaw."

Mrs. Crandall shook her head. "What a neanderthal philosophy," she murmured.

"Hey," her husband protested. "You don't think I'm an ape, do you?"

"I wonder."

"Well, I'm not. I'm a perfectly ordinary guy. And I used to get into lots of fights when I was a kid. There was this one kid on the block named Herbie Bell. Big for his age, you know, about six feet tall when he was twelve. I had to fight with him once and I'm glad I did. I couldn't see out of one eye for two weeks but I think I saw a lot deeper into myself after that."

"Did you win the fight?" Ben asked, beginning to feel a real kinship with his father.

"No. I got massacred." Mr. Crandall laughed.

"Let's not talk about this any more," Mrs. Crandall said, getting up and starting to clear away the dishes. "It's depressing."

Ben was only too willing to drop the subject. He had accomplished what he wanted to do and generated a certain rapport with his dad as a bonus. And now that he had him in a good mood, it seemed an appropriate time to launch into the discussion of something else he had wanted to bring up for a long while.

"Hey, Dad?" he said.

"Yeah?"

"Did you get a chance to read that thing I gave you this morning?"

Mr. Crandall cleared his throat, realizing that he had slipped the brochure under the blotter of his desk and had never really gotten back to it.

"I'm sorry," he muttered. "I meant to, but things are a little . . . tight at the office right now. It's a busy time of the year . . ."

Ben was genuinely hurt. The item he referred to was hardly a major work to read, just a couple of paragraphs and a few pictures to glance at. Hadn't it been important enough? All those thoughts rushed through his mind, but he knew enough to try hanging a guilt trip on his father. So he merely shrugged and looked away.

"Oh," he said. "Okay."

Mr. Crandall experienced a twinge of conscience. Several times during the day he had picked up the paper given him by Ben, but had been distracted. Now, seeing Ben's disappointed expression, he berated himself inwardly for not having taken the time.

"Can you tell me about it?" he asked.

Ben wasn't ready to give in yet. "Well," he murmured, "if you're so busy . . ."

"I'm not busy now," his father replied. "And I'd like to hear what it is. Honest."

The sincere tone in his father's voice impressed Ben. New excitement stirred within him, so that he was able to demur only a moment before blurting out his desire.

"Well," he said, "it's this thing called Space Camp. It lasts a week and you go to the Alabama Space and Rocket Center. They put you through all the weightless training and tests that the astronauts go through, and at the end there's a real simulated flight to another planet, and some kids get to be mission control and *some* kids actually get to be the astronauts."

Bill grunted his disapproval. "Sounds like another Disneyland rip-off," he said.

Mr. Crandall was less sarcastic than Bill but unable to endorse the idea with unbridled enthusiasm. "Well, that sounds great." He nodded. "Very educational and fun. We'll have to think about it."

"I'd like to do it this summer," Ben said.

"Oh. Well, let's be realistic about this. I mean, it doesn't sound exactly cheap."

"Probably costs an arm and a leg," Bill added archly.

"Please, Dad," Ben urged.

"Maybe," Mr. Crandall said. "We'll see."

Ben had seen too many dreams fade and disappear in the mist of we'll-see land. Now, while the iron was at least warm, he decided to pursue it. "If I save until summer," he said, "I can pay for half of it And if I get a part-time job, I can pay for even more."

"And if somebody leaves you a million dollars, you'll

have a lot left over." Bill smiled sardonically. "Well, maybe not a lot, but some."

The cross-arguments were beginning to get to Mr. Crandall, who, despite his assertion that he had been quite a battler during his youth, was not really a decisive person. Most of all, he wanted time to think about the suggestion, an interval during which Ben might even drop the notion in favor of something else.

Ben would not drop it now, though. "I've thought of something, Dad," he continued. "Remember those bonds Grandma gave me when I was nine or ten—"

"They're for your college education," Mr. Crandall said, his voice tinged wih anger.

"But suppose I become an astronaut?" Ben smiled. "Then going on that trip will really be a part of my education—right?"

"Wrong," his father returned.

"But—"

Mr. Crandall suddenly felt trapped by the conversation, no longer able to reason or appear conciliatory. "Listen," he said sharply, "now that you've pushed so hard, I've got to tell you that I don't really see the purpose of this trip. I mean, 'another planet'? What's that all about? You can't base the rest of your life on being able to visit other planets. It's like thinking about living in the fun house. It's a world that doesn't exist."

"Other planets don't exist?" Ben asked incredulously. "Is that what you're saying, Dad?"

Feeling cornered, Mr. Crandall started to grow even more truculent. "No, that's not what I said and you know it," he replied. "I said it's silly to be obsessed with visiting other planets. I don't know, I guess you're not as grown up as I thought you were."

Ben sighed and tossed his fork onto his plate. The battle was lost and he knew it.

"I think it might be better if you spent a little more time down here on Earth this summer," his father said. "Weren't you going to paint the garage? And how about that pile of dirt that's been sitting in the back yard for three months? You told me you'd haul it away if I paid you. Well, I paid you and it's still there."

"But, Dad—" Ben murmured.

"I'm sorry, Ben," Mr. Crandall interrupted coldly. "End of discussion."

Ben looked down at his plate. For a long moment, everyone was silent. Even Bill thought it appropriate to keep his mouth shut and not irritate his younger brother any further.

At least I didn't make a fool of myself by telling them about the dream, Ben thought.

It was much later that night. He lay on his bed, the lights out, staring at the science fiction posters and dragon models, which looked extra ominous in the moonlight. Some of the anger at his father had gone away, leaving a deep feeling of disappointment. He realized now that he had been counting on the Alabama trip.

"Ben?"

His mother was peeping at him through the doorway.

"Yeah, Mom?"

She came into the room, not turning on the lights. She walked silently to his bedside. Ben felt her weight next to him but did not turn his eyes from the wall.

"Ben?" she said softly.

"What?"

"I want to apologize for your father," she said. "He's been worried about work a lot lately and acts jumpy sometimes. He doesn't mean anything by it."

Ben didn't answer. It wasn't that he was pouting; he simply didn't know what to say. What did worry about work have to do with seriously considering something wholesome and educational? It sounded like a cop-out to avoid making a commitment and paying a few dollars. And if his father wanted to apologize, why didn't he do it himself? These and other angry thoughts crowded Ben's mind, but he decided it was fruitless to even bring them up.

"I guess you want to go to this Space Camp pretty badly," his mother said. Her eyes were full of sympathy, if not enthusiasm.

Ben nodded and looked at her intently.

"Nothing's more important than exploring the rest of the universe, Mom," he said. "I guess I want to be a part of that."

"You want to be an explorer, is that it? A modern-day Christopher Columbus . . ."

"Yeah. Why not? It's exciting that we can even think about exploring new worlds. There's gotta be something out there, Mom. New life, planets, people. And if they're there, they can probably help us. Maybe they know how to cure all our diseases and wipe out war and hunger—"

His mother smiled, enjoying the outburst of passion for what he considered a noble cause. But she was practical, too. Neither a grownup nor a boy could base his life on there being benevolent aliens somewhere in outer space waiting to be befriended and cultivated. He had to think about life here on Earth, look for goals that could be pursued in his own hometown or country. Someday Ben's passion would diminish and he would look back on this period in his life with amusement, but now he was deadly serious. His mother wanted to encourage him. She did not, however, want to lead him down a garden path.

"Where on earth do you get all this from?" she asked, looking around his room at the science fiction paraphernalia clinging to walls and dangling from the ceiling. "It certainly doesn't come from your father and me. We were both rotten in science."

"I know," Ben said.

She sighed and touched his cheek. "Ben, honey," she said. "It's great that you want to learn more about the universe and everything. You're interested in things and we're proud of you . . . and even if we don't know what you're talking about all the time, I do know it's important to go ahead and do what you want."

She got up and walked to the window. "Sometimes I wish I'd done some things," she said in a voice so soft it was almost a whisper.

Ben waited. Was she giving him the go-ahead on Space Camp or not?

"Well," his mother said finally. "I just hope you understand."

"That I can't go to Space Camp?" Ben asked, determined to solve it one way or the other.

His mother frowned. "I don't see how it's possible this summer," she replied. "There are too many variables . . . But let's not give up. Sleep tight."

She kissed him lightly on the cheek and then started for the door, as if she wanted to wrap up this unpleasant mission as quickly as possible.

"'Night," Ben said.

Alone again, he stared out the window at the stars and worlds beyond. Suddenly he felt uncomfortable and restricted in this room that offered only one tiny square for viewing the heavens. He needed space, vistas, a whole sky to look at. Getting out of bed, he grabbed his walkie-talkie and climbed the ladder from his room to the roof, enjoying the coolness of the night air on his face as he lifted it toward the limitless world above. Young as he was, he knew that while there were few things in life that could be truly counted on, the universe as a whole was consistent. It offered excitement, mystery, knowledge and opportunity to those bold enough to search for it. Ben was determined, now more than ever, to pursue his goals. Feeling that he was back in his element at last, he fell onto the sleeping bag he kept on the roof and looked up at the sky.

It was a crystal clear night. Directly above him, a plane moved from north to south, its lights blinking. The starry cloud of the Milky Way was visible, the most dramatic attraction of the sky until, quite suddenly, a falling star streaked downward. Ben closed his eyes and pictured an instant replay from close up. Now the churning, boiling mass of flame came twisting at him, no longer a beautiful, faraway wisp of light but an incredibly powerful and destructive force, a hundred times bigger than the sun, whirling through the universe. He wondered what it would be like out there during this episode.

A buzzing sound interrupted his fantasy. It was his walkie-talkie. Picking it up quickly, he hit the talk button.

"Yeah?" he said.

"It's working again," Wolfgang said simply.

"You're kidding!"

"Would I kid about a thing like this at midnight?" Wolfgang demanded.

"I guess not. How did it happen? Did it start all by itself?"

"Maybe you'd better come over."

"Sure. I'll be right there."

"Give me about ten minutes. I think my father's gonna make one more tour of the house checking for insects. Then he's off to bed."

"Right."

"And be quiet."

"Naturally. See you in a little while."

Ben's mood was totally different now. No longer was he depressed at his father's lack of imagination and understanding. The mystery generated by his dream of the night before was ready to yield new clues. Ben could hardly wait for the next act to begin.

Usually Darren slept easily, despite living in a house that was anything but peaceful. But tonight was different. Mona and his father had continued their argument of the day before, an exchange of invectives, threats and counterthreats that should have lulled him to sleep. At least that was the way it had happened in the past.

It was now past midnight, however, and Darren was rolling and tossing as if he had just awakened from a round-the-clock snooze. A few minutes before, Mona and his father had lapsed into silence, making Darren's wide-awake condition even more pronounced. In desperation, he got out of bed and did his homework, but even that failed to sedate him.

"What the hell's the matter?" he whispered.

A large part of the problem, he knew, could be traced to events that had taken place in the Muller home earlier that evening. Darren continued to replay them in his mind, although he had no desire to envision them again. He was nagged by the fear that a clever trick had been played on him, one so smoothly executed that he had absolutely no idea what had happened. Being more practical than philosophical, Darren did not ponder why Ben and Wolfgang had pulled the trick nearly as much as *how* they had done it. The circular holes in the books and wood and wall were so sharp and even! How had they managed that? For several minutes, he lay in bed wondering what sort of equipment was necessary to perform such a stunt. Finally, when the sound of heavy snoring told him his father was asleep, he got up, pulled on a shirt and tiptoed to the door.

The night air was cool and bracing, the stars unusually bright. Darren stood a moment on the back porch and looked around, rather enjoying this moment of solitude. Then, remembering why he had gotten up, he stumbled across the backyard toward a small, broken-down toolshed at the rear of the property. It was secured by a lock, the key to which was hidden under the cinder block foundation. Locating the key, Darren let himself inside and switched on the overhead light of his secret kingdom.

It was not much of a realm, or at least not a very elegant one. The single ten-by-ten room consisted principally of three work benches on which a variety of objects were stored. These consisted of old gasoline engines, secondhand tools, lathes, axles, buckets of machine parts soaking in motor oil and piles of nuts and bolts of every conceivable size and shape. The walls of the room were bare except for a two-year-old calendar and several notes Darren had written to himself.

Somewhere in the room was an old paperback book. He had seen it just the other day and had considered throwing it away. Now he was glad he hadn't, although the book was not in plain sight. He finally located it in a storage box, looked at it for a second, and then put it down on a clear area of one work bench.

"Now," he muttered. "Let's see how we can do this."

In the same storage box, he found a metal-punching tool approximately the same diameter as the hole that had appeared "miraculously" in the books and wood at Wolfgang's house. He checked the edge to make sure it was sharp. Satisfied, he put the hole-puncher on the book, found a four-pound hammer, lifted it well above his head, and then delivered a powerful blow.

When he lifted the hole-puncher, he was amazed and disappointed to see that it had barely made it through the cover. By page three of the book, even the outline of the blow wasn't visible. Examining the book carefully, he saw that the hole which had been made was rough around the edges rather than smooth, as had been the case at Wolfgang's.

"I don't get it," Darren muttered. "Even if they used something like this, it would take weeks to cut a hole through all those books."

He frowned, had a second and third bash at the book to see if it was easier once the cardboard cover was penetrated. It was slightly less difficult, each blow cutting through about a dozen pages. But when he tried to pull out the severed paper circle, the edges tore or separated in small, jagged sections.

"This looks like hell," he said. "I'd give ten bucks to know how they did it."

He looked at his watch. It was much too late to call either Ben or Wolfgang, but he was wider awake than ever. Shrugging into his jacket, he closed up the toolshed and returned to the house.

At the door, he paused and thought, one foot poised on the porch step.

"Nah," he said finally. "I'll never get to sleep. I'll take a walk instead."

Ten minutes later, as he trudged past one dimly lit house after another, he spotted movement in one back yard. A figure was balanced on the top of a wooden fence, one leg on each side. It remained in that position for a fraction of a second before swinging its right leg over and dropping silently to the ground. Darren watched, intrigued. What else could it be but a burglar?

Although he had no intention of trying to intercept the person, Darren reasoned that at least he could watch for suspicious activity and perhaps report it to the police. A tingle of excitement ran up his spine as he moved diagonally across the front yard in an attempt to keep the silhouette in view. Then familiar objects began to appear—a battered television set, a washing machine with a missing top, an oscilloscope, and beyond them, a gaping open garage door.

"Wait a second," Darren whispered. "This is that guy's house."

It was indeed the Muller's house. Now, at a better vantage point, Darren could see that the dark figure was that of Ben Crandall.

"Good," he said to himself. "Now maybe I'll find out what those guys are up to."

Creeping close to the house, he looked into the basement window. Inside, surrounded by his sophisticated equipment, his junk, and his talking mouse, was Wolfgang, obviously ready to begin some bizarre addendum to his previous experiment.

As soon as his father went to bed, Wolfgang switched on all the basement lights so that Ben would know it was all right to let himself in the back door. A few minutes later, following a somewhat scary run through the woods and along the creek bed, Ben climbed the fence behind the house and rapped lightly on the door before entering. Wolfgang was standing next to the Apple computer, staring down at it, his face tinged with the machine's blue illumination.

"Well," Ben said, still slightly out of breath from his run. "What is it?"

Wolfgang didn't answer. Instead, he looked in the direction of a thump and glared at Erhart, the cat, leaping down off the work bench. The cat had been toying with the catch of Heinlein's cage but had not succeeded in opening it.

"So what is it?" Ben repeated.

Wolfgang answered by putting his finger over his lips. "You're talking too loud," he said.

"I didn't realize—"

"Shhh."

Wolfgang looked upstairs and winced. "Calm down," he said. "You can't get emotional if you're going to study anything scientifically."

"Sorry. Was my voice that loud?"

"It had a sharp quality to it," Wolfgang replied. "The excitement carried."

"Maybe that's because I'm excited."

"Well, don't be. We have to be very cool and collected about this. It's something new and far out, but we can't allow ourselves to be thrown by it."

"I understand," Ben nodded. He exhaled deeply and forced himself to relax.

As if to underline the everyday quality of the experiment and keep himself from being carried away, Wolfgang began to pace around the basement, speaking very professorially. One could almost imagine an audience of fellow scientists taking notes as he delivered his lecture.

"Now what we have here," he said, "is, as near as I can tell, an electrically generated point of force."

"You said that before," Ben interrupted. "But I wasn't sure what you meant."

"It's simply a force that moves in response to electrical impulse. Think of it as a kind of laser, or a ball of energy that we can push around." He moved to the computer. "Now, by typing in coordinates, I can make this point of force move anywhere in three dimensions, even as far as slamming it through a few books and a concrete retaining wall. I shall now demonstrate how the point of force works."

He switched on the machine, which immediately began to make its familiar sound, and typed in some instructions. "There," he said finally, looking up in the air in front of the bench.

"Where?" Ben asked.

"Just above the work bench," Wolfgang replied, a slight edge of annoyance in his voice.

"Why can't we see it?"

"Because there's too much light."

With that, Wolfgang reached up to turn off the overhead lights. The entire basement was thrown into almost complete darkness, the computer being the sole light source. Then, as their eyes adjusted to the new darkness, Wolfgang and Ben were able to see the outline of a tiny bubble near the work bench. It hung stationary in the air, giving off a slight bluish glow. They stared at it with mouths open, as if they were seeing something from another world.

"God," they said together.

Despite his calm, even blasé, exterior, Wolfgang was every bit as awed as Ben. His throat felt as if a hard hot lump were obstructing his breathing and everything in his field of vision seemed to shake a little. Forcing himself to become more objective, he began to speak in his previous didatic tone of voice.

"Now then," he murmured. "I'm going to reference the point of force to this grid I did of my room on my graphics program."

He punched more keys and a simple overhead line drawing of the basement area appeared on the screen. When he typed in more data, a small X appeared in one corner.

"That's it?" Ben asked.

Wolfgang nodded.

"Make it fly," Ben smiled.

"Will do."

Wolfgang carefully typed in some information, looking at the bubble of light as he did so. Slowly, almost imperceptibly at first, it started to move, tracing a short horizontal line above the work bench.

Ben felt a rush of excitement. If people had done this before, he had never heard of it.

As the two boys stood watching the shifting bubble, Darren crept closer to the Muller house. A few minutes before, he had seen the basement lights go on and then, not long after that, off. Now he saw a weird, undulating illumination coming from the room and he wanted to know what it was. Edging across the lawn, he looked into the window. Wolfgang and Ben were standing as in a trance, staring at something in the air near them. The computer was on, its screen showing a bright diagram.

Darren shook his head and frowned. It looked as if the two strange characters were being hypnotized. For a moment, he experienced a sensation of panic. He was basically a tough and courageous young man, but this was something he didn't understand. If Ben and Wolfgang had invented some sort of computer voodoo and were now under its spell, that was perfectly all right with him. They could play with it, be captivated by it, do anything they wanted with it so long as Darren wasn't part of the game. Nevertheless, despite his nervousness, Darren remained rooted to the spot, fascinated.

Inside, Ben and Wolfgang continued to watch the bubble for another minute, content to change the coordinates ever so slightly and see their newfound creation respond. Then Wolfgang finally broke the silence.

"Would you like to see something else?" he suggested.

"Sure."

"I think I can change its size."

"All right!" Ben whispered.

"This variable ought to do it," Wolfgang said, punching some new data into the machine.

As he did so, the bubble grew slightly, its diameter increasing to about three inches. It looked like a softball suspended in the air.

"Great," Ben said breathlessly. "How far do you think you can go with it?"

"The sky's the limit," Wolfgang replied. "I guess we could make it as big as the world if we wanted to."

"Well, don't," Ben cautioned, suddenly fearful of the floating object.

"Don't worry."

As they watched the orb, a sudden noise caused them both to jump. It was Heinlein's scratching, followed almost immediately by the sound of his voice synthesizer.

"I would like . . ." it began.

The boys waited, expecting the usual cheese plea.

Instead, the synthesizer added, "to come out."

Wolfgang shook his head, turned back to the computer, punched more keys and watched the larger bubble move up and down.

Ben was thinking about something else, however. Heinlein had given him an idea.

"Sure," he said. "Why not?"

He went to the cage, took out the mouse and allowed it to crawl onto the tip of a broom handle he found sitting near the work bench.

"What the heck are you doing?" Wolfgang scolded. "Why play with him now?"

Ben grinned and moved the broom handle near the floating bubble.

"What are you doing?" Wolfgang demanded.

"Our first space traveler," Ben said with a smile.

"What?"

"Turn it off."

Still somewhat puzzled, Wolfgang turned off the force field. Ben raised the mouse until it was in the space last occupied by the bubble.

"Now you can turn it on," he said.

Wolfgang smiled. Now he understood. What an excellent idea—to see if the bubble could hold objects placed inside it or if they merely spilled through its skin. Heinlein hovered in midair, perfectly contained by the bubble. But an instant later, Wolfgang frowned.

"What's the matter?" Ben asked, noticing Wolfgang's hesitation.

"No . . ." he murmured.

He pressed some keys and looked at Ben. "Catch him," he said. "I'm turning him loose."

"But why?" Ben asked, even as Heinlein fell into his hands.

Wolfgang's mind was racing with pros and cons regarding the situation. On the one hand, it made sense to use Heinlein as the "first space traveler" in their new vehicle. The possibility of his being killed or injured was slight, especially in view of the fact that if anything untoward seemed about to happen, Wolfgang could simply cut him loose. On the other hand, suppose the bubble had something lethal inside, some gas or invisible substance that destroyed living things? Wolfgang was a scientist in every sense of the word, but he was not into testing animals without a very good experimental reason and under very controlled conditions. This situation qualified for neither category.

"Why?" he replied. "Because we might hurt him, that's why. We don't even know if that bubble will hold his weight."

"It did for a few seconds."

"And we don't know what sort of atmosphere is inside that globe."

"Okay." Ben shrugged, putting Heinlein back in his cage.

Outside the house, Darren stared in frozen disbelief at the sight of the floating mouse and continued to look at the bubble even after Ben had put the mouse back in its cage. Shaking his head in awe, he was completely taken by the display that defied gravity and logic. What were those guys into, anyway? Black magic, or just plain magic? He remembered seeing a show on television once in which a magician caused large animals to "disappear," but never had he seen anything quite like this.

"The heck with it," he whispered finally. "Even if they zap me, I've gotta find out what those guys are up to."

Reaching down, he rapped on the window and moved his face even closer to the glass.

"What's that?" Wolfgang said, taking his gaze from the bubble and looking around the basement.

"It's somebody at the window," Ben said in alarm.

Wolfgang's first thought was that it was his father. As soon as he had gone to bed, Wolfgang had locked the door to the basement in order to have complete privacy during the experiment. Was it possible his father had become so curious he had gone outside to spy on them? He had never done that before—at least not to Wolfgang's knowledge.

A moment later, Ben relieved his anxieties about his father by saying, "It's Darren."

"Darren who?"

"The guy who was here this afternoon."

"Oh."

Wolfgang wasn't sure that his father wouldn't have been a preferable interloper. At least he could trust him to keep everything within the walls of the Muller home. Darren, on the other hand, was an unknown quantity. If he immediately went back to school and blabbed to everyone—

As if divining Wolfgang's apprehension, Ben said quickly, "He's okay. He practically saved my life and he's a loner. He won't tell anybody."

"Are you sure?"

"Yeah. And if we let him in with us, he'll be even more dependable, I bet."

"Okay," Wolfgang muttered.

Ben tripped the latch on the basement window and Darren squeezed through.

"What's going on?" he asked.

"We're experimenting with something," Ben explained. "And why are you out so late, anyway?"

"I couldn't sleep. So I took a walk. When I saw somebody climb over the fence in back, I thought it might be a burglar so I followed."

"That was me," Ben said.

Wolfgang hit some keys on the computer, causing the bubble to bounce up and down at his command.

"Do you believe me now?" Ben asked, nudging Darren with his elbow.

"Believe you about what? I know crazy things are going on down here, but what's to believe or not believe?"

"Do you believe that we're working on something very scientific?" Wolfgang asked. "As I said, we've constructed a point of force which can be moved by putting new coordinates in the computer. That's what cut the holes through the books, not some trick we played."

"Okay." Darren nodded. "I believe you guys aren't into tricks. How's that?"

"Your apology is accepted," said Wolfgang.

"So how's that bubble stay up there?" Darren asked.

"A point of force is not governed by the ordinary rules of gravity," Ben explained. "Right, Wolfgang?"

"Right."

"Can you fly it around a little?" Darren asked, smiling.

"Sure!"

With that, Wolfgang returned to the computer and began punching new data into the machine. As he did so, the little opaque globule jiggled in place, then began to move through the air above the work bench in slow, graceful arcs. Darren and Ben could not restrain themselves from laughing, the sight was so outrageous. Even Wolfgang grinned and chuckled as he put the object through its paces.

"You see?" he said. "It's very easy to control and you can make it go anywhere."

Hoping to get a rise out of Ben, Wolfgang typed in coordinates that would cause the bubble to fly directly at his head, swooping away just in the nick of time. The maneuver worked too perfectly, however. When he saw the object whirling toward him, Ben emitted a little yelp and leaped backwards. He fell against Wolfgang, who in turn fell against the computer. Before he could regain his balance, Wolfgang's hand struck the keyboard, accidentally programming a line of random data into the machine.

"Watch it!" he yelled.

The warning was appropriate. As if possessed of a

mind of its own, the bubble suddenly began spinning in weird, disjointed flight patterns, making 180-degree turns on top of 270-degree ones. Up and down and backwards it flew, knocking over cans and tools right and left. The three boys had to fall to the floor or nearly perform backflips to avoid the dive-bombing object. Wolfgang, still worried about his parents waking up, made a valiant effort to catch as many falling objects as possible and was generally successful. Finally, all three found themselves prone on the cold basement floor, their necks twisted unnaturally so that they could watch the aerial show above them.

"Holy cow," Darren gasped. "If that thing hits us, can it do a lot of damage?"

"You gotta be kidding," Wolfgang shot back. "Didn't you see what it did to those books this afternoon?"

As he spoke, the force field zoomed toward the refrigerator, struck its side with a heavy rifle-like report, and then emerged through the opposite side, hurling several cans of fizzing soda out the hole after it.

"Holy—" Darren gasped, ducking so violently that his face struck the floor and choked off whatever was intended to follow.

"How long—?" Ben shouted to Wolfgang.

The bubble roared over their heads, hung a U-turn and then headed directly toward Erhart the cat. Crouching in a corner, the cat's tail was nearly as big as the animal itself, its eyes wide and whiskers bristling as the force field raced toward it. With a hiss and shriek of terror, it freaked out completely, rolling over, stumbling and jumping into things as the bubble pursued it across the room.

Wolfgang raised his head far enough to catch a glimpse of the computer screen. The X was zipping back and forth on the line drawing of the room, its pictorialized collisions coinciding with offscreen noises as it crashed into real-life objects in the room. Ducking just in time to avoid the force field, Wolfgang saw it strike a storage case, popping it open to reveal a shelf of expensive crystal glasses and decanters. Whirling in a tight circle in front of the case, it sent the glasses teetering on the edge of the shelf, their rims striking each other and sending forth a tinkly symphony of sound.

"No!" Wolfgang wheezed.

Hurling his body forward along the floor of the basement, he reached the storage case just as the delicate glasses plunged over the edge. Displaying remarkable dexterity and coordination, Wolfgang managed to catch all of them before they hit the floor.

No sooner had he placed the last one in position than another shotgun-like blast tore through the basement. Wolfgang looked up in time to see concrete shards falling to the floor from the hole where the force field had just cut its way out of the Muller home. There was a long moment of eerie silence, followed almost immediately by the squeal of car brakes, a dog barking and a crash. Wolfgang scrambled to his feet. So did Ben, both heading for the basement window in order to see what was happening outside.

"Look out!" Ben yelled.

The bubble, moving even faster now, was headed back into the house via the window through which they now peered.

Crash! Tinkle!

Wolfgang and Ben barely had time to pull their heads back before the force field blasted its way through the basement window, scattering glass everywhere.

"Turn it off!" Ben yelled.

Wolfgang raced back to the machine. Even as his fingers moved toward the keys, he wondered how the random pattern triggered by the accident could have produced such a prolonged sequence of maneuvers and destruction. Then the thought was erased from his mind as he concentrated to input the data that would bring the force field to a halt.

Pressing a series of buttons, he saw the bubble execute a few final acts of vandalism before finally coming to rest in the air above the work bench.

The silence that followed was broken only by the sounds of three long, overlapping sighs of relief.

"Of course," Wolfgang said at length. "I must have struck some keys that caused it to execute a repeating pattern or series of minor variations. Otherwise—"

The sound of footsteps upstairs caused Wolfgang to look apprehensively toward the cellar door. The basement was an utter shambles, as if a bomb or cyclone had struck it. He had no idea how to explain it, should his parents come down to investigate the noise.

"Wolfgang?" a feminine voice called.

"Oh, great, that's my mom." Wolfgang sighed. "God, I never get to have any fun."

"What's all that noise?" his mother asked.

"Nothing."

"Nothing? I'm coming down to see exactly what nothing is because it certainly sounded like something."

Wolfgang's face paled. "Don't come down," he called up the stairs. "I'll be right up."

"What's going on?" his mother persisted. "Are you alone down there?"

"Yeah, Mom. Just a minute."

Tiptoeing back to Darren and Ben, Wolfgang whispered to them. "Wait till I'm gone and then sneak out the back door, okay?"

Ben nodded.

"Wolfgang!"

"Coming, Mother!"

Wolfgang raced halfway up the stairs. His mother was standing on the top landing, wearing a housedress, her hair wild and very unattractive.

"What in God's name was going on down there?" she demanded. "It sounded like a car wreck."

"I was trying to determine the relationship between how large an object is and how much sound it makes when it strikes the floor . . ."

"At one o'clock in the morning?"

"That's the only time it's quiet enough," Wolfgang adlibbed. "Other times there's too much background noise from trucks and cars and stuff."

"I think you've lost your mind."

"It could be valuable research, Mom," Wolfgang said. "But if you want me to stop, I'll stop."

"Why don't you want me to come downstairs?"

"Because I made a mess. But if you give me fifteen minutes, I'll have it all cleaned up."

"You didn't break anything valuable, did you?" his mother asked, her eyes narrowing suspiciously.

"No, ma'am," Wolfgang said truthfully. "The crystal glasses are all okay."

"Come up here a minute."

Wolfgang disappeared up the stairs. Darren and Ben looked at each other. Ben tapped the computer thoughtfully.

"Well, what did you think?" he asked in a low voice.

"Interesting."

"Is that all?"

"Okay. It was mind-blowing."

"You're darn right."

"But what good is it?" Darren asked. "What are you going to do with it now?"

"Experiment," Ben replied, a playful gleam in his eye.

Chapter Four

"EXPERIMENT WITH WHAT?" DARREN ASKED AS HE AND Ben walked home. "Or who?"

Except for five or six cars far away on the interstate highway, there was no traffic on the streets and no pedestrians to be seen. A bit of a breeze was blowing, bringing with it some low-hanging clouds that blocked out most of the stars. Ben took a deep breath of the cold night air before answering, partly because it felt good and partly because he needed time to think about his reply. In fact, the most intriguing use of the force field, to his way of thinking, was neither scientific nor beneficial to mankind as a whole.

He wanted to see the inside of Lori Swenson's room.

The notion had struck him while he was lying on the basement floor at Wolfgang's, dodging the dive-bombing bubble. Whatever it was that carried the powerful object over their heads, through a refrigerator and concrete, was a perfect see-through space vehicle. One could go anywhere and see anything with it. Of course, as scientists they were duty-bound to undertake only noble missions, but as a sort of warmup exercise . . .

He looked at Darren and shrugged, deciding not to reveal his mundane but exciting plans for their discovery. Instead he said, "Well, we don't know what that thing can really do, how big it can get, how much weight it can support, how fast it can go. It's almost too much to think of right now. We'll start slow and find out what we have."

"Yeah."

Inwardly, Darren was imagining himself seated in the bubble, spying on the girls as they undressed for gym and showered afterward. The picture brought a sudden grin to his face and a chuckle.

"What?" Ben asked.

"Nothing."

"You were thinking of something funny."

Darren nodded. He had to admit that, of course, but he didn't have to tell why he was amused. "I was just thinking," he said, "of how silly we must have looked lying on Wolfgang's floor trying to stay out of that thing's way."

Ben laughed. Then, as they continued their brisk walk home, he went back to thinking about Lori.

The ordinary task of going to school, though never exactly enjoyable, suddenly became onerous to all three boys. Now they thought of little else but their next session with the force field. Instead of concentrating on their classes, they daydreamed of what might be possible or mulled over what had already happened. Two days were spent in further testing with the circuit board and computer in Wolfgang's basement. The bubble had been expanded and contracted, prodded and moved, until it became obvious that more space was needed. Wolfgang therefore set about devising a means of making the computer-monitor portable, fashioning a carrying case and power pack so that they could take their force field (or "the thing," as they called it) anywhere.

Today, Wednesday, was their first time in the open air and Ben was so nervous and excited he could hardly sit still. Two teachers commented on his squirming and a third threatened to send him to the principal's office if he didn't stop sliding back and forth in his seat. Somehow he got through the day, although he wasn't sure how.

An hour after school let out, the three boys could be seen running through a field and up the side of a hill overlooking the town. Ben and Wolfgang moved ahead, each carrying a walkie-talkie, several tools and a notepad. Behind them came the workhorse of their team, Darren, his biceps bulging as he lugged the heavy case containing the computer, monitor, and power pack. Every once in a while, he grimaced and made a sarcastic reference to their so-called "portable" unit.

"This is portable only if you're a pack mule," he said as they neared the top of the hill.

Wolfgang nodded. "I can see where it's a drag," he agreed, "but everything has to be together. I didn't know how else to arrange it."

"You could have put the power pack in one case and the computer in another," Darren suggested.

"Then we'd have had to buy a ton of cable. The heavy kind. Very expensive."

"Not half as expensive as a hernia operation," Darren replied.

"Maybe we can fix up something with wheels," Ben offered.

"Wheels wouldn't work on ground like this," Darren said, stumbling over the heavy ruts and avoiding several large rocks on the hillside.

"Well, let's do the best we can," Wolfgang said, by way of ending the conversation.

Arriving at the summit of the hill, they paused to look around. The air was chilly, the sky filled with heavy cumulus clouds, painted with mysterious shadows by the low-lying sun. At the bottom of the hill, the houses and other landmarks of the town seemed only vaguely familiar, viewed at this unusual perspective. Ben noticed that Lori Swenson's house was plainly visible, white and pristine.

"Well, let's start," Ben said.

To his annoyance, Wolfgang made no attempt to hook up the computer and start things rolling. Instead, he picked up a pad and flowpen and began to draw.

"What's that?" Darren asked.

"I'm making a rough sketch of the terrain in graphics mode for referencing," he replied.

"Oh," Darren said. "You're making a drawing."

"That's what I said."

"What are we gonna do when you're finished?"

"Never mind for now. I'll look for something we can experiment with."

Wolfgang finished the drawing, inserted it into the computer and turned away to ponder the situation. When he noticed Ben about to touch the keyboard, he quickly held up a hand.

"Don't touch that," he warned.

Ben felt a surge of resentment. Since he'd made the discovery, Wolfgang had become more and more dictatorial. He seemed almost to have forgotten that it was Ben who had gotten the ball rolling. Ben could also work the computer, although not as skillfully as Wolfgang. But that was only because Wolfgang was more familiar with the machine and had more hours of practice on it.

"Get Mr. Professor," Ben muttered to Darren as Wolfgang walked away. "It's my dream and I can touch it if I want. As a matter of fact—"

He reached out and turned the computer on.

"Come on, don't mess with it," Darren urged.

"I'm not gonna make any executive decisions," Ben said. "I just want to get things warmed up."

He touched the keyboard until the screen showed a circular display floating over the rough sketch of the landscape made by Wolfgang.

"That's where it'll be when it comes on," Ben explained, pleased with himself.

Darren was impressed. "Great," he said. "But it'll be bigger than that, right? Wolfgang will make it bigger when he comes back."

"What do you mean—Wolfgang?" Ben demanded. "I can do that as easy as he can."

Remembering Wolfgang's technique, he pressed several buttons and was gratified—and, although he wouldn't have admitted it, surprised—to see the orb enlarge.

"Cool," Darren said with a smile.

"Come on, Wolfgang," Ben said to himself rather than to his partner, who was still studying the lay of the land. He was visible on the computer screen now, a lone figure just below the bubble.

"The thing's not on yet, right?" Darren asked.

"Right."

"How do you make it come on?"

"Simple." Ben said. "Like this."

He pressed a switch.

With a loud crack, the force field expanded and moved downward, its lower rim encompassing Wolfgang on the screen and spinning the figure sideways.

"God!" Darren shouted.

They looked at the spot where the real-life Wolfgang had been. Now they saw a computer representation of his figure, canted at a thirty-degree angle, the feet slightly off the ground. Because the force field was soundproof, Ben and Darren could hear nothing from their friend, but each could well imagine the words and noises that were emanating from the shocked and frightened figure.

"You trapped him inside!" Darren yelled. "What did you do that for?"

"I didn't mean to!" Ben gasped.

Ben stared numbly at the console screen, which showed a vector graphic of Wolfgang inside the force field. He hadn't a clue how to help him.

"Do something!" Darren shouted.

Ben looked down at the keys, then at the spiraling graphic of Wolfgang. What had he done wrong? What could he do to rectify his mistake?

"God, I didn't know it could get that big!" Darren shouted.

"Me neither," Ben replied, awed. Then, catching sight of the soles of Wolfgang's sneakers, which were being buffeted about by the bottom of the force field, he added, "I could have cut off his toe or something."

"Turn it off, man," Darren urged. "Get him out! He's in trouble!"

"Yeah," Ben muttered. "I see."

On the brink of panic himself, he had no desire to stampede Darren, so he did his best to appear calm. He may have seemed cool on the surface, but underneath he was ready to snap; his brain had ceased to function clearly; all he could do was touch the keys, hoping he would trigger some magic combination that would free his friend.

The combination produced magic, but not the kind

Ben or Wolfgang needed. Instead of disappearing, the force field took off like a shot, moving through the grass so precipitously that it threw back a shower of green, hanging like a curtain in the late afternoon air. Inside the spinning globe, Wolfgang was turned upside-down, sideways, then upside-down again.

"Get him out!" Darren shouted, nervously hopping in place.

"Okay! Okay!" Ben yelled back, but his hands continued to hesitate above the keys. Now darker thoughts had taken over his mind. Suppose he accidentally caused the bubble to collapse with Wolfgang inside? Suppose he sent it someplace where it couldn't be retrieved? There were dozens of things he could do to endanger his friend. Why had he been so foolish as to operate a machine he knew comparatively little about?

"Go ahead!" Darren urged.

"I don't know what to do," Ben confessed.

"Well, you better do something."

Ben knew Darren was right. Grabbing Wolfgang's notepad, he flipped through the pages, trying to find a key to freeing him. Meanwhile, the force field was carrying Wolfgang along the surface at speeds of up to sixty miles an hour, banging stones and large logs out of the way as it tore from one side of the hill to the other.

Ben made a decision and punched a brief code into the computer.

Wolfgang promptly disappeared, he and the force field suddenly taking a sharp curve and plunging straight down into the ground.

"God!" Darren yelled.

He raced to the edge of the spot where the bubble had just entered the earth. The opening was six feet wide and as smooth as glass around the edges. A light dust shower was rising from the fissure as Darren peered inside. He strained his eyes but could see no sign of Wolfgang. It was like looking down a mine shaft or a very deep well. Only a faraway churning noise from deep in the bowels of the earth indicated that something was still going on.

"Where is he?" Darren screamed.

"I don't know," Ben replied, wringing his hands over the computer keyboard. He tried another set of figures, his fingers now almost unmanageable because of his panic and anxiety.

"I'm trying to bring him up!" he yelled. "It's like *Journey to the Center of the Earth* or something!"

"Will you get real!" Darren shouted back. "He's on his way to China!"

Ben felt his eyes burning as perspiration poured into them from his forehead. What had happened as a result of the last data he'd entered? Even the low rumbling beneath them had stopped. Was Wolfgang plunging ever downward into the molten center of the earth? Or was there still a slight possibility that he could be freed from the vertigo express Ben had unwittingly shipped him aboard? Now, at least, Ben had a nucleus of a plan. If the force field and Wolfgang appeared for the briefest moment, he would pull the power plug on the computer. That would send everything back to square one—he hoped. But even as he devised and congratulated himself on the idea, a new fear entered his mind. There could be only so much air trapped inside the force field. If Wolfgang didn't get out soon, he was in danger of asphyxiation and a horrible death.

"Come on," he breathed. "Come back, damn it, just for a second!"

As he spoke, his finger slipped and struck a digit on the computer keyboard. Darren, reconciled to his earlier fear that Ben was no expert with the computer, stared straight ahead with dread in his eyes. He had known Wolfgang only a few days, but during that brief time had done a complete U-turn on his feelings for the brainy little guy. He hadn't liked him much at first and he felt a twinge of guilt for that. Now he realized what Wolfgang was worth, both as a budding scientist and a person. It was a tragedy that he should be cheated out of what promised to be a very productive life.

"There's nothing you can think of to do?" Darren asked during the sudden silence.

"Just one thing," Ben mumbled. "But we have to wait."

Suddenly he cocked his head, straining his ears. Was the rumbling sound coming back? Darren, picking up the notion, did likewise, and was rewarded by hearing the low burrowing noise, increasing in volume every second.

"Here he comes!" he shouted. "He's coming back! It can't be anything else!"

"Don't veer off," Ben prayed. He looked down at the computer and took a good grip on the power cable.

The rumble was quite loud now and was rapidly approaching deafening volume. Darren and Ben both put their hands over their ears as they waited.

A second later, they felt the ground beneath them shake and start to bulge, giant cracks forming several yards away and spreading outward in a circular pattern. Darren wanted to jump, but he didn't know where; Ben experienced the same sensation of panic, but knew he had to keep his hand on the power cable. For him, there was simply no choice. He had engineered this harrowing problem with his stupidity. The only way to rectify his error was to stand his ground and give Wolfgang another chance to live.

Suddenly the ground humped up beneath them and exploded! Catching a glimpse of the force field as it roared past him, only inches from his ear, Ben ripped the power cable free from the computer. Then he was lying on the ground, staring at clouds and sky. The roaring sound had stopped and all he could hear was the normal sounds of civilization—traffic from the freeway and town.

"Wolfgang!" he yelled, leaping to his feet and looking around.

Neither his friend nor the bubble was anywhere to be seen!

"What the hell happened?" Ben whispered.

Darren was just a few feet away, his expression as terror-stricken as Ben's, his head swiveling upward in a circle as he sought to catch sight of the force field.

"He's gone again," Darren muttered.

"No!" Ben shouted, his expression somewhere between a laugh and a gasp. "There he is!"

He pointed off to the right, toward a thick oak tree. Wolfgang could be seen plainly, hanging from one of the top branches, his mouth open and working with almost uncontrollable laughter. It was the first time Ben had ever seen him in such an unguarded state; the sight caused him to start laughing, too, the recent panic evaporating completely.

He and Darren ran over to the tree and stood below the dangling figure.

"Are you okay?" Ben yelled.

Between giggles, Wolfgang managed to nod. He appeared well, physically, although Ben had considerable doubt concerning his mental status.

"What was it like?" Ben asked.

"Hey, let's get him down first," Darren suggested. "Hanging like that's gotta hurt after a while."

"He doesn't look like he's hurting," Ben smiled.

"I'm okay," Wolfgang called down.

Reaching one hand behind his back, he freed himself from a small branch, pulled himself into the Y of the trunk, and sat there a moment, getting his breath.

"Hurry up," Ben said. "I can't stand it, not knowing what it was like."

Wolfgang smothered the last few bursts of merriment and dropped to the ground. His face was slightly scratched and his hair mussed, but otherwise he looked little the worse for wear.

"It was fun, most of the time." He smiled. "Especially when it went underground. I could see it carving its way through dirt and stone and everything. We even went through somebody's septic tank, I think."

Darren and Ben chuckled.

"But near the end, I was having trouble breathing," Wolfgang continued. "It's airtight. At least we found that out, the hard way. So I almost passed out."

"How about when it turned you upside-down?" Ben asked. "Did that make you dizzy?"

Wolfgang shook his head. "That's something that was weird," he said. "I knew I was upside-down because that's the way everything looked, but there wasn't any vertigo. I couldn't even feel myself speed up or slow down."

"You couldn't!" Darren ejaculated. "That's incredible! You were going from zero to sixty in about two seconds."

"It didn't feel like anything," Wolfgang said. Then he grabbed Ben by the front of his shirt. "Do you realize what this means?" he cried, his eyes very wide now, his expression verging on the maniacal.

"You say it," Ben replied.

"Traegheitslosigkeit," Wolfgang said.

"What?" Darren asked.

Wolfgang said the word phonetically. *"Tray-kites-low-zick-kite,"* he smiled.

"Say again," Ben murmured.

"Troglodytes?" Darren offered.

"No, guys. *Traegheitslosigkeit.* It's German for 'no inertia.' "

"No inertia," Darren repeated. "That's great. I'm not even sure what inertia is."

"Inertia is what keeps things the same," Wolfgang explained. "Objects that are standing still tend to remain standing still and objects moving tend to keep moving in the same direction . . ."

"Sounds like my house," Darren said.

". . . unless they're changed by an external force," Wolfgang continued.

"What are you saying?" Ben asked.

"That this force field isn't affected by the laws of inertia," Wolfgang said. "When you're sitting in a car and it suddenly stops, inertia is what throws you forward through the windshield. When you're sitting in a car that suddenly zooms forward, inertia is what causes you to have your head snapped back. Get it? But in that bubble I was turned every which way at all sorts of speeds and I couldn't even feel it. So—no inertia to fool with. That's what makes travel in that thing so easy."

Darren smiled. "Yeah," he said. "If we had something to sit in, all three of us could fly around in that thing, right?"

Wolfgang nodded.

"We could look in the top of the girls' gym."

Wolfgang directed a disgusted look at Darren, but Ben welcomed Darren's comment. For one thing, he knew that Darren was an ace mechanic and builder; if he showed that sort of interest in the project, he could be very useful. Also, looking in the girls' gym wasn't that far removed from peeking into Lori Swenson's bedroom.

"Great," he said. "I mean, it would be great to fly around together, wherever we went."

Darren's mind was already racing ahead, considering ways and means of constructing a practical space vehicle for the three of them. As the bits and pieces of the plan formulated themselves, he poured them out.

"It would have to be on supports so the field wouldn't break pieces of it off every time we turned it on," he said, his eyes gleaming with excitement. "And of course we'd need to breathe in there."

"My dad's got a scuba tank," Wolfgang offered.

"How much air does it hold?"

"I think about forty-five minutes."

"So if we hooked up three masks, that's like fifteen minutes of air each."

"Fifteen minutes," Ben said. "That doesn't seem like very much. I wonder how much breathing time you get now."

He looked at Wolfgang.

"Don't ask me," his friend said. "I wasn't exactly looking at my watch the whole time I was in that thing."

"I wasn't either."

Ben stared down the bottom of the hill, toward the familiar house he had never entered. A scheme was forming in his fertile mind.

"Why don't we try to find out?" he suggested.

"Find out what?" Wolfgang asked.

"How much time there is with no air tanks—just in the bubble itself."

"Why?"

"Because if something goes wrong, say if the air tank goes up, we'll know how many minutes we have—"

"Before what—before we die?"

"No. We'll know how long we have to perform some emergency operation."

"All right," Wolfgang conceded. "I guess it makes a little sense."

"And since you know how to operate the computer better than I do—" Ben began.

Darren burst into laughter, a loud derisive guffaw.

Ben reddened. "Since you know how to operate the computer better than I do," he repeated, "I'll be the subject and you be mission control."

"Okay," Wolfgang said. "We'll do it tomorrow."

"Why not now?" Ben asked.

"It's getting dark."

"That's even better. Nobody can see us."

"Yes, but it makes things difficult."

"Why? The computer gives off enough light to see the keys, doesn't it?"

Wolfgang looked at Ben suspiciously. "What's the big hurry, anyway?"

"No hurry," Ben replied evenly, but he knew right away his attitude betrayed him.

"Bet he wants to look in the girls' gym," Darren taunted.

"And see what?" Ben retorted. "There's nobody in there and hasn't been for two hours."

A light went on in Wolfgang's eyes.

"I get it," he said, smiling.

Ben looked away.

"What's he want?" Darren asked.

"He wants to look in Lori's window."

"And see her undressed, huh?"

"No," Ben interjected. "I just want to know more about her, that's all."

"Well, what better way to find out?" Darren laughed.

"He says he wants to look at her record albums and see what she reads and stuff like that."

Darren just laughed.

"Okay," Wolfgang said. "If this will end your acting like such a creep every time you pass her house, let's do it."

Ben shrugged, trying not to look satisfied. "Okay," he said. "You talked me into it."

Ten minutes later, Wolfgang had the computer programmed and ready. Ben stood on a mound of earth about a foot high, waiting to be encapsulated. He took a deep breath and whistled an unidentifiable tune that came out past dry lips, a wheezy tribute to his nervousness. Wolfgang's plan was to place the bottom edge of the force field below Ben's feet so that when it was activated it would cut through the mound of earth, rather than come close to Ben's feet. A signal had been devised so that when he felt himself growing faint from lack of air, Ben would be able to have the bubble removed immediately.

"Let's go. Okay?" he called to Wolfgang.

His friend nodded, fed data into the machine and, a moment later, Ben was enclosed in the force field.

The experiment to measure the amount of air in the sphere went without a hitch——there was little that could go wrong under the circumstances. Wolfgang merely allowed the bubble to remain stationary while Ben breathed in a normal manner and consulted his watch. After a few minutes, he noticed an increase in the temperature and shortly after that, he began to feel lightheaded. His watch showed that just over five minutes had passed. Signaling to Wolfgang, Ben breathed a sigh of relief and pleasure as the force field disappeared and cool, fresh air rushed in.

"How do you feel?" Wolfgang asked.

"Fine."

"Take a couple of deep breaths and then we'll send you off."

Ben nodded. He was eager to fly away and see his beloved Lori, but he was quite apprehensive, as well. He had gone too far to back out, however, so he piled the dirt beneath his feet, stood on the mound and waved at Wolfgang.

"Ready," he said.

The force field appeared around him, destroying the dirt mound and nearly sending Ben sprawling. He quickly regained his balance and indicated that he wanted to take off. A moment later, he saw the ground begin to fall away beneath his feet as he rose in the direction of Lori's house. The course was a bit erratic, so he lifted the walkie-talkie provided for just such a purpose and began issuing instructions to Wolfgang.

"A little more to the right," he said as the bubble neared Lori's window. "Okay, that's it. I can almost see in. Good. Now straight ahead."

On the ground below and perhaps an eighth of a mile away, Darren watched as Wolfgang manipulated the bubble by punching new instructions into the computer. He was amazed that anyone so young could be so skillful.

"Great," he said. "But he's gonna be disappointed."

"Why?" Wolfgang asked.

"It's too early for her to be undressing."

Wolfgang shot a disgusted look at Darren. It was all right for Ben to be kidded by Wolfgang himself; after all, the two of them were longtime friends. For Darren to insinuate such vile motivation on Ben's part was not very nice.

"He just wants to see what her room looks like," Wolfgang said defensively.

"Sure," Darren laughed.

Inside the bubble, Ben experienced a surge of excitement as *she* suddenly came into his field of vision. She was seated at her table next to the bed, talking on the telephone and eating dessert.

"Oh my God, there she is," he sighed.

He was pleased to see that Lori was seated in such a way that her direct gaze was turned away from him. He could therefore watch her with little danger of being seen. Lifting the walkie-talkie, he spoke with a calm, almost objective voice.

"She's talking on the phone," he reported. "And eating some . . . it looks like Boston cream pie."

"Wow, what a scoop," Darren replied on his own walkie-talkie.

Ben was too enraptured to notice the sarcasm. He continued the description of her room and the objects in it with awe and admiration.

"She's got some stuffed animals on her bed, and those look like Duran Duran records by her stereo," he reported.

"What else?" Darren asked. "This is really terrific information. I'm getting all excited."

"There's a picture on the wall of two horses jumping a fence."

"Out of sight!"

"She's got her own television, too. A portable right next to the bed."

Darren put his hand over the walkie-talkie and rolled his eyes at Wolfgang. "Boy, he's got it bad," he said.

"Idiotic," Wolfgang agreed, the expansive descriptions having sent him over the edge.

"Oh-oh!" Ben's voice interrupted them.

"What is it?" Darren asked.

"She almost saw me," Ben replied. "She turned and

hung up the phone—thought she looked right at me, but I guess she didn't."

"Isn't that enough?" Wolfgang muttered. "What else is there to see, for God's sake?"

"You want me to tell him we're hauling him back down?" Darren asked.

"No, we'll give him another minute to drool."

"She's writing in a small brown book," Ben reported. "Looks like a diary."

He leaned forward in the force field, hoping to get a glimpse over Lori's shoulder at the writing. It was already quite warm in the bubble and he was starting to feel a little lightheaded. But he couldn't go back now, while he was on the verge of seeing something really personal about Lori. Suppose she wrote about his fight with Steve?

"Get me closer!" he yelled into the walkie-talkie.

Wolfgang complied. The field took a sudden lurch forward, breaking a branch off the tree outside Lori's window and bumping into the sill.

Ben gasped. This would blow everything! In the excitement of planning this spy mission, he had not anticipated what might happen if Lori saw the force field suspended in the air outside her window. Only now that discovery threatened did he realize what an unsavory thing he was doing. Panic gripped him as he hurled himself backwards away from the window.

"Turn it off!" he yelled. "Turn it off!"

The terror in Ben's voice caused Wolfgang to react violently. Instead of guiding the force field gently to earth, he simply repeated Ben's last-ditch action of a quarter hour earlier—he pulled the power cable loose from the computer. As he did so, the bubble vanished.

Ben hung in the air for what seemed an eternity, his

body curled into a near-fetal position, his eyes bugged as he continued to stare at Lori. Then, a microsecond before he plunged downward into some bushes near the side of the Swenson home, Lori looked in Ben's direction. Leaping off the bed, she raced to the window and looked down at the fallen figure below.

"Who is that?" she called out.

Ben rolled over and removed his face from the boxwood.

"Ben?" Lori cried. "Is that you?"

There was nothing to do but admit it, of course. Ben gulped, trying desperately to think of any possible reason why he should be here. No really logical ones came to mind, so he decided to stall.

"Yeah," he muttered. "I guess it's me."

Understandably, Lori got right to the point. "What are you doing down there?"

"Nothing, really."

"Nothing!" Her tone indicated that she wasn't about to accept such evasiveness.

"Well," Ben explained. "I saw a cat in your tree and I thought I'd help him down."

"And did you?"

"Uh, yeah."

Her expression softened a bit. "Do you always help cats get down out of trees?" she asked.

"Not all the time," he replied. "But this one was special because it was outside your window. You know how witches sometimes take over cats' bodies? Well, it occurred to me that the cat might be a witch. So in order to protect you, I climbed the tree . . ."

She smiled, but Ben wasn't sure whether it was a smile of pleasure or derision. But at least the explanation period seemed to be over.

"I can't believe you would do such a thing," Lori said. "You could have gotten yourself killed."

"But for a good cause," Ben replied, trying to sound casually gallant.

By this time, he had extricated himself from the bush with its sharp branches and was standing on the ground, looking up at Lori. He felt a bit less ludicrous.

"Oh, by the way," Lori said. "I'm sort of glad you dropped by—"

They both chuckled at her little joke.

"Why's that?" Ben asked.

"Oh—because I won't have to mail out your invitation now."

"Invitation?"

"Yes. My birthday's in a couple of weeks and I'm having a party for our class, so you're invited."

"I am?"

"Sure, and you can bring your friend, too. What's his name?"

"Wolfgang."

"No. Darren. The guy who helped you take on Steve and those bullies."

Ben nodded. The way Lori said it made his massacre sound noble and uplifting.

"Really?" he replied, unable to keep the rampant happiness out of his voice. "Okay. That's great. I'd love to come and so would he."

"Okay. See you then."

She smiled and started to pull her head back into her room.

"Wait a minute," Ben called up. "See us when? You didn't say when or where. I guess it's here but—"

"My mother's calling me," Lori said. "I'll mail you the invitation anyway, okay?"

"Yeah."

"See you tomorrow."

Then she was gone.

Sighing deeply, Ben smiled, stepped backward in order to get a last glimpse at the girl of his dreams, and tripped over the fallen branch.

Chapter Five

"LET'S NOT MAKE TOO MUCH NOISE," DARREN CAU-
tioned. "I don't want to wake up Pop and Mona."

The three boys were standing outside of Darren's
house, which was completely dark except for a single
light in the living room.

The words were hardly out of his mouth before
shouting voices interrupted the silence of the night. At
the same time, lights went on in the bedroom, hallway,
dining room, and kitchen. Whenever a fight started in
the Woods household, Mona darted nervously from
room to room, turning on lights and shouting obsceni-
ties at Darren's father as she went. The soprano and
baritone voices blended in a traveling cacophony of
invective that Darren and his friends listened to for a
minute or so. Then Darren led them away from the
house.

"The heck with it," he said. "I'll show you the sketch
tomorrow. Let's go to Wolfgang's and see what kind of
building materials he's got."

After their successful experiments of that afternoon,
Darren had remembered that the night before, just
prior to going to sleep, he had made a drawing of a

space vehicle that the three of them might use. At the time, it had been a purely fanciful thing, but now it seemed distinctly practical. When he had suggested that they go home with him and look at it, the boys had agreed with alacrity.

That was before they discovered the Woods home was again in a state of siege.

A few minutes later, they entered the garage of the Muller house. It looked like the remnants of a decade's worth of scavenger hunts. From the outside—the only view Darren had had of it to this point—it seemed bad enough. Inside, hemmed in by the junk crammed from floor to ceiling, Darren was doubly impressed by the amount of energy that must have been expended just to get so much material into the garage. He looked around at the electronic equipment, old machines, furniture, sheet metal and wooden carts with something close to awe.

"There's got to be lots of stuff here we can use as building material," he said.

Ben, meanwhile, was less concerned about their upcoming travel plans. He had already taken a trip to seventh heaven, compliments of Lori Swenson, and was still basking in the glow of her smile and invitation.

"I think she really likes me," he whispered.

"Will you shut up about her?" Wolfgang retorted. "I'm tired of hearing it."

Ben merely smiled and looked away. Wolfgang could try to rain on his parade but it wouldn't do any good. The memory lingered on.

Mentally constructing their vehicle, Darren was oblivious to the minor squabble going on nearby. "Here's an old car seat over here," he said. "And some washing machine doors—we can use them for portholes —and some heavy wood we can use as bracing." He looked at Wolfgang. "Once we get this built, how fast will it go?"

"It depends."

"On what?"

"A lot of things. From an aerodynamic point of view, our force field presents a lot of opportunities—"

"How fast?" Darren repeated.

"—Inside this field, you have no inertia, no resistance to acceleration. You can start, speed up, and stop without slowing down. It's almost like the thing is on tracks."

"How fast?"

"It's all a function of how much power we put into it. The more power, the more speed."

"Answer me, will you?"

"I'm trying to. What I'm saying is, I guess the sky's the limit. She'll be able to go almost as fast as we want, as fast as we have power for. She's running on this now."

He pulled at some wires inside the power pack and held up a transistor radio battery.

"That's it?" Darren gasped. "We made the thing go fifty-sixty miles an hour and cut through concrete and dirt and stone with a single crummy battery?"

Wolfgang nodded proudly. "I pulled it out of my radio and it was kind of worn down. Otherwise we might have gotten even more power."

Darren's eyes were gleaming. If one tiny battery could move the force field along the way it had traveled this afternoon, a heavy-duty car battery might get it to the moon in a couple of minutes.

"I know we can build something to hold us," Darren said after a moment, "but I'm not exactly sure what it should look like."

"I've been thinking about that myself." Wolfgang smiled. "This is the way it's got to be."

He moved to a corner of a work bench and picked up a model. It was egg-shaped, constructed basically of parts from an old balsa wood airplane assembly kit. Darren and Ben stared at it for a long while, each picturing himself inside the strange-looking vehicle.

"Interesting," Ben said noncommitally.

"The oval is one of the strongest structural shapes," Wolfgang explained. "That's why eggs hold together so well without breaking."

"Eggs break easily," Darren said.

"Not considering the thickness of the shell," Wolfgang pointed out. "If you had that same thickness in other objects, nothing would be intact."

"Okay," Darren said. "There's only one major problem as I see it."

"What's that?"

Darren took the model and applied a small amount of pressure inside it, whereupon the bottom dropped out and the shell fell apart.

"It's pretty weak if you're sitting in it," he explained. "I mean, the oval may be strong from the outside but once the chick starts kicking, it's all over."

"Well, we should be able to counter that," Wolfgang replied.

"Sure. I'll build this thing for you so it's good and strong, but we'll have to do it my way."

"And what's that?"

"Oval on the outside but with lots of good, strong support on the inside."

Wolfgang nodded.

"Too bad we can't find something like that that's already built," Ben mused.

"Like what?" Wolfgang asked.

"I don't know. I remember seeing a futuristic car in a magazine once—"

"Good thinking, but no cigar."

"Wait a minute!" Darren smiled, snapping his fingers. "You guys just gave me an idea."

"You're not gonna steal somebody's car," Ben cautioned.

"No."

"Then—"

"Want to take a walk?"

Wolfgang and Ben looked at each other. It was late and neither of them had done a bit of homework, but they were wired on their problem and wanted to get it settled.

"Okay by me," Ben said.

Wolfgang agreed and a few minutes later the three would-be astronauts were walking across town past the less prestigious neighborhoods toward that section of their community known sardonically as "junkyard villa." For nearly a half mile, from the edge of town to the freeway, was a corridor of anchor fence which enclosed one junkyard after another. No one could say exactly where the debris came from or where it went, but as none of the dealers went out of business, it was presumed that it went somewhere for a good price.

Soon the boys arrived at a gate and sign that read: ROGER'S RECLAMATION CENTER—IF YOU CAN FIND IT I CAN SELL IT. Beyond a chain-link fence lay a fantastic mess of shadows and silhouettes, an armageddon of broken machines, car bodies, and unidentifiable hulks.

Wolfgang leaned against the fence and peered inside. Even without seeing a suitable object, he agreed that if any place contained what they needed, this was it. But he didn't like the idea of poking around the lot during the middle of the night.

"This Roger," he said to Darren. "Do you know him? Is he a friend of yours?"

"Yeah. He's a nice old guy. He won't notice if we borrow something."

As he spoke, a ferocious-looking guard dog sprinted up to the fence and leaped against it. His teeth were bared and a succession of angry snarls emanated from his throat. Wolfgang recoiled.

"Maybe Roger won't notice if we borrow something," he said, "but what about him?"

Ben shook his head nervously from side to side. "Not me," he muttered. "I'm not going in there with that thing. He looks like he attacks freighters."

"Don't worry," Darren said. "He's all right."

"How do you know?" Wolfgang asked.

"Because I've made friends with him."

"He doesn't look like your friend."

"Sure, he is. Here, Bozo . . ."

The dog stopped snarling but continued to regard the three boys with fierce eyes.

"Watch this," Darren said.

As he reached into his pocket, he moved closer to the fence. Wolfgang and Ben followed timorously, remaining a full step behind.

"His name is Bozo," Darren explained. "I always come over here at night to get parts, so I kept bringing things to make friends with him. You know—bones, meat, stuff like that. But nothing worked. Then I finally found out what he likes. Hey, Bozo . . ."

Removing his hand from his pocket, Darren held up a piece of chewing gum, unwrapped it and stuck it through an opening in the fence. Bozo grabbed it and began chewing. As he did so, his eyes glazed over, an expression of total ecstasy taking over his face.

"Incredible," Wolfgang muttered.

"Doesn't he swallow it?" Ben asked, still regarding the dog a bit nervously.

"No, he just wears it out," Darren replied.

"It'll ruin his teeth." Ben smiled. "Maybe you should start him on sugarless gum."

"No," Darren said. "He only likes Doublemint. He's pretty weird."

He led them to a crack between two fence poles and began to slip his body through.

"You sure he'll just sit there and keep chewing?" Ben demanded.

"Yeah. He's done it a million times. Come on."

Wolfgang and Ben slipped through the opening and followed Darren, both of them keeping careful watch on the guard dog as they moved along. As Darren had predicted, the animal continued to sit, chewing stupidly, the effort making his mouth curl in strange configurations. He seemed to be sneering at them, but as long as he made no more attack overtures, it was all right with them.

Darren was apparently well acquainted with the junkyard; he walked quickly between rows of old machines and lines of cars toward his destination.

"How about that?" Wolfgang asked once. "There's a car in there—"

"No good," Darren interrupted. "I'm telling you, there's a gold mine down the line. We'll find something that's perfect. Unless, by some quirk of fate, Roger sold everything in stock."

Presently they entered a section full of old amusement park rides. Signs proclaimed: THE WHIP, TUNNEL OF LOVE, RAM-JET, and beneath each was a pathetic bundle of debris.

"All this stuff came from carnivals and amusement parks," Darren explained. "Roger even has some old rides and a couple of merry-go-rounds. All the good working stuff's over there. The really run-down stuff is here. A bunch of rats live in them, so watch out."

"Let's skip those," Wolfgang growled, looking down at his feet.

"Here's the stuff I thought we could use," Darren said, pausing at one pile of rubble.

The boys looked off to their left. All three of them spotted the object immediately. The effect on Ben and Wolfgang was almost electric, their eyes widening and smiles of glee and surprise illuminating their features. Darren, knowing what was coming, smiled complacently, his main emotion being relief that the object was still there.

It sat atop a scrap metal heap, forming a clean silhouette against the moonlit sky . . . a 1950's-style, bullet-shaped compartment from an old Tilt-a-Whirl ride. In the semi-darkness, it was possible to see large areas where rust had eaten away the metal, but some of the originally bright reds, blues, and silvers shone through.

Wolfgang was speechless.

"It's beautiful," Ben said, breathlessly.

"I knew you'd like it," Darren said with a smile.

"Let's see it up closer," said Ben, starting to climb the pile of debris. As he did so, a dark form raced out from beneath the mound, moving directly toward Ben's feet before veering quickly away.

"Yipe!"

Ben leaped a foot in the air as he dodged the rat, which seemed as large as a raccoon. Wolfgang, reacting a bit late but with total commitment, danced away with a shout of terror.

"It's just a rat." Darren shrugged. "They don't attack you unless there's nothing else they can do."

"Maybe he thought that was his only choice," Ben replied. "Who am I to read rats' minds?"

"Once we get up top, it'll be all right. They usually hang around the bottoms of things."

Darren put his foot on the pile, kicked at it a couple of times, and then walked upward toward the compartment. When he was halfway up the heap, Ben gingerly picked his way after him, followed a moment later by Wolfgang.

The ascent was a brief but significant one for the young men. Thoughts of reaching the summit of Mount Everest crossed Ben's mind as he approached the battered prize at the top. The notion that all three of them were a little wacko never occurred to him. Nor did it occur to Wolfgang or Darren.

Arriving first, Darren waited impatiently for the others.

"I've never looked inside," he said, reaching for the door handle. "I just saw it from a distance, so it might be in really terrible shape."

He swung the door open and the boys saw immediately that the outside was definitely the better side. Inside, the seats were torn almost to shreds, the walls contained long, deep gouges, and some supporting boards stuck out at odd angles. But the inside dimensions were nearly perfect, appearing to be about six feet in diameter. Moreover, the overall condition of the walls looked solid.

"This is perfect," Ben said, his mind envisioning what it could look like after a lot of hard work.

Wolfgang was less sanguine. "It stinks in here," he said, wrinkling his nose.

"What do you expect?" Darren asked defensively. "You'd stink, too, if you'd spent a couple years sitting on a pile of crap like this."

"It'll do, though." Wolfgang admitted. "It's too spherical, maybe. Not egg-shaped enough, but the principle's the same and it'll do fine. But how do we get it home?"

"We roll it," Darren said.

"Yeah. I guess that's the only way."

"You guys stand below and I'll shake it loose from the pile, okay?"

Ben and Wolfgang did as suggested, placing their hands against the clammy and foul-smelling exterior of the compartment while Darren pushed it free of the network of upraised parts holding it in position. For perhaps five minutes, he continued to shove, growing more and more impatient because he had no stable place to stand and push. It seemed that most of his effort went into shoving his own body backwards. But finally the compartment rose up, cleared a board beneath it, and broke loose from the pile.

Wolfgang and Ben were unprepared for the sudden movement of the compartment down the steep incline. Ben slipped and fell sideways, then threw himself clear of the huge object as it scraped its way down the pile. Wolfgang stood his ground for a moment before following Ben's example.

"Watch it!" Darren yelled.

Gaining speed, the ship rolled free of the pile of scrap metal and smashed into the fence. The huge blob came to rest a few yards away, causing a large bow to form in the chain-link wall. Rushing up behind it, Wolfgang and Ben worked it loose and began wrestling it toward a break in the mounds of rubble. Darren trotted up to assist them, but keeping the compartment moving in a straight line was not easy. Guiding it around a corner was even more difficult.

"This is going to be tricky," Wolfgang said. "We'll just have to be real quiet."

"Easier said than done," Ben remarked.

Despite its generally round shape, the ship moved only grudgingly. It was also quite noisy, rumbling along the concrete with a sound roughly equivalent to that of a Conestoga wagon with chipped wheels.

"We'll wake up the whole town," Ben yelled.

"That's too bad," Darren retorted. "We're not doing anything illegal."

"*Borrowing* from a junkyard?" Ben said. "Disturbing the peace?"

Darren shrugged.

At the main entrance, Bozo the guard dog was still chewing his Doublemint, his jaw teeth exposed on one side of his mouth like a very bad ventriloquist. Darren swung the gate open and led the way out.

Ben and Wolfgang pushed while Darren guided the compartment, running from side to side and yanking it forward on course. On the level stretches, their work was relatively simple, although several times they had to wrestle the blob off the street in order to accommodate oncoming vehicles. Moving uphill was rather more difficult, the ship having one flat section which continually resisted their efforts to roll it forward with a fluid motion. As a result, when the flat section hit the ground, the compartment tended to stop and skid, usually sending one or more of the boys slightly over the top until its forward movement was reestablished.

Going downhill proved to be the biggest problem of all. The ship wanted to roll, but not in a straight line: No sooner was the long, sweeping arc to the right corrected than it began another long and equally sweeping arc to the left. Like skiers snowplowing across a slope, they moved with agonizing and noisy slowness, the compartment crashing and banging against curb, telephone pole and trash cans as it ended each pendulum-like movement. Only constant pressure and dexterity kept it from smashing into parked cars.

Nor was the physical work the hardest aspect of the job. Even more debilitating was the mental anguish of accompanying this avalanche of sound. Light after light blinked on as they thundered past the lines of small suburban homes.

"I just hope nobody calls the police," Darren murmured, shortly after one man appeared on his porch. Clad in pajamas, he shook his fist at them as they slowly moved away.

Then, just after turning one corner, the inevitable happened.

"Look out!" Wolfgang cried.

As he fell, he released his grip on the compartment just as they cleared the brow of a hill and began to start downward. Ben and Darren hurled themselves forward to block the ship, but it rolled out of control away from them, taking off down the hill at a terrific speed. Even worse, it chose this particular time to steer a remarkably straight course directly down the fall line. As it proceeded, it smashed into a row of empty trash cans, which started rolling after the ship like a herd of smaller creatures following their mother. The noise was deafening.

Darren, Wolfgang, and Ben, in hot pursuit, all suddenly stopped at the same time.

The rolling ship was approaching the intersection below just as a police car moved toward the same junction from the right.

"God!" Darren yelled.

He hurled himself behind a hedge and quickly looked up to see what was happening. The other two followed suit.

The police car arrived at the intersection first, proceeding through it five seconds before the thundering globe rolled past. Because their windows were still slightly steamy from the coffee they had just bought, the cops saw only a dark form move behind them in the moonlight.

"What the hell was that?" asked the driver, looking in the rearview mirror.

"What?" said the other.

He turned his head just in time to see a moving shadow, but could not make out what it was. A few seconds later, he saw three boys racing through the intersection as if being pursued by demons.

"Three kids," the second officer said. "I guess there must have been a fourth."

"Looked too big for a kid," the first cop said. "Looked more like a rhino or a small tank."

"Want to go back?"

"Guess not. No sense spilling the coffee."

"No. Still, it's awfully late for those kids to be out. And maybe something's chasing them."

"Unlikely. They're just in a rush to get home, if you ask me."

"Okay, let's forget it."

As the three boys raced through the intersection, Wolfgang yelled forward to Darren.

"That was the police, wasn't it?"

"Big deal!"

"They saw us!"

"So what?"

"They probably think we're running from a crime or something!"

"Nah!"

"Suppose they come back?"

"They won't. It's too much trouble."

"Great!" Wolfgang wheezed. "I'll bet I go to Juvy before I can even drive."

"There's the creek!" Ben yelled.

They were now on nearly level ground and had closed the distance between them and the ship to less than twenty yards. But as Ben and Darren dodged their way between the rolling trash cans, followed by Wolfgang, they saw the outline of the police patrol car turn the corner and start back their way.

"They're coming back!" Wolfgang yelped. "I knew it! They're gonna get us!"

Ben and Darren barely heard him. Sprinting ahead as fast as they could, they managed to catch up with the compartment, but could not stop it completely. Rolling forward with inexorable force, the huge sphere crashed over a waist-high concrete wall, hung suspended for a long time in midair, and then flipped over into the creek.

"Get it!" Ben yelled.

He and Darren took a step forward just as the headlights from the police car turned the corner. Diving behind a row of bushes, they pressed themselves flat against the ground until the cruiser slowly moved away. As soon as the car was gone, they got up and looked around for Wolfgang, crossing back over the road and calling his name.

"Where the heck did he go?" Darren asked, puzzled.

"Damn it!" a muffled voice cried.

A moment later, the mud-soaked figure of Wolfgang staggered up from the culvert, where he had thrown himself in order to avoid detection. Blackish gray muck clung to the front of his shirt, trousers, and face, only his eyes showing clear and white through the mess.

"Boy, you look terrible." Ben sighed. "Maybe you better go home and change clothes."

"Not yet," Wolfgang said. "First we better make sure the ship's all right."

Darren nodded and the three of them walked down to the edge of the creek. The compartment had come to rest near a mud bank about ten feet down the creek, the water being too shallow to float it very far.

"It looks like she's okay," Wolfgang said. "Where are we going to work on her?"

"I better not try it at my house," Darren replied. "If my dad gets in a bad mood some night, he's liable to cut it to pieces."

"I used to be pretty sure my folks were behind everything I did," Wolfgang said. "You know, they're scientists themselves. But lately they've been acting strange. They think I'm into something weird, I'll bet."

"I wonder where they got that idea," Darren said, smirking.

Wolfgang and Darren looked at Ben.

"Sorry, guys," he muttered. "It won't fly at my house. My dad's been pretty crabby lately and he thinks my idea about going to Space Camp next summer is really crazy."

"Well, then I guess we better work on it here," Wolfgang suggested. "We can cover it up with limbs and nobody'll see it . . . I hope . . ."

"Yeah." Darren nodded. "Maybe it's best that way. Parents are liable to ruin everything . . ."

For the next two weeks, Darren, Ben, and Wolfgang spent most of their waking time either at work on the spaceship or thinking about it. Inevitably, their progress with the ship led to deterioration of their work at school, but there was nothing they could do about it other than adopt a saner attitude toward their space mission. That, of course, was quite impossible. Each of them was absolutely possessed to find out how far their homemade vessel could carry them.

One afternoon, walking from school, they compared notes on their miserable performances in class.

"I was just about out," Ben recounted. "I guess Mr. Rossiter must have seen me nodding off because suddenly he asked me to tell the class something about carbon dioxide."

"That shouldn't have been too hard," Wolfgang said.

"Not normally. But I just wasn't with it."

"What did you say?"

"Lori Swenson told me later I said, 'well, carbon dioxide is what you breathe on Mars . . .' and then I rambled on about how there might be life underground."

Wolfgang chuckled.

"I got three D-minuses in a row on those history quizzes," Darren muttered.

"Too bad," Ben said.

"That's nothing," Wolfgang continued. "The worst thing of all happened to me. During English class, I just couldn't keep my eyes open, so I scrunched down behind Melvin Lewis—this big guy who sits in front of me—and fell asleep. That was second period. Well, the next thing I knew, it was dead silence and I opened my eyes. I looked around and saw my whole class was gone and another class was there. It was fourth period! Mrs. Gore had let me sleep and told everybody to get up and leave quietly just so she could embarrass the hell out of me. You should have heard that class laugh!"

"What a great trick!" Darren said enthusiastically. "I didn't know Mrs. Gore was so sharp."

"I'd like to unzip her face," Wolfgang grumbled.

"Hey," Ben interjected. "At least you got some decent sleep. That's more than I got."

Temporarily freed from the onus of school duties, they experienced a surge of new energy as they approached the creek bed home of their space vessel, which was rapidly nearing completion. The interior had been completely refurbished, a support built for the power control panel, mattresses nailed to the walls for padding, and new seats added. Repainted from stem to stern, the ship no longer smelled of mold and rat droppings; in fact, it had a wonderful aroma of newness about it. Some of the colored lights from the amusement park aspect of the vessel had been retained and two new brilliant white car headlights had been mounted on poles so that they could be aimed from inside the ship. After the hull was repainted to its original colors, Ben stenciled a large silver lightning bolt along the side. All agreed the ship was beginning to look absolutely stunning.

"We're gonna have to start thinking about a name for the ship," Darren said. "I'm tired of calling her 'the thing' and I don't want to even think about calling her the *traegheitslosigkeit*."

"What's so difficult about *traegheitslosigkeit*?" Wolfgang asked archly.

"Nothing if you're part Kraut," Darren retorted.

"Well, I suggest—oh-oh," Ben began.

"Oh-oh?" Darren repeated, puzzled.

"Over there."

He gestured with his head toward a tiny figure standing not far away from them. It was Wolfgang's six-year-old brother, Ludwig, wearing a jacket over his pajamas.

"You're supposed to be in bed," Wolfgang said sternly. "It's after eight o'clock."

Ludwig ignored him, looking instead at Darren and Ben. "What are you guys doing?" he asked.

"You go back to bed right now or I'm calling Mom," Wolfgang threatened.

"What is that thing?" his younger brother persisted, moving closer to the ship.

"It's a school project," Ben adlibbed.

"What kind of project?"

"A terrarium," Wolfgang said.

"A what?"

"A terrarium. We're going to fill it up with dirt and put snakes and tarantulas in it."

Ludwig shook his head, not buying it at all. "You

112

can't fool me," he said evenly. "It's a spaceship. Anybody can see that."

"You get to bed or I'm calling Mom!"

"You call Mom and I'll tell her you're building a spaceship!"

"You tell her that and I'll tell her who put Silly Putty in the toaster."

The look on Ludwig's face showed that Wolfgang had the more powerful ammunition. Slowly his determined expression melted into one of compliance. "Please let me look," he asked pathetically.

"Later," Wolfgang promised. "If you're quiet and don't say a word, we'll show you everything."

"When?"

"Soon."

"You're sure you'll do it?"

Wolfgang nodded. Impressed by his brother's sincerity, Ludwig trundled back toward the house.

"That's the last thing we need," Darren muttered. "Some kid to go spreading this around."

"He's right," Ben said. "Maybe we better work through the night. Tomorrow's Saturday and we don't have school. I'll feel a lot better once we get this thing off the ground. And once it's off the ground, we can put it anywhere."

"Yeah," Darren agreed. "I'm not crazy about keeping it here anymore. It looks too good, for one thing. Some nut's liable to steal it."

"I agree," Wolfgang replied. "Let's get to work and maybe we can have a dawn launching."

With a round of subdued cheers, the three pitched in with renewed energy. The night passed quickly. By the time Darren had tightened the last bolt, the first flush of dawn light was beginning to penetrate the trees surrounding the creek bed.

Wolfgang and Ben sat on the bank, munching baklava and sipping Coke. While their creation obviously wasn't the work of Lockheed or Douglas, to them it was an impressive and beautiful combination of engineering and art.

"Well," Darren exclaimed, tossing the crescent wrench high in the air and slapping his hands together. "What do you say to a little spin?"

"Now?" Wolfgang asked.

"Why not?"

"I think it would be better if we waited till it got dark," Ben offered.

"So do I," Wolfgang said.

Darren shrugged. The others hadn't advanced any reasons for waiting but he was beginning to see them by himself. There was a great deal of preparation to be made and it would be better if their first mission took place under cover of darkness.

"Okay," he said. "Let's go down the checklist of things we need and we'll all meet again at seven-thirty."

"Maybe we should take turns guarding the ship," Ben suggested. "It would be a shame if something happened now that we're so close."

Wolfgang and Darren agreed. Shifts were assigned and the boys split up, Darren remaining with one walkie-talkie and a crowbar to use as a weapon, if necessary.

Twelve hours later, they reassembled, each carrying a knapsack loaded with gear. Their equipment included flashlights, a compass, binoculars, an air tank, harnesses, food, and helmets. Ben, in charge of procuring the latter, held up a motorcycle helmet, bicycle head protector, and a green U.S. Army helmet, without liner, for his friends' inspection.

Wolfgang was not impressed. "Come on!" he said,

rolling his eyes. "You expect me to make history wearing something like *that?*"

"It's all I could find," Ben explained. "Take the one you like best."

"I don't like any of them."

"What would you suggest then?"

"Never mind," Wolfgang snapped, selecting the motorcycle helmet, which had at least a little class.

Then, turning to Darren, he said, "Did you bring the power source, a dry cell or something?"

Darren smiled, put down his knapsack and lifted out a truck battery.

"Good grief!" Wolfgang muttered. "Where did you get that monstrosity?"

"Out of my dad's truck. He won't need it until tomorrow morning."

"Just a small one would have done, Darren."

"Yeah, but once we get up there, we're liable to want to hit the moon or something."

"I don't know what we might do with this much power," Wolfgang said, frowning.

"Well, let's find out," Darren said.

"Yeah!" Ben echoed.

"Well, I guess we're about ready," said Wolfgang.

Darren reached into his knapsack and pulled out a brown paper bag.

"Not quite," he said. "First we gotta toast and christen this spaceship."

Ben and Wolfgang nodded enthusiastically.

Darren pulled a bottle of beer from the bag, twisted off the top and took a swig, a bit too nonchalantly. He then passed the bottle to Ben, who took it and, acting equally cool, had a drink. Looking around as if he were afraid of being caught, Wolfgang quickly upended the bottle and downed a mouthful. It was the first drink of beer for Ben and Wolfgang, both of whom thought it tasted awful; being partners in crime made it all right, however, and they grinned wickedly at each other.

"Now then," Ben said, taking the bottle from Darren, who seemed about to chugalug it. "Let's think of a name for our space vehicle. I suggest calling her the *Enterprise.*"

"No." Wolfgang sneered. "That's too Trekkie. We'll call her the *Einstein.*"

All at once the three of them began hurling names back and forth.

"Young Voyager!"

"Explorer!"

"Santa Maria!"

"Mayflower!"

"Challenger!"

"Frontier!"

"Apogee!" suggested Wolfgang.

"What the hell's that?" Darren demanded.

"The farthest point from the earth by a satellite."

"That's not bad but nobody'll know what it means."

"So they ask."

"Wait a second," Darren said. "How about *Thunder Road?*"

Ben and Wolfgang looked at him, their expressions blank. Actually, they were quite impressed, almost stunned by the appropriateness of the name, but Darren thought they were merely lukewarm.

"It's from a Bruce Springsteen song," Darren saw fit to explain.

"That's a great name," Ben said finally.

"Yeah," Wolfgang agreed.

Darren smiled, somewhat overcome by the power of his own genius.

"I christen thee *Thunder Road,*" Ben announced, raising the beer bottle and dashing it against the nose of the ship. Wolfgang ducked aside to avoid getting covered with beer. Darren applauded.

They stood a moment in silence, watching the beer trickle down the front of the *Thunder Road* as each of them inwardly prepared himself for the adventure or disaster that lay ahead.

"Okay," Darren said finally, clapping his hands like a quarterback leading his team out of the huddle, "Let's do it . . ."

They climbed into the ship, shut the hatch and strapped themselves into their seats. Against the inside wall was bolted a yellow compressed-air tank; air hoses were attached to three mouthpieces dangling over the seats.

"We don't need air yet," Wolfgang said. "Wait until I give the order before using the mouthpieces."

"Aye, sir," Ben said.

Darren merely nodded. Ben thought he looked a little silly in the bicycle head protector. He tried not to imagine how he looked in the oversize army helmet.

"I'm going to take it very easy at first," Wolfgang continued. "If we stay fairly low and keep the speed reasonable, we'll be safer. We're not sure how the ship handles yet. Something might go wrong if we're not careful and we could all get killed."

Ben frowned. "Stop talking about getting killed all the time, will you?"

"It's a possibility. I can't help it."

"Then think it but don't say it so much."

"Yeah," Darren chimed in. "You're making me nervous, too, Wolfgang."

"Sorry. But if I'm the captain, I've gotta be allowed to say what I think. We were operating before on a transistor radio battery. Now we're being powered by a heavy-duty truck battery. That's quite a jump in power. What if the ship falls to pieces?"

"She'll hold," Darren replied. "I went over every bolt myself. She's a good strong ship."

"Let's not sit here debating, okay?" Ben interrupted. "Let's blast off."

Wolfgang nodded, took a deep breath, sat back and braced himself. Reaching into his pocket, he then withdrew a paper and unfolded it.

"Systems check," he announced.

Ben and Darren waited expectantly.

"Air pressure," Wolfgang began.

"Check," Ben replied, noting that the tank showed "full" on the gauge.

"Battery power."

"Check," Darren said, without moving.

Wolfgang leaned forward to look at him, his expression seeming to ask where and how Darren got the information validating their power source.

"My dad drove it home today," Darren said smiling. "It's got to be okay."

"Exterior illumination," Wolfgang continued.

Darren flipped the outer lights on and off. "Check," he responded.

"Drive system response . . . check," Wolfgang said, turning on the computer himself. "Harness strength."

Ben tugged at the seat belts they had installed.

"Check," he replied, his voice betraying his growing irritation. "Come on, let's go."

"Just a minute," Wolfgang persisted. "Supplies."

Ben lifted a bag containing some potato chips, soft drinks, Cheetos, candy bars, pretzels, and a package of Band-Aids.

"Check, check, check, check, check," he grated. "Now come on, let's go!"

Wolfgang swallowed hard. He had reached the end of the checklist. There was no other way to stall, at least not without looking like a coward. Clearing his throat, he forced a certain authority into his voice as he delivered a final word to the crew.

"We'll be able to talk briefly after the field is on," he said, "But breathe through those air hoses most of the time. We'll use up the oxygen pretty fast. Ben, you keep track of the time and air expended."

"Check," Ben replied.

Wolfgang reached forward, checked his data one last time and fed information to the computer.

"Field on," he announced.

He flipped a switch on the console in front of them. CRACK!

They felt a jolt as the wooden supports attached to the bottom of the *Thunder Road* were snapped in half by the force field. They had expected that. What happened next was totally unexpected. Suddenly the interior of the ship was thrown into utter chaos as everything that wasn't tied down or securely fastened began to float about the cabin. Bags of chips, tools, pens, binoculars, the compass, and various bits of paper flew into the air, bouncing off each other and the faces of the crew.

"What's going on?" Darren yelled, ducking to avoid a Swiss army knife and banging his head in the process.

"Wait!" Wolfgang yelled.

The barrage of flying objects continued for another thirty seconds while Wolfgang located the button he wanted and pressed it. Immediately everything clattered to the floor of the ship.

"What was that?" Ben asked during the sudden silence that followed.

Wolfgang shook his head indecisively. "I think we just went into reverse gravity."

"What's that?" Darren asked.

"I don't know," Wolfgang muttered defensively. "I got it back to normal, didn't I?"

"Yeah, but was it luck?"

"Of course not."

"Then why did it happen in the first place?"

"Maybe I just forgot," Wolfgang replied irritably.

Darren and Ben looked at each other, their expressions apprehensive. Was this the same guy who was preaching to them about safety and discipline, the expert who was going to be controlling the ship?

"Well, let's go," Ben muttered.

"Is the force field still on?" Darren asked, looking out the window. "I can't see it."

"It's there." Wolfgang replied. "When it's this big, it's less concentrated, less luminescent."

He fed more data into the computer, which promptly produced a display showing four views of the creek bed from ground level.

"Here's my launch area graphic," Wolfgang explained. "Since the power source and computer are inside the field instead of outside, I'm going to plot our movement relative to an imaginary stationary point." He looked at the two blank faces of his crew. "In theory this should work," he added, hoping that this quasi-confident endorsement would cheer them up.

Darren looked out through the porthole. For the first time since their mission had been conceived, he felt a bit queasy. Ben and Wolfgang had been airborne in the force field while he had not. That gave them a certain advantage over him. Even more to the point was the fact that Darren had gotten sick during the one extended airplane trip he had taken—a twenty-minute flight over the Grand Canyon several summers before. True, the air currents that day had been fierce and he'd been younger, but he couldn't rid himself of the fear that he would embarrass himself now. There was also no denying the fact that this trip involved considerably more risk and danger than a short sightseeing flight.

But it was too late to back down, nor did he even think about bowing out of the mission. He was simply a little bit scared. A few minutes in the air without mishap would correct everything.

"Let's go!" he said.

Wolfgang was still typing instructions into the computer. "Just a second," he whispered.

Completing the feed, Wolfgang leaned back, took a deep breath, and waited.

Slowly the *Thunder Road* began to rise from the ground. The ends of several small branches scraped against the invisible globe as their perspective changed. Objects formerly at eye-level receded into the bottom of their field of vision, and the tops of trees, once high above them, soon appeared only inches away. It was both fascinating and frightening. Darren was glad it wasn't possible to look directly downward. He was almost happy when he spotted a loose bolt near the edge of the cockpit. Hand-tightening it gave him something to do, his mind less opportunity to harass him. Had he glanced at Wolfgang, he would have seen that the captain of the *Thunder Road* was staring directly ahead, his eyes wide in fright and head quivering slightly.

After rising thirty feet above the ground, the *Thunder Road* slowed to a halt. Silhouetted against the clear evening sky, it hung incongruously over the back yards of a half dozen homes with contiguous property, a spherical smudge on the starry background.

"What's happening?" Ben asked.

"Nothing," Wolfgang answered. "I programmed us to get up this high and then stop. No sense going too high or too fast right away."

They looked down. Plainly visible below them was a dog on the back porch of a house. Looking up, it began to whine, then leaped to its feet and ran into the yard, barking at the ship in the air. In another yard, a second dog awakened and joined the chorus, followed by a third and then a fourth. Running in circles, hopping into the air, banging their bodies against fences, they soon orchestrated a relentless wail of noise that spread throughout the area. At first, the boys found it amusing.

"Hey, look at all those dogs," Darren cried, chuckling at their antics.

"We're driving them crazy," Ben said.

If it was true, the dogs were also transferring their craziness to the residents of the area. One by one, the houses went from dark to light as one homeowner after another got up to investigate the cause of all the dogs' commotion. The atmosphere inside the *Thunder Road* presently changed from amusement to concern.

"We better get out of here before somebody reports us," Ben cautioned.

"Can't just yet," Wolfgang replied.

"Why not?"

"I programmed in two minutes of stationary observation. Thought we might want to just look around awhile."

"Seems like a long time. I mean, two minutes just to look around in one spot?"

"Hey," Wolfgang replied defensively. "It seemed logical at the time, okay? Now leave me alone."

More lights were blinking on beneath them. Even more dogs had joined the yelping refrain drifting up to them and now a few people were visible in doorways.

"People are coming out," Darren said. "Isn't there anything you can do to get us out of here in a hurry?"

"How about canceling the previous order?" Ben suggested. "You ought to be able to do that."

"It takes almost as much time as we have left,"

Wolfgang replied. "We can wait another thirty seconds or so, can't we?"

"Not if it's a gun that guy's holding," Darren said, pointing.

He looked off to the right toward a silhouetted figure that was indeed holding something resembling a rifle. After a few seconds, the figure seemed to spot them and lifted the weapon.

"Get us outa here!" Darren yelled.

Wolfgang began typing furiously. As soon as he finished, the *Thunder Road* moved almost imperceptibly. But the houses fell away beneath them so rapidly it reminded Ben of the newsreel shots taken from rockets as they rose from their launching pads. Yet the motion was so minimal! It was almost as if the distance had been increased optically rather than via the actual movement of their vehicle.

"Damn!" Darren whistled. "This baby can really dig out when she wants to."

"Yeah." Wolfgang smiled, feeling more at ease.

Continuing to type, he eased the *Thunder Road* out of her rapid ascent and brought the ship level. He then dropped to just above treetop altitude and began searching for familiar landmarks. One thing he did not want to do on their very first mission was get lost and have to land in a strange neighborhood. To his chagrin, however, the houses and streets blended together into a mishmash of suburbia that looked completely unfamiliar. Yet they could not have come that far from home. Deciding that the change of perspective was most responsible for his disorientation, Wolfgang continued to strain his eyes for hometown features.

"Look!" Ben said. "There's the drive-in."

Wolfgang was relieved to see the familiar structure which was nicknamed the "passion pit" in honor of generations of necking couples. Now the venerable theater specialized in showing movies that no one had ever heard of, even on home video. The feature this evening was a low-budget Italian-made sci-fi thriller with spaceships on strings zooming at each other.

"Let's get lower," Darren suggested.

Wolfgang nodded, punched some instructions into the computer, and smiled as the *Thunder Road* began to lose altitude. Whatever happened now, he thought, their first mission was already a success.

Chapter Six

BILL CRANDALL LOOKED AT ANDREA OUT OF THE CORNER of his eye and decided that she looked terrific even while eating pizza. They had been going together now for nearly a month but he still experienced wonderful twinges when she put her hand on his arm or glanced at him in that special way. After careful consideration, he decided he liked her eyes best of all her features; they were extremely large, nearly black, and alive with energy and feeling.

Now, leaning back comfortably opposite her in the front seat of his car, he saw wonderful highlights dancing in her eyes as she finished the pizza and returned her gaze to the movie screen in front of them. She watched the picture only a moment before sliding over to him and leaning her head on his shoulder.

"Are you interested in this?" she asked provocatively, looking up at him.

"Not really," he said.

"I don't even know who those people in black are," she said as a group appeared on the screen. "Do you want to tell me?"

"No," he said.

"Good."

He could smell the aroma of her hair, hear her light breathing, and wanted to kiss her very much. He was about to tilt her chin in order to do so when she suddenly spoke.

"How do they get such terrible special effects?" she asked.

"It's what's known as a traveling matte," he explained, torn between enjoyment at being the expert and disappointment at not kissing her. "When it's well done it looks pretty real but when it's cheap it looks terrible."

"How do you know all that?" she asked breathlessly.

"All these films use them," he said. "It's standard procedure."

As the battle of the onscreen space vehicles continued, the young man and woman felt the electricity growing between them. Soon they forgot what they were watching ahead of them, having only eyes for each other. Barely an inch separated their lips when a sudden movement distracted Andrea, causing her to look once again at the movie screen.

"What's that?" she whispered.

With a sigh Bill resisted the urge to plunge his lips onto hers, partly because she had turned her head slightly and he would have come down at an odd angle. He looked at the screen and grunted. A large and slightly out-of-focus spaceship seemed to have appeared from out of nowhere. But while all the other ships were launching missiles furiously at each other, this new one simply hung in the middle of the interstellar no-man's-land, not firing in either direction, a sort of disinterested or baffled referee. It differed from the others in both size and shape, being dumpier and less streamlined, like something from a 1930s movie.

"Boy," Bill growled. "That looks so fake. You can tell it's not flying."

"It looks different . . . somehow," Andrea said. Her voice sounded apprehensive.

"It looks different because it's even cheaper than the rest." Bill laughed. "What a phony!"

As he spoke, the new space vehicle suddenly made a sharp right turn and swooped directly at the car. Bill and Andrea went tumbling backwards in a shower of Coke, ice, and pizza crust.

Inside the *Thunder Road,* the rapid and unprogrammed movement caused Wolfgang to gasp and reach quickly for the keyboard. Because of the lack of inertia inside the ship, there was no backlash or lurch. Ben and Darren, peering through the porthole at the drive-in screen, saw their field of vision widen but were not aware that anything unusual was happening.

"Great!" Ben smiled, watching the duel of onscreen spaceships. *"Starkiller!* I haven't seen this yet. I hear it's terrible!"

"It's kind of hard to see through this porthole, though," Darren said.

"Yeah, but it beats sneaking under the fence, doesn't it?"

"Hey, what happened?"

Darren, looking downward instead of directly at the screen, suddenly noticed that they had passed within inches of several parked cars.

"What's going on?" he yelled at Wolfgang. "We're practically on the lot. Why are we moving around so funny?"

Wolfgang stared at the computer monitor and scratched his head.

"Will you get us out of here?" Darren cried, exasperated. "We're right in front of the—"

"Do you *mind?*" Wolfgang shot back. "I've never done this before."

"I thought you had everything under control."

"So did I, but—"

As he continued to type instructions into the computer, the board started to make strange noises none of the boys had ever heard before. Figures began to appear on the side of the screen.

"What are those?" Darren asked. "And what's that funny noise?"

"No idea," Wolfgang replied.

They heard a gasp from Ben, who was staring out the porthole. After narrowly missing his brother's car, the *Thunder Road* was in the process of buzzing other vehicles on the lot, shearing off several radio antennas as it moved along.

Fifty yards away, at the drive-in snack counter, Steve Jackson and his friends were playing their usual game with the attendant. The modus operandi was for one of them to distract the girl behind the counter while the others helped themselves to candy from areas out of her field of vision. Now, in accordance with that plan, Steve bought some popcorn and looked down with a carefully studied expression of pain and puzzlement as the girl dropped change into his palm.

"Hey," Steve said. "That was a twenty I gave you, not a ten."

"It was not," the girl replied.

As she spoke, angry and distracted, Steve's pal leaned over the counter to pilfer a dozen candy bars.

"I want to see the manager," Steve demanded, hoping to give his friends at least one more shot at the goodies.

"He's not here."

"Then get him."

Inside the *Thunder Road,* which was rapidly bearing

down on the snack bar, Wolfgang continued to punch instructions into the computer. Nothing he did seemed to have any effect on the endless lines of instructions pouring forth so fast it was nearly impossible to read them, much less interpret their meaning.

"Watch it!" Ben yelled from the porthole, alarmed at their course.

"I'm not doing it!" Wolfgang yelled back.

"Then who is?"

"I don't know. It must be programming itself. Or I fed it some data it can't deal with. It's like it's trying to carry pi to infinity."

"Stop!" Ben shouted as the *Thunder Road* roared toward the candy counter. "Stop it!"

"I can't! I'm no good under pressure!" Wolfgang half yelled, half sobbed.

Together they watched through the porthole as the snack bar came closer and closer.

The girl behind the candy counter, meanwhile, had just finished telling Steve Jackson exactly what he could do with his demand for more money when her eyes suddenly widened with terror. Steve, misinterpreting her over-his-shoulder glance as a sign of weakness or at least confusion, decided to apply clinching arguments to his plea. The worst that could happen would be that she would say no again while his buddies glommed more candy bars.

"Hey," he said emphatically. "That twenty was a present from my sick mother. I wouldn't lie about a thing like that. So help me, it's the truth. If I'm lying, I hope I get struck by lightning or hit by a freight train."

An instant later, the *Thunder Road* blasted its way into the snack bar, wrapped in a huge awning previously hanging in front of the concession booth. The frighteningly close block letters read: GET MORE OUT OF LIFE: GO TO THE MOVIES. After a moment of panicked immobility, the girl leaped out of the way as the spiraling force field ripped through the wall in front of her and proceeded to tear its way out the rear partition of the building. Steve Jackson was pushed into a popcorn machine and his cohorts cata-pulted backwards into the restrooms, where one of them came to rest with his head lodged in a toilet. Amid a shower of popcorn, flying Pom-Poms, twisted candy bar wrappers and various bits of other barely recognizable debris, the *Thunder Road* emerged from the back wall of the snack bar with a loud crash, a flying shishkabob of junk food and demolished building parts. Those persons who got a good—although neces-sarily brief—look at the missile saw only a huge round shape, a sort of colorful blob with something resem-bling a crude lightning bolt etched down its side. Some later described the object as a meteor but most, because of its regular shape and presence of what one person claimed was a porthole, reported it definitely as an alien spacecraft of the flying saucer type. One eyewitness who maintained that the object was a refur-bished Tilt-a-Whirl car was quickly dismissed as a prankster not worth questioning further.

Inside the *Thunder Road,* the imminent meeting with the snack bar caused Ben to close his eyes and brace himself. From chin to toe, his body stiffened in readi-ness for the crash, but to his surprise, the high-speed collision occurred without the slightest increase in sound. No massive jolt or even a shudder was felt as the ship zoomed through the concrete, glass, and wood of the concession booth as smoothly as a jetliner entering a fluffy cloud bank.

Striking the awning first, the front section of the vehicle, including the porthole, was partially enfolded in the canvas by the time it crashed through the front wall and entered the customer service area. As it continued through the snack bar and zoomed out the rear wall barely ten feet off the ground, the *Thunder Road* shucked its cover of flapping promotional material, revealing its true shape and colors to a bevy of terrified, scattering witnesses.

Fortunately, no one was struck directly by the flying object or crushed against a hard surface. Even Steve Jackson was knocked through the open doorway of the popcorn machine, rather than forced through the plastic side. But the cries of terror would have convinced anyone that a true calamity was taking place.

When the expected turbulence failed to shake the ship, Ben opened his eyes and peered through the porthole. At first, it was covered with a dark shape, only a small triangle of light showing near the bottom.

"What's going on out there?" Wolfgang yelled over his shoulder. His eyes remained glued to the keyboard and monitor, which continued to display data of its own creation. Line after line of arcane figures, numbers and abbreviations flew by, as voluminous and recognizable to Wolfgang as the parts list of an aircraft carrier.

"I don't know," Ben shouted back. "I can't see a damn thing."

"What do you mean, you can't see anything? Is it dark out?"

"Something's covering the porthole. I guess we got wrapped up in something."

"Damn!" Wolfgang muttered. All he needed now to complicate his problems was lack of visibility.

"There!" Ben shouted. "It's gone!"

As soon as the awning slipped away from the nose of the *Thunder Road*, Ben could see the receding opening in the concession stand through which they had just passed. It was as smooth and precise as the tiny holes punched in Wolfgang's books and shelves by the smaller version of the force field. On the periphery of the opening was a scattering of debris and, outside that, groups of people staring with wide, wild eyes. Most were standing as if rooted to their spots, but a few sat or lay on the ground where they had fallen to avoid the terrifying flying object.

"I hope we didn't hurt anybody," Ben murmured. Until this moment, the *Thunder Road* had been little more than an elaborate toy to him; now he was amazed by not only its scientific potential but by the amount of harm their toy could inflict if not used properly.

Darren was even more impressed and upset by the impromptu assault on the snack bar. To him it was proof that Wolfgang's knowledge of the vessel was sketchy at best. After looking at the shattered building they had just tunneled through, he gritted his teeth and turned on the captain.

"Move over, Ex-lax," he shouted. "You don't even know how to steer this thing."

He started to reach for the computer. Wolfgang slapped his hands away.

"What are you doing?" he yelped. "Get your paws off! You don't know—"

"And neither do you, jerk! You just took us right through the snack bar."

"I didn't!" Wolfgang protested.

"Then who did?"

"It wasn't my fault! I didn't do that. I don't know what happened!"

"I think they were going to tear it down anyway," Ben said philosophically.

"I don't want to fly with this jerk," Darren continued, glaring at Wolfgang.

"Okay," Wolfgang replied. "Then suppose you take over, sport."

He removed his hands from the keyboard, indicating that Darren should take over.

After a moment of hesitation, Darren looked away. The fact that he hadn't the vaguest idea how to correct the *Thunder Road*'s erratic behavior helped mollify his anger. He suddenly realized that, like it or not, their future was in Wolfgang's hands.

"Try to figure out something, will you, genius?" he muttered.

Wolfgang returned his gaze to the console and keyboard, his expression tight-lipped and thoughtful. Finally, as he continued to feed the machine data that would block what was already being programmed by some unknown force, the long lines of mysterious signs and figures stopped.

"What did you do?" Ben asked, noticing his partner's mixed relief and puzzlement.

"I'll tell you later," Wolfgang replied, not wanting to admit he was as much in the dark as Ben or Darren.

Striking the keys, he was gratified to see that the monitor began displaying what he was feeding, rather than the chicken-scratchings shown previously. Hopeful that they might have escaped from a chaotic and potentially disastrous episode, he programmed them to gain some altitude and execute a sharp left turn. Instantly the *Thunder Road* followed his instructions, the lines of cars and curious people falling away beneath them, even the large theater screen reducing to postage-stamp-size in the distance.

"I think we're back on course," Wolfgang said, breathing a sigh. "She's doing what I tell her now."

"Great!" Ben smiled.

Darren's mood also brightened. "Good work, Einstein," he said, giving Wolfgang a pat on the shoulder. "I'm sorry about before. Now let's see what this crate can really do, okay?"

Wolfgang shook his head. "How about letting me get my bearings first? I want to be able to think straight before I really put this thing through the paces. I'm not sure I'm confident yet. You said yourself I don't even know how to steer her."

"That was before. Everything's great now."

"But I'm not sure everything's great. I never found out why it malfunctioned."

"But we only have so much air," Darren protested. "It would be nice to give her a real spin before we have to land."

He looked at Ben for confirmation.

"Yeah," Ben said.

"I agree with both you guys," Wolfgang replied. "But first let me make sure I know what's going on."

"You said yourself she's doing what you tell her."

"Yeah. Now. But before it was different. And later it might be different. I want to be sure everything's under control. That was scary back there. I didn't know where those figures were coming from and I still don't."

"All right," Darren said. "Test it a minute or so. Try some spins and stuff. If she works, let's really fly."

"I'd rather go back," Wolfgang murmured. "It will be a lot better to check this out on the ground."

"Come on," Ben urged. "No time like the present. Why sit on the ground when we can be testing the *Thunder Road* under real conditions?"

"Yeah," Darren nodded. "Let's see what she can do."

"Are you serious? I'd say she's done more than enough already!"

"I don't mean go through buildings and like that. I mean speed. Let's see how fast she can go."

Wolfgang sighed. He really wanted to take a more reasoned approach to this experiment. A battery of questions whizzed through his mind as he hesitated. Suppose the computer was malfunctioning intermittently? That meant that what had gone wrong before could go wrong again sometime in the future. Suppose he was feeding data incorrectly, causing it to program itself into violent random patterns? Wouldn't it be much saner and safer to test both the computer and himself on the ground, using a smaller force field that could be observed? He likened their situation to that of a ballistics expert testing a new projectile. Anyone knew that the true expert performed his tests on a firing range so that he could stand on the side and study the results. Only a maniac would test his projectile by using himself as a human cannonball.

"No," he said finally. "This is crazy. Not only that—I'm the captain and I say—"

His decree ended in mid-sentence as a white light suddenly poured in through the porthole, startling and temporarily blinding the three boys.

"What the hell!" Darren shouted.

"What's that?" Ben shouted.

The answer was not long in coming. Abreast of the *Thunder Road* and slightly above it, two officers of Police Helicopter #2 struggled to maintain their composure as their high-powered spotlight landed on the unidentified flying object and gave them their first clear sight of the ship. Charlie Drake, veteran of the crew, had been flying law enforcement missions for a dozen years and had seen nothing like this. The younger pilot, Gordon Deems, nearly lost control of the chopper when the *Thunder Road* popped into view.

"Holy mackerel!" he said with a whistle. "What the hell do you think that is?"

Charlie Drake had no idea whatever. It seemed to be a mixture of space-age sophistication and pop art. Whatever its origin, it sent a quiver of fear and excitement through his body, but he managed to suppress any outward symptoms of panic. Holding the microphone to his mouth, he first reported the unknown object's position to police headquarters as a precautionary measure, then pressed the button switching on the external P.A. system.

"What are you gonna do?" Gordon asked.

"What does it look like I'm doing?" Charlie replied. "I'm gonna go by the book. Talk to them first, and then if they resist arrest, use sterner measures."

"That P.A. system's been acting up lately," Gordon said, trying not to show his trepidation. "They might not be able to hear it."

"They'll hear it all right. Get closer to them so I can order it down."

Gordon applied more power, kicking the chopper twenty yards or so ahead of the bulbous globe that moved smoothly and silently in a parallel course.

Angling the spotlight as they moved, Drake kept the object illuminated as he lifted the microphone and barked his first order.

"Attention!" he shouted. "You're flying an unauthorized vehicle with no pre-filed flight plan. That is a violation of Federal Aviation Agency procedure. We're ordering you to land immediately."

The unidentified object showed no inclination to do as ordered, continuing its path directly northwest. Charlie repeated the admonition with the same effect.

"Maybe there's nobody in it," Gordon suggested.

"Don't be silly."

"It could be a satellite or something sent here by other people just to observe. Right?"

Charlie shook his head disdainfully.

"I'm serious," Gordon said. "Or, if it's not a remote-controlled thing, the people inside might not be able to understand English. In fact, it would be damned unusual if they knew one word. They probably think we're saying hello instead of ordering them to land."

"Well," Charlie replied, the muscles of his jaw

working overtime, "we have ways to fix that. If they don't understand they're supposed to land, we'll just *force* them to land."

Gordon's heart did a flip-flop.

"Do you really think that's the best course of action?" he stammered. "I mean, if they're from another planet, this could disrupt the whole first meeting between our world and theirs. Not only that—if they're smart enough to get here first, they're also smarter than we are, which means they'll probably have weapons that'll make ours look like peashooters."

He thought he'd made a very telling argument, but Charlie wasn't impressed.

"Then we'll neutralize their superior intelligence by shooting first," Charlie said.

Gordon took a deep breath, causing Drake to regard him with a mixture of scorn and concern.

"Calm down," he said. "That thing, whatever it is, just terrorized an entire community. It frightened people and destroyed private property. It's our job to order it down and find out who or what's in there."

"Yeah, but if we get killed, nobody'll ever find out much about it. But if we just kind of follow along and don't antagonize them—"

Charlie turned away and pressed the P.A. button again.

"Attention!" he barked. "This is Sergeant Drake of the Air Police. We repeat, you're in violation of federal and municipal ordinances. We're ordering you to land immediately so that this matter can be handled peacefully. If you continue to ignore these orders, we will be forced to open fire as a means of—"

Inside the spaceship, the three boys watched the officer's lips flap but heard no sound.

"I'll bet he's ordering us to land," Darren said. "He'll blast us away if we don't get outa here."

Wolfgang nodded as he finished programming new information into the computer. Fortunately, he had started to work as soon as the helicopter pulled abreast of them, realizing immediately their need to escape.

"I understand," he said now, not looking up from the keyboard. "And I'm doing my best to comply."

As he fed the last item into the computer, he smiled with a confidence that he hoped was justified.

"Now here's what it means to have no inertia," he said simply.

As he watched the alien vessel apparently ignoring their ultimatum, Gordon Deems's lips were so dry he was sure that uttering a single word would cause them to split apart. Not that he had a single word to say that was appropriate, other than "help." Deep within himself, he wanted to hit the throttle and move as far away from the spaceship as possible. He was too well-trained a policeman for that, however, having learned to conquer his pangs of fear by saying nothing and following orders when they were issued by a more decisive partner. Now Charlie Drake was that partner and Deems simply did as he was told. He didn't even have the strength to argue anymore. He just wanted to get it over with.

"All right then," Charlie Drake announced over the P.A. system. "That was your last warning. At the count of three, unless you land immediately, we intend to open fire . . . One . . . two . . . thr—"

Suddenly, to Drake's amazement and Deems's delight, the alien ship was gone. One second it was just below them; the next it was a dot at the end of a blur moving away at terrific speed.

The occupants of the *Thunder Road,* meanwhile, were thoroughly enjoying themselves. Wolfgang's escape data had worked perfectly, sending the ship into three ninety-degree turns and a power climb that left the police helicopter floundering far behind. Darren and Ben, though restricted by the vessel's space limitations, were doing their best to hop up and down in place.

"Did you see that?" Darren shouted. "They just disappeared! I'll bet those cops are taking gas."

"Way to go, Wolfgang!" Ben yelled, pounding his friend about the head and shoulders.

Wolfgang smiled. He was pleased, not only at his crewmates' approbation, but by the fact that now things seemed to be going right for a change. It bothered him that he still didn't know the cause of the recent malfunction, but he tried not to dwell on it. If he could work with the force field on the ground for a while!

"Thanks, guys," he said. "Now let's go home and take a break."

The suggestion did not sit well with Ben and Darren, who were still celebrating their escape from the police and wanted more action.

"No . . . no . . . no," they pleaded. "Let's stay up just awhile longer."

Wolfgang had to admit that tooling along a mile above town was enjoyable. Their ship was homemade but it didn't seem uncomfortable at all. "You'll notice we're not even cold," he said.

"I was wondering about that," Darren replied. "How come? It should be cold up here, right?"

"It is—outside. But the force field insulates against everything."

"Great. How's my dad's truck battery holding out? She's pretty good, isn't she?"

Wolfgang checked the performance figures on the video screen. "It's ridiculous," he said with a smile. "We're traveling at ninety or one hundred miles an hour and I'm not even using one percent of our portable power yet."

Ben withdrew his gaze from the porthole and the landscape whipping by beneath them. "Think we got enough power to make it to the moon and back?" he asked.

"Easily," Wolfgang replied. "But not tonight."

"Why not? You chicken?"

"No. It's our air supply. I'm worried about that. That one tank is all we have."

"Yeah," Ben nodded. "We gotta do something about that. Fifteen or twenty minutes isn't enough for some of the missions I had in mind."

"Well, just keep them in mind until the next time we fly," Wolfgang said. "And keep a lookout for recognizable landmarks below. We don't want to get lost."

"So what's the big problem?" Darren asked. "If we're lost, we just land, open the bubble for a new batch of air and then take off again."

"That could become very time-consuming," Wolfgang cautioned. "And there might not be a convenient place to land where we run out."

"Okay, okay," Darren muttered.

"Anyway, we're still all right," Ben interjected. "I just spotted Rucker's Mall over to the left at nine o'clock. We can follow Mason Boulevard all the way home from here by heading south."

"Where's the cop chopper?" Darren asked.

"Don't worry about him. He's so far back, I can hardly see him."

"Well, let's go! Let's show him some real speed!"

Wolfgang nodded and fed more data into the computer, hitting a few keys too fast but apparently doing no harm. The *Thunder Road* responded to the new influx of orders by taking off like a bullet.

Charlie Drake cursed when he saw the alien vessel shoot forward with a new burst of speed. After the series of rapid turns and display of accelerative power, the vessel had slowed down a bit, following a straight course that they were able to track. This led him to hope that losing the invader completely was not necessarily inevitable. If he could remain close, perhaps the assistance of ground radar and additional helicopter crews could be used to alter the situation.

"I'm going to call Frank Martin at the airport," he said.

"Good idea," Gordon replied.

Hitting the switch, Charlie was soon on the radio to Frank. "Listen," he said in a staccato voice, abandoning formal radio procedure in the interest of speed. "This is Charlie Drake. We're two miles west of Chambers Crossroads, tracking the alien ship . . ."

"What alien ship?" a voice crackled.

"—the alien space ship that demolished the drive-in theater. We need a radar fix and tracking on her and some more choppers."

Back at the municipal airport, chubby and balding Frank Martin sighed and adjusted his headset. So far it had been a very pleasant evening. A portable color television set on the table next to his desk was showing his favorite crime drama; Max Caldwell had just returned from the all-night eatery with some fresh coffee and jelly rolls; the climax of the drama was just about to begin. In short, everything was perfect—and now this. If it had been anyone other than Charlie Drake on the horn, Frank might have displayed more concern or paid more attention. But Drake was well-known as a sort of flying vigilante, a one-man posse out to round up all the outstanding and available crime in one evening. It was reassuring to see a law enforcement officer take his job seriously, but sometimes Charlie simply overdid it. He tended to see violators lurking in every shadow, which could be very irritating to co-workers who just wanted to get through the evening.

"I didn't hear anything about damage to the drive-in theater," Frank replied, matter-of-factly, trying to keep one eye and ear on the TV set.

Charlie didn't like his disinterested tone of voice.

"Well, it happened," he shot back.

"What happened?"

"I'm telling you—this alien vessel tore through the snack bar. Went in one side and came out the other. Tore a hole eight to ten feet in diameter."

"Anybody hurt?" Frank asked in an obligatory manner.

"You can check with the ground police if you want to hear a newscast," Charlie replied acidly. "Right now we gotta get that ship to land. We ordered it to come down but it's got too much speed. Just clear run away from us."

"Where is it now?"

"My guess is it's in sector five, near coordinates A-fifteen. And moving fast."

"Roger. Wait."

Frank Martin put his feet back on the floor and flipped his control observation panel to the appropriate sector. Nothing was visible.

"Sorry," he said into the microphone. "Ain't nothing there. Not a mini-blip even."

"Must be moving too fast. Try sector eleven."

Frank sighed. "You sure it's another UFO, Charlie?" he asked.

"What do you mean, *another* UFO?"

"Well, you've seen more than a couple that never turned up." Frank smiled. "We still get a kick out of that time you called about that weather balloon. And what was that other one—a satellite? We were getting ready to attack NASA . . . "

Across the room, Max chuckled appreciatively, encouraging Frank to continue his needling.

"Personally, Charlie," he said, "if you ask me, I think you're getting too much caffeine in your system. That extra tenseness is making you see things that don't exist."

"This is a real spaceship, dammit," Charlie shot back. "I got a witness here in the person of Gordon Deems. Now suppose you start tracking that sucker."

Still smiling, Frank Martin flipped from one observation sector to the next without success. Then, as he slid sector twenty-two into position, he saw a red blur dart off the edge of the screen.

"Just a second," he said.

Switching to the next adjacent panel, he saw the tiny blip skim from one edge of the square to the other side in about ten seconds. Then the radar screen was clear again.

"What do you see?" Charlie demanded.

"Must be equipment malfunction," Frank replied. "I thought I saw something but it was going too fast."

"That's it, dammit!" Charlie yelled. "Find that alien ship or she'll get away!"

Frank hit another button, which compressed their entire enforcement area into one panel. On this chart the blip was plainly visible, moving from southeast to northwest and nearly off the edge.

"I guess you're not crazy after all," Frank admitted, his eyes widening and a knot beginning to form in his throat. "There's something out there, all right, but you ain't gonna catch her in that glue-footed chopper. And maybe even an air force jet won't catch her . . ."

"Notify Greenville . . . that's where she's heading."

"Yeah. But now something crazy's happening . . ."

"What?"

"Hard to explain. An erratic pattern . . . looks like she's blown her cork . . . gone out of control. And the blip's getting smaller, like she's heading straight up."

"Dammit," Charlie grumbled. "I'll bet that son-of-a-bitch is heading for Jupiter or something."

Inside the *Thunder Road*, everything seemed efficient and quite ordinary, if one could discount the fact that a glorified Tilt-a-Whirl car was now flying along at several hundred miles an hour with no visible means of propulsion. Even the normally nervous Wolfgang had started to relax, joining his two crewmen in watching the lights below. All were impressed with the ship's effortless motion and speed.

"This is really something," Darren said after a while. "I couldn't even feel us speed up."

"Where should we go?" Ben asked, his eyes gleaming with excitement. "How about Australia?"

"No," Wolfgang replied. "We have to go back home in a minute."

"One minute?"

"Yes. That's about all the time we have. We probably have more but there's no sense cutting it too close."

Looking out the porthole, Ben saw no recognizable landmarks. "Can you find our way back?" he asked.

Wolfgang nodded. "No problem," he said. "At least I don't think so. I fed a set of homing coordinates into the machine so all I have to do is hit one key and we automatically head there. So even if something happens . . ."

"Like what?"

"Like, we all pass out or start to feel woozy. All I'll have to do is hit that key and we'll head for home. It could save our lives."

"There you go again," Ben said, frowning. "Talking about dying and stuff."

"Well, when you're this high off the ground and moving this fast and on limited air, you have to consider the possibility of something happening."

Ben shrugged and returned his gaze to the porthole.

He then did an abrupt double take—for one moment the ground lights were flashing by in a smooth line, the next they were gone, replaced by stars and dark sky.

"Hey!" he shouted, turning back to Wolfgang. "Did you just do something?"

"What do you mean?"

"Did you change course?"

"No, why?"

"You're not trying to surprise me by going to Australia after all?"

Wolfgang shook his head.

"Then I think something's wrong," Ben said soberly.

Before Wolfgang could answer, the computer started making a strange trilling sound, the same noise it had made when they'd gone out of control earlier.

"Oh-oh," Wolfgang muttered. "Looks like it's doing it again."

Ben and Darren watched with worried expressions as the monitor once again began filling up with enormous lines of numbers and signs. Wolfgang's fingers were nowhere near the keys.

"What do you think it is?" Ben asked. "It's got to be something, doesn't it?"

"See for yourself," Wolfgang replied.

"What does that mean?"

"It means, I don't know what the hell it is, that your guess is as good as mine. Maybe better."

"Tell it to stop. Type in something."

"I tried that before."

"Well, try it again. I'm sure you can think of some magic formula. How did you stop it before?"

"I didn't. It stopped itself."

"Come on," Darren said. "Fix it."

"That's easy for you to say," Wolfgang growled. But he put his fingers on the keyboard and typed in the most precise cease-and-desist orders he could concoct. The screen continued to display line after line of mumbo-jumbo.

"It won't respond to my instructions," Wolfgang said, somewhat unnecessarily.

Ben, who had returned his gaze to the porthole, suddenly gasped.

"What is it?" Darren asked.

"I can hardly see the ground! We must be a hundred miles up!"

Darren took a glance and immediately gave way to panic. "Get . . . us . . . the . . . hell . . . down!" he ordered, his voice sounding gutteral and constricted.

Wolfgang could only shrug helplessly. He tried hitting the single key that would return them to their home coordinates, but the computer refused to acknowledge his command. As he watched the screen with mounting despair, the vertical displays of data were replaced by smaller, more complicated-looking, even less identifiable rows of horizontally moving objects, as if the program had achieved a new plateau.

"What is it doing?" Ben asked, noticing Wolfgang's jaw drop.

"I don't know, okay? It must be getting commands from somewhere else!"

"From Earth?"

"I don't know!"

"Great!" Darren rasped, leaning his cheek against the ship's bulkhead.

Wolfgang went back to the keyboard, his fingers poised above it just in case the figures paused for a second. He would need only a split-second to enter the single-key rescue code—if the orders ever stopped.

"Oh, God!"

The voice was Ben's.

"What is it?" Wolfgang yelled, not daring to take his eyes off the screen.

"We're outa air," Ben whispered, tapping the needle on the tank next to them.

If the gauge was accurate, it was indeed true that a new problem existed—the ultimate problem of where their next breaths would come from.

All three of the boys turned ashen white as they looked at the gauge on the tank.

It read EMPTY.

Chapter Seven

"IT CAN'T HAVE HAPPENED. NOT THAT FAST. IT'S JUST plain impossible."

"I tell you, it's true, Charlie. I talked with Greenville, Tamago, and West Lawrence. They followed the blip in a perfectly straight line the same as I did, and all three of them saw it disappear *upwards*. Not off the chart, but *up*."

"To what altitude?"

"Forget it, Charlie. That little devil's out of sight, higher than you ca—"

"Tell me!"

"Would you believe five hundred miles and still climbing?"

"No."

"Well, that's all the higher we can track it. It's probably halfway to Mars by now."

Inside the *Thunder Road*, the occupants would have gladly welcomed the opportunity to surrender to Charlie Drake and take their medicine. Now they were so far above the earth it seemed they would never get back. The fact that they were either out of air or dangerously low meant only that their demise would be mercifully brief rather than protracted and agonizing.

Considering the circumstances, the crew members behaved with extraordinary calm. Darren simply stared ahead, his eyes fixed on the porthole. Ben and Wolfgang looked at the computer console, their expressions vacant as they watched the lines of incomprehensible figures roll by.

"Maybe the gauge is wrong," Ben mumbled finally. "We could have more time than we think."

"You mean like a minute or two?" Wolfgang replied. "That'll help a lot."

Ben opened his lips to continue the discussion, then closed them. Talking would only use more energy, depriving them of precious seconds.

NO ACCESS, the video screen read. Wolfgang was still trying to find a method of breaking through the impenetrable curtain of material being fed to it. Again and again he hit the keys, only to draw the inevitable and infuriating response, NO ACCESS.

"Damn!" Wolfgang finally yelled, pulling his fist back as if to strike the screen.

"No!" Ben cautioned, grabbing his friend's arm in midair.

Wolfgang sighed and tried another series of typed instructions. NO ACCESS, the machine replied.

"How about the single key bit you told me about?" Ben suggested.

"I tried that already."

"How about if you—"

"Shut up! Let me concentrate!"

The barrage of NO ACCESS responses was definitely getting to Wolfgang, who felt as if his sanity was slowly slipping away. Not only was he running out of gimmicks to try, but his brain was finding it harder and harder to even function, much less be brilliant.

"Come on," he pleaded, holding the screen gently between the palms of his hands, like someone trying to reason with a petulant child. "Listen to me. Just give me one chance, will you?"

The NO ACCESS sign remained.

Ben glanced out the porthole. Below them, land masses were plainly visible, but no individual lights stood out. We must be a thousand miles up, he thought.

"I . . . can't . . . breathe," Darren said softly, almost matter-of-factly.

Ben was also beginning to experience some light-headedness but he tried not to acknowledge it. Closing his eyes, he tried forcing himself to think of something pleasant—like Lori Swenson and her party the next night—but that started a train of thought that was even worse than contemplating their imminent demise. What would she think, he wondered, when he never returned? Would she notice at all? When his parents realized he was gone, how much mental anguish would they suffer? Would one or both of them dedicate a large part of their lives to visiting or calling every police department or bureau of missing persons? Only now did he realize how thoughtless he had been to exclude them so completely from his life. If only he had thought to leave a note . . . that might have spared them some suffering . . .

His eyes were closed only a few seconds when he felt a new terror. His sense of equilibrium seemed to be going fast. With his eyes closed, he felt himself drifting in all directions, floating upside down, trapped in a pounding, pressurized blackness. Because that was the worst state of all, he opened his eyes again. But everything in the *Thunder Road* suddenly looked different. Darren, though only a few feet away, seemed to be seated at the end of a long corridor filmed through a fish-eye lens. Wolfgang's head and features were elongated, his body twisted surrealistically. And then Ben realized that every breath he took was causing him terrible pain.

"We're suffocating!" he gasped. "Do something!"

He heard Wolfgang yelling in frustration but couldn't make out actual words. Sweat was pouring down his friend's face, even popping off his forehead like some character in an animated cartoon.

"Help . . ." Darren moaned.

"Shut up, both of you," Wolfgang grunted. "What can I tell it? What can I tell it?"

"Tell it to go backwards," Ben mumbled.

"I tried that already . . . I don't know what to do anymore . . . it's over . . ."

They heard nothing but their own constricted breathing sounds as the three thought of their impending doom. Then Darren looked at Wolfgang. His arm slowly rose and one finger came forward in a slow-motion crooked pointing gesture, his mouth hanging open like that of a drunken man about to make some terribly significant observation on life.

"Try . . . switching . . . something on . . . the circuit . . . board," he moaned, driving the words out with great difficulty between long, labored silences.

"That won't w—" Wolfgang said. Then he shook his head, not bothering to finish.

"When a . . . car doesn't . . . work . . ." Darren continued, "you don't . . . keep driving . . . it . . . you look . . . under . . . the . . . hood . . . right?"

Wolfgang slowly looked up. His eyes, unfocused and insensate, began to come alive.

"Maybe . . ." he muttered. "Maybe . . ."

Reaching for the computer, he ripped off its cover and examined the small, complex breadboard of circuitry.

"Maybe if I . . . reverse this diode," he gasped.

"Hold your ears . . . this may . . . cause a sort . . . of bang . . . it's going to . . . turn off for a second . . . and the change . . . in pressure . . . aw, the hell with explanations . . ."

He pulled out the small power diode as Ben and Darren looked on, their glassy eyes curiously lacking a sense of either jeopardy or involvement.

WHAM!

Whatever atmospheric problem caused a change in pressure sent a loud explosion reverberating throughout the ship. Sharp as it was, however, the boys continued to stare ahead, only a blink indicating that the noise had penetrated their semiconscious state.

As the force field momentarily released its hold around the *Thunder Road,* the car skipped out of its upward rush. Stale air whooshed out of the vessel, to be replaced by the thinner, colder air of the upper atomosphere. Chilled by the sub-zero temperature, the boys shuddered to life.

"What . . . ?" Darren mumbled.

"So cold . . ." Ben stammered.

"It'll warm up," Wolfgang said softly. "Body heat . . . and I think something good may have happened."

Immediately after shutting off the force field, he had turned it on again and slightly enlarged its size, hoping that during the fraction of a second he would be able to wipe the programming slate clean and recapture the *Thunder Road* in a new bubble. The maneuver involved terrible risk, chiefly that they would be left stranded in space with no insulating shield around them. But as they were in danger of suffocating anyway, it seemed a risk worth taking.

Apparently it had worked. As soon as the operation was completed, the computer screen went blank. Wolfgang exhaled hopefully. At least the gibberish was gone. Turning the diode around so that its connectors were reversed from its original position, he was gratified to see the screen light up with its normal Apple-type graphics.

He looked out the porthole. Their upward motion seemed to have stopped.

"Yeah . . ." he said as he breathed.

Reaching for the computer keyboard, he quickly punched the single digit that would return them to their home coordinates. Then he fell back in his seat, exhausted.

"What's happening?" Ben asked, moving only his eyes to look at Wolfgang, his expression very white.

"We're heading back, I think."

"Just falling?"

"Falling to our home coordinates."

"We won't burn up first?"

"Shouldn't."

"We won't smash into a million pieces?"

"Shouldn't."

"Why not?"

"No inertia. We'll just stop at the coordinates . . . same as if we're going two miles an hour."

"If the coordinates are right."

"Right."

"Can you see Darren's face?"

"Yeah."

"Is he all right?"

"I don't know. He's out."

"Please, God, don't let him be dead."

"He'll be okay."

"How do you know?"

"He's tough. Now don't talk. Save your oxygen."

Ben and Wolfgang leaned back. Through the porthole they could see land masses returning. The *Thunder Road* was falling faster than they could possibly have imagined—not relying on the dictates of gravity, but actually tearing its way through the Earth's atmosphere as if racing to the finish line.

"Look . . ." Wolfgang gasped, pointing. "There are . . . clouds . . . and lights."

The horizon was tilted at a forty-five-degree angle but plainly showed, by the size and intensity of lights, that the ship was less than a mile from the ground. Ben leaned forward to look out, but Wolfgang placed a hand gently against his chest and smiled.

"Never mind," he said. "I take it back. Don't look out. The speed'll scare the hell out of you."

Ben closed his eyes.

"Let me know when it's over," he said.

As they continued to move downward, the horizon was replaced by the shapes of tree tops.

"It's over!" Wolfgang whooped.

Tearing himself free of the straps, he looked out and saw that they were once again neatly nestled in the woods by the creek bed. Reaching for the keyboard, he quickly deactivated the force field.

Cool air rushed into the *Thunder Road* and with it, fresh, abundant oxygen. Ben inhaled deeply, smiled, and then looked at Darren. His big friend seemed to be breathing . . .

"Great!" Ben shouted, as Darren's eyelids fluttered and opened.

"Where are we?" Darren asked thickly, like someone emerging from heavy sedation.

"We're home."

"How did you do it?" he asked, looking at Wolfgang with a stunned, happy expression.

"I programmed the EPROM to take us back to our beginning coordinates . . . if the system ever rebooted. Anyway, it's over. We made it. We're alive."

Ben started to chuckle.

"What's so funny?" Wolfgang asked.

"I was just thinking that it was *great!* That was really incredible. Next time—"

"Listen, Ben," Wolfgang interrupted. "I'll admit that was exciting, but you have to admit it was just too risky. Next time we need to be more scientific. I'm not getting in that thing again until we find out where it was getting those numbers. Then I'm gonna run tests, hundreds of tests . . ."

They were standing on the ground next to the vessel, which looked none the worse for wear, following its trip of several hundred—possibly thousands—of miles.

"You're chicken," Ben said smiling.

"I am not. It's just that using a scientific method is a lot smarter than suffocating to death or getting needlessly squished."

Darren, still shaking his head groggily, dropped to the ground next to them.

"What about you?" Ben asked. "Do you want to go up again soon? Maybe tomorrow?"

Darren looked away. His complexion, which had been regaining some of its color, suddenly began to whiten again.

"Uh . . ." he murmured.

Ben looked at his two friends with frustration and scorn. "I don't get it," he said. "We have our own spaceship! We're the three luckiest guys in the world. We can go anywhere, visit the moon if we want, and you act like it's a curse or something. What about the *Thunder Road?* Are you just going to let it sit there and rust?"

"Yes!" Wolfgang replied sharply. "That's exactly what's going to happen, until we find out exactly what went wrong up there."

He turned away. Ben looked at Darren, who was in

the process of pulling his father's truck battery out of the spaceship's hatch. Feeling Ben's eyes on him, Darren shrugged as he hefted the battery onto his shoulder.

"Sorry, man," he said. "I want to live."

"Come on, Dar—" Ben pleaded.

"Soon as we get the bugs out, count me in."

With a shaky little wave, he left.

Ben stood for a moment, watching as Wolfgang and Darren departed by different directions. Then he kicked the bottom of the *Thunder Road*, winced in pain, and stumbled off toward his own house.

". . . On the local news scene, almost one-hundred Central City residents reported seeing a large flying object last night. According to eyewitness accounts, the unidentified aircraft appeared first in the southwest, where it hovered several hundred feet off the ground. One resident, Dayton McComber, said he frightened it off with a shotgun blast . . ."

"Hey, Charlie, where you goin'?" Gordon Deems asked, shouting above the noise of the chopper blades. It was near the end of their shift and he was ready to fill out their reports and get some sleep.

"I'm gonna take one more look around," Charlie Drake called back over his shoulder.

"What for?"

"That spaceship."

Gordon took a few steps after him. "But it's gone, Charlie," he protested. "You ain't got a snowball's chance in hell . . ."

"See you in an hour or so . . ."

"Wait a minute. We gotta fill out these reports. I need you. I can't go home unless—"

But he was speaking to empty air. His jaw firmly set,

the indomitable Charlie Drake was already inside the helicopter and cleared for takeoff.

". . . *Approximately ten minutes later, the unidentified flying object buzzed the Elk Ridge Drive-in Theater. After sweeping at treetop altitude, the missile or vehicle may have gone out of control, tearing through the theater snack booth and leaving this six-foot-diameter hole. Police said no one was hurt, although one young man swallowed the equivalent of four packs of bubble gum and had to be treated at Mount Zion Medical Center . . .*"

"Turn off that television set," Mrs. Muller shouted into the kitchen. "You know I don't like television at the breakfast table."

Ludwig flipped off the set. As he took his eyes off his troublesome brother, Johann placed a grapefruit seed in the hollow of a spoon and let it fly at Ludwig's head.

"Keep your projectiles to yourself," Mr. Muller warned, looking over the edge of his paper.

The family sat in silence for a minute, barely noticing Wolfgang when he trundled into the room, his eyes red and bleary. Slumping into a chair, he poured some cereal into a bowl and waited for Ludwig to finish using the milk. As was his annoying habit, Ludwig was letting the milk fall very slowly, almost in single drops.

"Come on," Wolfgang muttered.

Ludwig smiled, continuing his delicate project until his Mother glared at him and he released the carton.

"There's been quite a lot of activity in this town last night," Mr. Muller announced, flipping the pages of the morning newspaper. "There were numerous UFO sightings, many of them at the drive-in, where people are investigating who is responsible for the destruction of a concession stand . . ."

"Wolfgang!" Mrs. Muller said loudly.

"What?" he nearly yelled.

A single, terrifying thought raced through his mind: How could she have known? Was it reported in the morning paper? Biting his lip, Wolfgang looked at his mother, trying to appear innocent.

"What?" he asked in a softer voice.

She walked to the table, reached forward deliberately, and pinched his cheek.

"Your color is not good," she stated. "You should not stay up so late."

Wolfgang exhaled, relieved.

"What were you doing?" Ludwig asked.

"Nothing you'd be interested in."

"Did you go up in the terrarium?" his brother continued, smiling knowingly.

"No," Wolfgang replied.

"No?"

"The same answer as to whether Mom knows who put the Silly Putty in the toaster."

"What's the meaning of this conversation?" Mr. Muller demanded. "It doesn't make sense."

"That's right, Father," Wolfgang replied. "It doesn't make sense at all."

"*. . . A police department helicopter reportedly caught up with the UFO and ordered it to land. But the object either did not understand the order or refused to obey. Trackers at Central City Airport said the ship moved away from the helicopter at a 'very rapid rate of speed.' When questioned later as to just how fast the object was moving, Frank Martin, an air traffic controller, said he had not been able to measure it accurately and preferred not to make even an educated guess. Meanwhile, several persons have come forth to state that they saw people inside the craft. We'll have more on this aspect of the strange events of last night after these messages . . .*"

"Liars and headline-hunters," Charlie Drake muttered as he turned down the radio volume. "Nobody could have seen inside that crate. I was the closest person to it and I never got a look."

He was flying at slow speed over the northern suburbs, generally following the creek bed, when he spotted a streak of color beneath the trees. It was probably a large hunk of wood or plastic, but he decided to check it out anyway. Clues had a habit of showing up just when you least expected them . . .

Doubling back, he saw nothing at first and began to think it had been his imagination. Then, his eyes fell on a familiar, round object poorly hidden under a few branches. Smiling, he dropped down to get a better look.

"Looks like it," he said. "Yeah, it sure does look like that sucker . . ."

. . . Laurie Tompkins."

"Tell us what you saw, Laurie."

"A face looking out a window . . . a round window like they have on ships."

"I see. And what did it look like?"

"I told you . . . it was round."

"I mean, what did the face look like?"

"Well, it was really mean-looking and ugly. Kind of greenish . . ."

Ben nudged Wolfgang and smiled. "That must have been you she saw," he said.

"No. More likely Darren."

"Where is he, by the way?"

"Trying to make out with some girl. I don't think he was having much luck."

"Come on, you guys," Lori Swenson said, suddenly sweeping into view. She was dressed casually but looked absolutely stunning. "Come on," she repeated.

"Get up and circulate. This is my party and I want everybody to have fun."

"Listen to the cruise director," Wolfgang whispered.

"I can have fun just looking at you," Ben said with a debonair flourish.

"Oh, brother," Wolfgang muttered.

About a dozen boys and girls, most of them dressed smartly in designer jeans and shirts, stood near the television set, watching the newscast. In the background, Duran Duran on the stereo competed with the TV and normal party chatter, most of which also dealt with the extraterrestrial events of the night before. Lori frowned. This was obviously not what she had in mind for her party.

"How about if I turn that off?" she suggested, reaching for the television set.

"No, don't!" several kids implored her. "We want to see if there's any more."

Lori withdrew her hand and walked away, mumbling to herself.

Ben and Wolfgang eyed each other, enjoying over-hearing bits of conversation in which they figured.

". . . Everybody saw it," one boy said. "I was talking to Pete last night on the phone and we both looked out our windows at the same time. It was up there, all right . . ."

"You saw the UFO that blew up the drive-in?" a girl asked, thrilled.

Ben and Wolfgang saw that she was talking to Steve Jackson, who was helping himself to hors d'oeuvres along with his cronies. Lori Swenson stopped to glare at the boys as they stuffed their faces.

"God," she said. "For someone who wasn't even invited, you guys are sure putting it away."

Steve took no notice of the sarcastic comment,

enjoying the notoriety of being an actual eyewitness to the scene.

"You should have seen it," Steve said to the enthralled girl. "It was huge. Fifty feet across, at least, with these glowing lights."

"Didn't you run?" the girl asked, her eyes wide with admiration.

"No. I mean, what was the use? Might as well stand and fight, I thought. So I reached around for anything and grabbed this mop. I started swinging it and yelling 'Hey, man, get out of here,' and it just took off . . ."

"Were there people inside?"

"Yeah. Just like that girl said on TV—really mean and ugly-looking."

Ben and Wolfgang listened with straight faces to the fantastic commentary. Neither could have gone into a court of law and testified that Steve's story was a lie from beginning to end, but they knew definitely that the *Thunder Road* wasn't fifty feet across. As for the aliens being 'mean and ugly,' that was a matter of opinion generated by fear and the desire to tell a good story. The excitement did stimulate Ben in particular. All this talk filled him with a craving to fly another mission, as soon as possible. Why, they could even do it as soon as the party was over.

Nudging his sidekick, Ben mentioned his proposal. Wolfgang glowered at him.

"Crazy," he said. "You're just plain wacko."

"Why do you say that?"

"Because we've got so much study to do before we can just take off again."

Ben pounded his fist against his knee. "Come on!" he urged passionately. "You're supposed to be a scientist! We've got to go up again! There's something out there we don't know anything about—"

"Something? There's millions of things!"

"That's what I mean! With all that stuff to be studied and places to be explored, it's just plain stupid to sit here on Earth . . ."

"I agree, but we've got to make sure, be one hundred percent certain—"

"Certain of what?" Lori asked as she passed by, carrying a tray with punch glasses.

"Uh . . ."

"Never mind." She smiled. "Have some punch. Are you sure you're having a good time?"

Ben took a couple of glasses and handed one to Wolfgang. "Oh, yes," he answered.

"Then why don't you spread yourself around? Mingle with the others."

"We will," Ben said. "In a minute."

She smiled and whirled off. The two erstwhile spacemen sat in silence for a moment, watching the other party guests. Not far away, Darren was trying to pick up a girl, but was obviously having a hard time of it, judging from the girl's expressions and body language. After a minute, she walked away from him. He shrugged and moved on to the next girl.

"At least he's not thinking about flying another mission," Wolfgang murmured.

"He may be," Ben replied. "You can't tell."

"Well, it doesn't look that way to me. He's probably just glad we're alive. I don't think you realize how lucky we are."

"To be alive?" Ben shot back. "You call this being alive? I mean, *this* is as good as it gets!"

Wolfgang looked at him and frowned. He simply couldn't understand how someone could have so close a brush with death and be eager to fly again. If a year, even six months, had passed, that would have made sense. The human mind eventually obliterates or at least diminishes many fears and anxieties, but it takes time. The guy who was ready to face death again only hours later had to be a maniac.

"Come on," Ben pleaded softly.

"Even if I wanted to," Wolfgang said firmly. "We almost ran out of air last time, and that's an insurmountable problem. There ought to be a way—"

He paused, suddenly realizing that Ben wasn't listening to his carefully reasoned statement. He was staring at Lori Swenson, who looked particularly animated and stunning as she talked with a group of girlfriends.

"—There ought to be a way to blow up Pittsburgh and then make downtown Dallas into a parking lot, don't you think?" Wolfgang continued.

Ben nodded, still staring at Lori. "Yeah," he said, "I guess you're right."

"What did I say?"

"I forget, except that it made sense. You always make sense, Wolfgang."

"Hmmmph."

"Look at her," Ben said. "God, if she only knew."

"Only knew what?"

"That I'm America's newest astronaut. That I did something nobody else has done before. I bet if she knew that, she'd look at me differently."

"Yeah? Well, you'd better not tell her."

"Why not?"

"Because the cops are still looking for the people who tore up the drive-in, that's why."

"Lori wouldn't turn me in."

"Maybe not, but she'd sure spread it around a lot. And it would get back to the police."

"Not if I swore her to secrecy."

Wolfgang grabbed Ben's arm and squeezed. "Listen,

big shot," he warned, "there are two other guys involved in this project. What would you think if we each told another girl?"

"Who?" Ben asked.

"It doesn't matter." Wolfgang gestured to a tall blonde standing next to the punch bowl. "How about if I tell that one? She looks nice."

"You don't even know her," Ben protested.

"It makes just as much sense."

Ben snorted, shrugged, but continued to look longingly at Lori.

His soulful gaze was not lost on Lori's girlfriend, Marni. Speaking out of the side of her mouth, she said, "Don't look now, but Ben Crandall's staring at you again. He's practically drooling."

Lori looked at her with an expression of total boredom. "Please," she murmured. "I mean, who cares?"

"Come on, Lori, don't you think he's cute?"

Lori couldn't help changing her field of vision so that she was able to see Ben from the corner of her eye.

"I guess so," she admitted. "He's not the cutest, but he's not the worst either. He's all right, but I wish he wasn't such a . . ."

"A what?"

"Oh, you know, a space cadet."

Ben looked at Wolfgang, nudged him with his elbow. "I think they're talking about me," he said.

"No," Wolfgang replied. "I can read lips."

"Then what did they just say?"

Wolfgang hesitated a moment. He could not read lips, of course, but if Ben believed he could, it made sense to use the power to turn him off Lori Swenson.

"Well," he said, "I'm not sure you'll enjoy hearing what they said."

"Tell me," Ben ordered.

"All right. The girl next to Lori asked her why she didn't kick Steve Jackson and his friends out of the party, and Lori said she thought he was cute. A little bit loudmouthed, but cute."

Ben's jaw dropped several inches. "No," he muttered. "She didn't say that. She couldn't think that."

"Maybe I read her wrong," Wolfgang said with a shrug.

"No," Ben said. "You're right about nearly everything. What else did she say?"

"She said he was sexy."

"No! How could she think a thing like that? He's a total creep!"

"Hey, I'm just reporting what she said, not explaining what goes on in her mind."

Ben sat for a moment, his eyes downcast. Wolfgang felt a major twinge of guilt at deluding his friend, but comforted himself with the knowledge that he could always set things straight when it was no longer necessary to maintain secrecy. Nearly a minute passed before Ben spoke.

"That settles it," he said finally. "I'm going to do it. Right now."

"Do what?"

"I'm going to tell her."

"Tell her? Are you crazy? We can't tell anyone, least of all a girl who's crazy about Steve Jackson. That's worse than being a communist."

"She's not crazy about him. Just thinks he's cute and sexy. There's still time to head her off at the pass. I'm going to tell her how I *feel*."

"How you feel?" Wolfgang repeated. "Not what we did last night?"

"No."

"Okay. There's a big difference. But if she doesn't

165

feel the same about you, you won't do anything desperate, will you—like telling her about the flight?"

"No."

"I still think it's better if you just keep your mouth shut. Girls don't want to hear how guys *feel* about them. If you *feel* anything about them, they know it. It's like when somebody's run over a skunk in the road. You don't have to see the skunk to know what's happened."

"I still want to tell her." Ben sighed, starting to get up. "If I died without her knowing how I felt, I'd be miserable the rest of my life."

"Boy," Wolfgang muttered. "Why would you want to go up again when it's obvious that lack of oxygen has given you *brain damage?*"

"I'll be back in a few minutes."

As Ben got up, Darren strolled over toward them. For a moment, Wolfgang toyed with the notion of telling Darren that Ben was a security risk in the hopes that together they might either talk or physically coerce him out of his romantic insanity. But Darren's expression was so thoroughly bummed-out that Wolfgang decided against it. The hell with it, he thought, if Ben spills the beans, that's simply the way it was meant to be.

"No luck with the girls?" Wolfgang asked.

"No. Zero. Sub-zero."

"I think I know what your problem is."

"What?"

"Instead of hitting on all those young, inexperienced cuties, you should be going after somebody who's done it. Like her."

As he spoke, Wolfgang pointed to a rather chunky but voluptuous girl nearby.

"Done it?" Darren repeated.

"Yeah. You know—gone all the way." Wolfgang sounded a bit awkward saying the words.

"She's gone all the way?" Darren asked, tilting his head toward the girl in question.

"Absolutely."

"How do you know? It sure as hell isn't because you went with her yourself."

"No," Wolfgang replied. "I know because of scientific observation."

"Tell me about it."

The girl moved a few steps away, providing Wolfgang with a flash of inspiration.

"It's the way she walks," he said.

"Yeah?"

"After they've gone all the way, their walk changes," Wolfgang explained.

"You mean they bounce because they feel good?" Darren smiled.

"No, nothing like that. It's some scientific change. I saw a film about it once."

"What kind of film was that, anyway?"

"It wasn't a dirty film. It was for doctors. One of my father's doctor friends had it."

"You're not kidding me?"

"No. I'm just trying to help you out."

Darren pursed his lips thoughtfully. "And you can see that one's done it, huh?"

"Not a doubt in the world. As a matter of fact, she's done it a lot. Should be easy for you."

"Great."

He got up.

"Don't say you know she's done it," Wolfgang cautioned. "That wouldn't be cool."

"Then what should I say?"

"You'll think of something. Just be more confident.

Look at her like you're an animal and she's an animal. She'll pick up the vibes."

"Okay, I'll do it."

He walked off jauntily, following the girl outside and across the lawn. Wolfgang watched as Darren waited patiently for the girl and a friend to finish their conversation. Then, as the second girl left, he smiled debonairly and launched into his spiel. Wolfgang couldn't read his lips, but he could tell even at a distance that Darren's manner was more intimate, perhaps even lecherous. The girl listened carefully, didn't seem to mind his familiarity—at least for nearly a minute. Then her hand suddenly came up and cracked Darren solidly across the cheek. His debonair expression faded. Turning on her heel, the girl walked away from him and into the house.

Darren, his eyes firmly fixed on the grass at his feet, walked slowly back to Wolfgang.

"Thanks," he muttered.

"What did you say?" Wolfgang asked. "It looked like it was working for a while and then you suddenly lost it."

"I couldn't think of anything else to say," Darren mumbled, "so I said something about knowing that she did it . . ."

"You didn't! What kind of dummy are you?"

"A first-class one, I guess," Darren muttered, his eyes downcast.

Wolfgang shook his head and thanked the powers that be for his lack of involvement with women. As far as he could judge, it brought only heartbreak, anxiety, and frustration, in addition to being very hard on the work schedule. An object case was Ben, who only minutes before had been solely dedicated to flying a second mission; now he had forgotten all that and was undoubtedly making a fool of himself at the altar of Lori Swenson.

In fact, Ben was already berating himself for his obvious feelings for Lori, but he had gone too far to turn back. She had spotted him as soon as he moved away from Wolfgang and had seemed to make a conscious effort to avoid him. Ben should have taken that as a harbinger of things to come. Instead, he gently pursued her, following his dream princess from conversation to conversation until she had no choice but to stop, face him, and smile.

"Yes, Ben?" she said. "How's the party going? Having a good time?"

He nodded. "Great. Uh . . . could I talk to you for a second?"

"Sure," she said, not moving.

"Uh . . ."

"What is it?"

Ben glanced around at the other partygoers. "Uh, could we move over there?" he asked.

When Lori nodded, not very enthusiastically, he led her to a more private section of the back yard. Seeing the two leave, Marni and several others giggled significantly.

When they were sufficiently isolated, Ben smiled at Lori and tried to think of something pleasant that would break the ice.

"That's Duran Duran," he said finally, "You've got their new album, right?"

"Sure. You brought me all the way over here to ask me that?"

"No. There's something more important."

"Good. Because I can't stay away from my guests very long. You know how it is. I'm the hostess and I have to keep things moving."

"Sure." Ben nodded. "I understand. I just wanted to give you this for your birthday."

He reached into his pocket and withdrew a small box.

"Here," he said. It sounded rather weak and uninspired but he wasn't about to make a speech.

Lori smiled and opened the box. Inside was a ring with a gray, jagged pebble set in it. She stared at it for a long time, not sure whether it was a joke or not.

"I've never seen a . . . stone like this," she said finally. "I mean, it looks like a real stone."

"It's a martian rock," Ben explained.

"Really?" she asked, more interested now. She was no space junkie, but she knew if the stone came from Mars, it must be more valuable than it looked. Not that Lori was a gold digger who put a dollar value on every present she received. Ben's going to the trouble of getting her a true martian rock must mean he really cared for her.

"Well," she said. "That's really sweet. I've never seen a martian rock before."

"It's not actually real," Ben murmured. "But it's supposed to look exactly like the rocks they found when they took pictures on Mars."

"Thanks," she said.

She could see the look in his eyes—warm, nervous, crazy in love with her—but he didn't seem dangerous or threatening in any way. Earlier, when Steve Jackson had gotten her in a corner, Lori had fought down the desire to yell for help, so potentially violent did he seem to her. Ben, on the other hand, was a truly gentle type. Thus, when he leaned forward to kiss her, she didn't recoil or even look around for someone who would help her out of an embarrassing situation. She let him put his lips against hers, not moving or encouraging him by returning his embrace, but not totally unmoved, either. After a few seconds, she even closed her eyes and began to get involved in the kiss. It was not, however, her most passionate response, and she saw the disappointment in Ben's eyes when he released her.

"Uh . . . thanks," he said.

"I'm sorry, Ben." Lori smiled. "I just don't feel that way about you. I like you a lot . . ."

"Oh, no," Ben muttered. Though quite young, he knew that once the word 'like' entered a relationship, 'love' was practically impossible.

"It's okay," he said, trying hard to be gentlemanly and not show his pain. "I like you a lot, too. Maybe if I grow a few inches."

"Don't be silly," Lori said, slapping his shoulder lightly. "It's not a matter of height."

A few seconds later, she excused herself and went back to her guests. Ben hung around the area a while longer, not wanting to return too quickly to Wolfgang, who would undoubtedly ask questions, either directly or by implication. When he did go back, he found Darren and Wolfgang only too willing to leave the party.

"That's it for me," Ben said.

"Maybe we should thank Lori first," Wolfgang suggested.

"It's all right. I already took care of that."

Ten minutes later, after the silence became nearly unbearable, Wolfgang finally asked, "So what's the story? What happened?"

"I'm going to kill myself," Ben said simply. After due consideration, he had decided it was the only logical method of ending his pain.

"Don't take it so hard," Wolfgang said with a shrug. "She's only a girl."

It wasn't the kind of consolation Ben wanted. Turning on Wolfgang, he spoke in an angry, defensive voice. "What the hell do *you* know about it?" he demanded. "Just shut up for once in your life, okay?"

Wolfgang was shocked, but not intimidated. "You amaze me, Ben," he said evenly. "One minute you're trying to talk me into a suicide mission because it 'feels good,' and now you're going to kill yourself because Lori Swenson won't mate with you."

"Mate with me?" Ben shouted. "Is that what you think?"

"Sure," Wolfgang replied. "It's purely biological. No logic involved at all."

Darren looked across at Ben. "Hey, you got farther than I did. At least you got to kiss the girl. All I got was a slap in the chops."

"You too?" Ben snapped. "Forget it! See if I talk to you guys again!"

"That'll be too soon for me!" Wolfgang shouted after the departing figure. "Why don't you take Lori Swenson with you next time? You can make out on the moon!"

"Where you going?"

"Car pool."

"Why? Your shift was over six hours ago."

Charlie Drake merely shrugged, not particularly anxious to explain his comings and goings to the desk sergeant, who was a notorious gossip.

"I'm on the track of something interesting," he said, trying not to make it sound *too* interesting.

"Yeah? What?"

"Look, Wilson, pardon me, will you? I'm in sort of a hurry."

"Sure. No offense."

Drake quickened his pace until he arrived at the police car pool, where he signed out an unmarked car and headed for the spot where he had seen the spaceship. He had taken a chance by not landing his helicopter as soon as he spotted the familiar object. He had reasoned that doing so would attract attention and possibly alert the operators of the vessel. On the other hand, returning to headquarters for a car would give them time, if they were nervous, in which to hide the ship and possibly escape detection forever. After debating the issue with himself, Drake decided he would rather tackle the problem on foot, with an assistant. He therefore drove to Gordon Deems's apartment and rang the bell.

Deems's wife came to the door. She didn't look happy to see him.

"Yes?" she asked.

"Is Gordon in? I could use him."

"He's asleep."

"Oh. Well, I won't bother him then. It's not a matter of life or death."

Charlie was pleased to see the woman smile with something close to gratitude.

"You want me to give him a message when he wakes up?" she asked.

"Yeah. Tell him I've found the spaceship."

"Spaceship?"

"That's right. He can contact me on the radio and I'll fill him in later."

"Fine." Mrs. Deems nodded, looking at him with a slightly suspicious glance.

"Thanks." Charlie said, hurrying off.

A few minutes later, as he struggled down a steep embankment through the wet and heavy growth bordering the creek, he could dimly make out a saucer-shaped object partially covered with dead tree limbs and leaves.

"Yeah," he whispered. "That's it, all right."

Arriving at the vessel, he stared at it for fully a half minute before gently opening the hatch. He was surprised at how tiny it seemed, close up. Looking inside, he quickly saw that the interior was unoccupied. Some breather masks and a kid's jacket were the only clues available, but as he examined the jacket, a slow smile spread across Drake's features.

The owner's name and address were neatly written on the label.

Chapter Eight

THAT NIGHT BEN WENT TO BED EARLY, NOT TO DREAM BUT to forget.

The argument with Wolfgang and Darren, following the rejection by Lori, was simply too much for his brain to assimilate. Frustration piled on top of frustration was not his concept of enjoyment, yet he knew that if he could get through the next twenty-four hours, he stood a good chance of being all right.

Fortunately, he was still tired from the exertions of the previous evening, so it was no hardship to get into bed soon after he got home.

He was asleep in less than ten minutes. Not long afterward, the dream began. He was standing on the plain with the crystalline surface and green clouds blowing overhead, but this time he was not alone. Sensing another presence, he turned and saw Wolfgang and Darren, each standing on one side of him. The sight of them filled him with instant, irrational anger. How dare they invade his dream! This was his imagined landscape, a world he had invented or which had been devised expressly for him. It was his to enjoy and interpret and he resented their being here, especially in view of their hostile attitudes.

"Hey!" he shouted, fully intending to order them out of his dream once and for all.

Wolfgang's expression had lost none of its recent arrogance and brusqueness. "I *said* I'm not talking to you!" the erstwhile friend retorted.

Darren, true to his nature, seemed more ill at ease then anything. "What the hell is this?" he asked, looking around suspiciously. "Where is this place? I don't like the looks of this."

Suddenly Ben's proprietary attitude melted. He took a few steps and felt the sense of weightlessness he had had before. This was a golden opportunity—not something to be squandered because of petty differences. If he had been able to absorb most of the diagram's contents by himself during the first dream, think of what three of them could do! But first they had to be educated.

"Look," he cried. "We can get the missing part of the diagram this time! Come on!"

"Come on what?" Darren asked.

"Jump!" Ben replied.

To demonstrate, he took a few short steps and then hurled himself upward. The effort sent him soaring far above their heads and both boys pivoted to look at him, amazement etched into their features.

"You can do it!" he shouted down to them. "Just throw yourselves up in the air!"

"That's all there is to it?"

"Yeah! Nothing to it!"

Hesitantly, Wolfgang and Darren followed, executing the maneuver so perfectly that they were next to Ben in an instant. As they floated toward the green clouds above them, all three turned their bodies experimentally, enjoying the feeling of being able to hover.

"There!" Ben said, pointing to the ground.

As before, the crystalline surface, seen from a height, formed a circuit-board pattern of schematic lines, right angles, and U-turns.

"Is this what happened the first time?" Wolfgang asked. "Is everything the same?"

Ben's feeling of hostility returned. Why was he yammering on like this when they had so much to memorize? Didn't he understand that they might get only one good look at the diagram?

"Shut up and let me concentrate!" Ben shouted. "I'm the one who has to remember it."

"Why can't we all remember it?"

"Because this is *my* dream! When I wake up, you'll be gone and no help at all."

"What makes you so sure?" Wolfgang demanded. His voice sounded exactly as it had that afternoon, haughty and superior.

"I'm sure," Ben replied. "I've been here before and you haven't. You dream about dumb things, like being naked at school. My dreams are useful."

"Your dreams aren't so great," Wolfgang said with a sneer. Ben suddenly had the feeling that Wolfgang wanted to end the dream to make him wake up. He experienced a sharp, sinking sensation that caused him to gasp.

"Come on, cut it out," he warned. "I might wake up at any second."

As he spoke, he could feel his body start to slip, rather like lying atop a balloon that was being rapidly deflated. He forced himself to look at the diagram, to memorize something new before he fell to earth and awakened. But his rage and panic were stronger than his scientific discipline. He saw images, but nothing stuck or formed a memorable pattern.

"See! You've ruined it!" he shouted up at the smiling Wolfgang. "I'm waking up!"

Then the diagram was becoming larger, less distinct, as the ground rushed up to meet him. Throwing his hand above his face and curling into the fetal position, Ben felt his mouth open and a scream emerge from his throat a split-second before impact.

It was something between a shout and a scream and seemed to come from above. Only after he lay there for half a minute, sweating profusely, did Darren realize that the sound had come from his own throat.

He closed his eyes and tried to reconstruct the dream. It was fascinating and frightening, something about flying above a ground that seemed to be covered with neon lights. Ben and Wolfgang had been there, and everyone had been shouting at each other. Why? He shook his head. Whatever perverse logic the dream had was already beginning to fade into his subconscious much faster than he could remember it.

"Damn . . ." he muttered.

Wolfgang's scream was more a grunt of satisfaction. As soon as the lights went out on the strange plain and came on in his bedroom, he leaped out of his bed, found a pen and paper and began to write.

For a minute, his fingers flew across the page, reconstructing the schematic diagram he had seen in his mind only seconds before. Then, as the image began to fade, he frowned, hitting himself in the head as if to jar more data loose.

"Come on!" he shouted. "Come on!"

His walkie-talkie began to buzz, but he didn't answer it for ten seconds. By that time, he was resigned to the fact that no more information could be gleaned from his memory.

"What is it?" he said into the walkie-talkie. "I just had a dream weirder than yours."

There was a long pause on the other end. A wrong number on a two-party walkie-talkie? Then Ben's voice, soft and a bit faltering, could be heard.

"You mean . . ." he said, "you were dreaming the same dream?"

"Yeah. The one you had that got us started on this little project."

"I had it again tonight," Ben said.

"So did I," Wolfgang replied. "Except it was the first time for me."

"That's incredible . . . Tell me about it."

"We were floating above this schematic diagram," Wolfgang said. "Because our mind likes to humor us and make things seem normal, it didn't show just a schematic. Instead it made the diagram appear as a fairly normal landscape. But I saw through that right away. It's a trick, I said. So as soon as I rose above the diagram, I started memorizing."

"How much did you get?"

"Maybe all of it. Or nearly all."

As he spoke, Wolfgang continued, adding embellishments to the sketch he had made of the diagram, the conversation with Ben somehow furnishing him with details he thought he had forgotten a minute before.

"It's weird," Ben said.

"You're telling me. I've never heard of two people having the same dream at the same time."

"What about Darren?"

"I don't get you."

"Maybe he had the dream, too," Ben suggested.

"Impossible," Wolfgang said. "That's stretching the laws of probability to the limit."

"I think we're dealing with something a little more definite than probability," Ben said.

"It's too bad he doesn't have a walkie-talkie," Wolfgang said.

"Maybe we should go to his house."

"Right now?"

"Why not?"

"You're too crazy to move," Wolfgang said. "I don't understand why you're so impatient all the time. There's still a lot of testing to be done. We have new information now from the second dream, so why not give me a chance to see what it means?"

"We might be killed in an accident tomorrow," Ben said ominously.

"Hey," Wolfgang retorted, "how come *you're* talking about death now? Usually I'm the one who brings that up."

"Because it's to my advantage," Ben replied frankly. "I want to see this thing through. We were on the news. People and cops are looking for us. Anything could happen. I want to blow this planet and find out what's out there."

The passionate outburst got to Wolfgang. He didn't agree with all of it, but some of Ben's urgency impressed him.

"We'll start to work first thing in the morning," he promised.

"We'll start to work now," Ben corrected.

"But most of the equipment is at Darren's."

"So we'll wake him up."

A half hour later, Ben and Wolfgang, walking toward Darren's work shed, were suprised to see the lights on. They tapped lightly on the door.

Darren waved them inside.

"I've been waiting for you," he said.

"What?" Wolfgang asked.

"Ever since I woke up from the dream, I knew

something was cooking. I'm not sure what we have to do, but I knew you'd be sure."

"You had the dream, too?" Ben asked.

Darren nodded.

They questioned him about it briefly, until they were satisfied that it was the same experience.

"I think it's fate," Ben said quietly. "Somehow we're being ordered to keep moving forward on our project. It would be wrong to ignore what we've been through."

Wolfgang opened his mouth as if to protest, then thought better of it. Pulling a sheet of paper from his pocket, he spread it out on the work bench.

"I've worked out some revisions to our power plant that I think should be made—based on new material from the dream we've all experienced," he said enthusiastically. "I'd like to test it first, but since both of you guys are so eager to get started, let's go."

Charlie Drake was getting cold. For the past hour, his stomach had been growling up a storm, but that could be suppressed with will power. Talking yourself out of freezing to death was another matter.

After examining the "spaceship" and finding the kid's jacket inside, he had faced a decision. Should he go to the address and confront the youngster, who may or may not be directly involved? Or should he stake out the vessel in the hopes of catching the whole cast of characters, possibly even aliens from another star system? Because he was first and foremost a lawman, his instincts told him to track down the kid whose jacket was in the ship. He would undoubtedly lead Charlie to the rest of the gang or at least provide beneficial clues. But there was another part of Charlie Drake that complemented his basically hard-nosed attitude: he wanted to believe in a better world and universe. Just a few nights before, he had seen *The Man From Planet X* on television. A week previously, it had been *The Day the Earth Stood Still.* Now scenes from both movies raced through his mind, challenging him to consider the possibility that visitors from another world might not be the same as violators of the law here on Earth. Instead of asking himself which course of action would be more likely to bring about an arrest, he began to ask himself which modus operandi would be least likely to offend the aliens. He did not, after all, want to cause an intergalactic misunderstanding. There was even a part of him which cherished the idea of being some sort of universal goodwill ambassador. Yielding to his altruistic side, he therefore decided to remain at his post. When the aliens approached to take off again in their ship, he would step forward and convince them en masse that he was a man of peace.

"But I sure hope they don't take too long," he muttered. "My butt's about ready to freeze off."

Unaware that their ship was being carefully watched, the three boys worked long into the night, Wolfgang completing a new circuit board with a soldering gun while Darren welded a small metal box onto the side of the computer-power pack combination. Ben sat across from Wolfgang as he worked, unable to resist asking questions.

"You say you don't even know what problem this is going to solve?" he asked.

"I said don't talk," Wolfgang responded nervously. "I have to concentrate."

Biting his tongue as he soldered the final connection, he tossed the gun on the work bench and carried the circuit board over to Darren.

"Hook it up to the central board through the new box," he said.

Ben, who had followed Wolfgang across the room, watched as his friend sat down at the controls.

"Maybe it's a—" he began.

Wolfgang silenced him with a dark look.

"Let's see what it does first," he said. "Then we can talk about it and you can go off the deep end."

"You're just scared because you can't explain what's going on," Ben said. "You like to be in control and now you're dealing with something—"

"You're right. I'm not scared, but it does seem like the whole thing is getting out of control. And I don't like that, not a bit."

In fact, Wolfgang was terrified. He was convinced that some outside source had sent them the key to their problem in the form of new information. But suppose he and Ben and Darren, as mere mortals, were not capable of interpreting or using the new information correctly? Or perhaps the outside source had miscalculated in some way. It was like giving a can of food and a can opener to a hungry savage, presuming that the savage would be able to put two and two together and open the can. But wasn't it possible the native would injure himself with the can opener or just not be able to figure it out? Of course. Thus Wolfgang worried about the consequences of their new information and tests. But they had come too far to turn back now.

"Here I go," he said, pressing the power switch.

A second later, Ben and Darren felt a tremendous explosion of air. Falling to the ground, they shrieked with fear and pain as the torrent of wind seemed to push into every pore of their bodies, pounding against their eardrums, eyes, rushing up their nostrils and into their mouths. The sides of the flimsy shed were pushed outward by the force, which came directly from the power pack. For a long moment, Ben lay with his face pressed against the floor; then he slowly opened his eyes to see what had happened to Wolfgang.

"Holy—!" was all he managed.

Wolfgang was gone!

The chair in which he sat was hopping in place several feet away from the power pack-circuit board, but was completely empty. Had Wolfgang been transported to another world or merely blown out of the shed?

"Get me down!" a hoarse voice shouted, answering Ben's questions. "Turn it off!"

Ben and Darren glanced toward the sound at the same time. It came from directly above them, about fifteen feet in the air. There, bobbing up and down on an invisible mattress, was Wolfgang, his expression a mixture of terror and delirious pleasure.

"Pull the plug!" he shouted, the terror obviously having won out.

Darren leaped forward, grabbed the power cord, and yanked it from the wall socket. The wind gradually began to die down, allowing Wolfgang to drift slowly back toward them. Reaching up, Ben helped his friend land softly, noting that his face was flushed and his breath quite labored.

"Are you all right?" Ben asked.

"Yeah, I think so."

"Shhhh!"

Darren had rushed over to quiet them, shoving both boys under some nearby bushes. Ben was surprised for a moment, until he realized that the shed in back of Darren's house had just blown apart. Aside from disturbing the neighbors and attracting the police, they had to worry about waking Darren's father, not the most tolerant character. But as they squatted quietly, they heard only 'normal' night sounds—a dog barking down the block, some faraway traffic, and drunken snoring through an open window at the back of Darren's house.

"Okay," Darren whispered finally. "I guess we didn't wake him."

"So tell us what happened," Ben said, looking at Wolfgang.

Wolfgang smiled. "The new information will allow us to break the air barrier," he said excitedly.

"What's the air barrier?" Darren asked.

"It's what almost killed us last time," Wolfgang replied. "We've got to have more than fifteen or twenty minutes of air to breathe or we'll never be safe."

"You mean that's solved?"

"Yeah. This is our air. That thing's producing oxygen, maybe out of carbon dioxide, I don't know, but the main thing is, if we turn down the volume of air produced so it equals the amount we're breathing inside the field, we'll be able to go indefinitely."

"You figured that out while you were hanging there in space?" Darren asked, impressed.

"Of course. What else was there to think about?"

"Besides," Ben said, "it's not a matter of logic now. It's a feeling. I know you guys feel it, too."

"Yeah," Wolfgang admitted. "Ever since I woke up—"

"It's like that feeling in the dream when we were being pulled up," Darren continued. "It never stopped."

"Somebody's calling us," Wolfgang murmured.

"They've been calling us since the beginning," Ben said. "Who knows from where?"

The three stood on the wet grass of Darren's back lawn, their heads tilted upward toward the Milky Way. The world out there seemed mystical, beckoning, endless, challenging, all the things they had not found here on Earth, in school, on television. As one, they felt they were being offered their great opportunity to participate. In what, they were not certain. Perhaps that was part of the allure. In any event, they responded with equal fervor.

"We're never going to find out who or what's out there if we stand around here," Darren said.

"I'm with you," Ben whispered.

"No one flies that ship better than me," Wolfgang said resolutely.

The three joined hands.

"Blood," they said together.

"I'll prepare her for liftoff." Wolfgang smiled. "We'll meet in a half hour. That'll give us time to get some things for the trip."

Charlie Drake had had a change of heart, perhaps precipitated by his freezing feet and butt. No longer was he enchanted by the romantic notion that visitors from outer space were going to use him as a catalyst or intermediary for universal peace and cooperation. Now he was just plain cold and tired. Yet to give up would be making a mockery of his entire day's work.

"I got a clue," he muttered. "What's the matter with me? Follow it up, man."

Taking one last look at the makeshift spaceship, he sidestepped up the embankment toward Ben's house.

"I hope the little fellow's alive," he said, the thought suddenly crossing his mind that the aliens had taken the jacket's owner hostage or disposed of him in some way. That threw a new light on his mission, of course. A minute before, he had decided to track down a boy because his jacket was at the scene of a mystery; now he realized he might have to deal with frantic, weeping parents. Was he prepared to deal with this possibility? He had never enjoyed that segment of the policeman's job which required him to commiserate with victims' survivors, much preferring the hunt for offenders. Confronted with this new development, he hesitated and then shrugged.

"Can't shirk my duty," he murmured, striking out across the pavement toward his primary suspect's house.

Doing his best to avoid waking his snoring father, Darren moved about his bedroom on tiptoes, a tiny flashlight providing all the illumination he needed. He had decided to travel light, reasoning that he and his companions would return from their journey before he needed a large number of conveniences. Either that or . . . he preferred not to think of the second reason for taking only the barest essentials. In any case, the *Thunder Road* had little space for amenities, so Darren opted to take only his Walkman cassette-radio. On the way out of his room, he paused before the mirror and somewhat irrationally made sure his hair was brushed and neat. He saw a bruise on his cheek, a memento of his having incurred his father's anger by awakening him from a sound sleep.

"Here's looking at you," he said to the silhouetted image of himself. "Maybe we'll meet here again sometime. If not—"

Shrugging, he waved good-bye and disappeared into the hallway.

Several blocks away, Wolfgang was going through a similar process of selection and elimination. He was rather more scientific than Darren with regard to which possessions should accompany him. Written material was high on his list of priorities—science texts, language books, and a large chemical chart of the elements went into his backpack. To these he added a globe and calculator, which so overloaded his bundle he was barely able to lift it.

Ben's knapsack also contained lots of written material, including a dictionary and a desk encyclopedia. A pair of leather gloves, a collapsible cup and a harmonica also went into the bag. After tightening the strap securely, he stood in the center of his room a long moment, thinking of other possible items people from another planet might be interested in seeing. While doing this, he remembered the terror he had felt during their previous mission when it had suddenly occurred to him that no one on Earth would know what had happened to him. Going to his desk, he found a clean piece of paper, quickly wrote down his major possessions, assigned them to appropriate people, wrote 'This is my will' at the top of the paper and signed his name at the bottom.

Then, walking briskly but softly through the house, he paused for a moment near the kitchen, where his father and mother were sitting, talking in hushed tones. He could not make out what they were saying. It probably wasn't important, but for some strange reason, Ben wanted to hear what might be the last words they ever spoke in his presence. After straining his ears for thirty seconds, he whispered 'good-bye' in their direction and started out of the house.

He had just rounded the front of the building when an adult figure suddenly loomed from the shadows near the porch. For a moment, Ben thought it was his father, but he saw almost immediately that the form was too tall and bulky. An instant later, before he could react, the figure stepped toward him and grasped his shoulder with one of its huge hands.

"Is this your jacket, kid?" the man asked, holding Ben's coat in the other hand.

Ben realized at once it was a policeman. No sound emerged from his throat.

"You were up in that UFO, weren't you, kid?" the cop continued.

Ben's legs were galvanized by a sudden wave of panic. Twisting his upper body, he managed to slip out of the man's grasp and sprint down the end of the yard toward his bike. The cop followed, losing ground every step as he shouted after Ben. Whether his words were a promise of immunity, a threat, or mere imprecations remained unknown to Ben, only guttural half-syllables reaching his ears.

Leaping onto his bike, he pushed it several feet through the soft mud until gaining the driveway several yards ahead of the policeman. He attained getaway speed only a split-second before the huge hands were about to encircle his body.

"Damn!"

Charlie Drake stifled a second curse as the young man wheeled away from him. He had promised the boy that he wouldn't be punished. Why hadn't he listened?

The truth was that for the first time in his career, Charlie was more interested in the activities of an 'offender' than in punishing him. If the kid had only known how much he yearned to just talk with him—

Shrugging, Charlie retraced his steps to his parked car and located Gordon Deems on the police radio.

"Yeah?" his partner asked. "What's going on? You been working round the clock, Charlie?"

"That's right."

"What on?"

"The UFO."

Gordon rolled his eyes. Charlie seemed to have developed an obsession and obsessions were generally a pain for somebody who just wanted to get through a shift with as little trouble as possible.

"Listen," Gordon began, "we'd better stick close to the freeway tonight. There's lots of drinking and driving going on—"

"Forget that," Charlie interrupted. "I know this is weird, but could you meet me at the corner where Elm cuts across the creek?"

"Sure," Gordon said with a sigh.

He put down the microphone and started to follow Charlie's orders. At the same time, Deems breathed a silent prayer that his partner's insanity would turn out to be temporary.

Ben barely paused at the confluence of Elm Street and the creek, doing a wheelie at the curb and plunging down the bank into the soft earth that soon gave way to sand and then water. As his wheels sank into the goo, he tossed the bicycle aside and ran toward the dark form which he knew as the *Thunder Road.*

Wolfgang and Darren were already at the launch site, their expressions a mixture of irritation and anxiety as Ben approached, panic-stricken.

"We gotta get outa here!" Ben shouted. "Some guy knows about us."

"What?" Wolfgang shot back. "Who? Who is the guy, anyway? A cop?"

"I don't know," Ben panted. "He's probably a cop. He tried to grab me outside my house. He'd found my jacket."

"What jacket?"

"The one I took on our last trip."

"That means he was here! He must have seen the *Thunder Road.*"

"Right!" Ben exclaimed. "He's probably on his way back here now. We've got to get going!"

Ben and Wolfgang's faces were filled with panic, but Darren remained impassive.

"So what?" he said. "We'll kick his butt! This is our property. I want to see him put a hand on it."

"That's not the proper attitude," Wolfgang replied. "He may have friends or a partner."

"So? We'll kick their butts, too."

As he spoke, he reached down to grab a rock from the stream bed.

"Wait a minute," Wolfgang pleaded. "Let's not panic . . . Maybe we should just abort the mission."

"Now who's panicking?" Darren shot back.

"What?" Ben chimed in. "Abort the mission? Are you crazy, Wolfgang? If we're found out now, there may never *be* another mission!"

"He's right," Darren said.

"No way we're gonna abort this mission," Ben continued. "It's too late. Get in."

But Wolfgang stood his ground.

"Think a minute," he urged. "What is it we're actually doing here? We're trusting our whole lives to some kind of theoretical, maybe imaginary, auto-pilot and we don't even know what it is! Or where it's gonna take us."

"But explorers never know what they'll find," Ben argued. "That's why they do it. To find out the truth. To be there first."

"Sometimes they do it just to be on TV," Darren added irreverently.

"Not Columbus," Ben returned. "There wasn't any TV then. Or Magellan or the rest of those guys."

"You know what I mean," Darren muttered. "They wanted to have their friends call them and say what a great thing they did."

Ben suddenly felt that their dream was slipping away into a morass of irrelevancies. "Come on, you guys!" he yelled desperately. "This is *it!* You gotta believe in something! Or nothing means anything."

Darren shook his head. The plea had gone by so quickly he really hadn't understood what Ben had said.

"Okay," Wolfgang said. "Tell us then. Who are they? What is it they want with us? Huh?"

"I don't know," Ben shrugged. "Does it matter?"

"You bet it matters," Wolfgang replied. "What if they want to *eat* us? Huh? Or inject us with larvae that'll digest us from the inside? Or . . ."

The debate was getting to Darren, especially now that it had drifted into the realm of their being eaten by aliens.

"Let's just go," he muttered.

With that, he lifted the hatch of the *Thunder Road* and prepared to step inside.

"Aaaahhhhhh!"

A grotesque figure, made even more terrifying by the darkness, leaped out at him.

"Shit!" Darren yelled.

Grabbing at the undulating form, he wrestled it out of the spaceship and onto the ground. Halfway down, the monster started to giggle. Darren angrily reached toward the sound and felt his hand touch rubber. A moment later, he had ripped a mask and set of rubber claws from Wolfgang's younger brother, Ludwig.

Recognizing the voice, Wolfgang raced to the scene.

"Ludwig," he snarled. "I'm going to kill you."

His brother was neither cowed nor impressed by the threat. "I'll wake up Mom," he countered.

Realizing that time was short and their means of dealing with the recalcitrant Ludwig quite limited, Wolfgang decided to descend to blackmail.

"I'll let you play with the Mechanical Arm," he promised, trying to smile.

"I don't take bribes," Ludwig replied. "I'm going to tell Mom."

"Tell her what?"

"That you're fooling around out here."

"So what?" Wolfgang demanded, quickly losing patience with his brother. "We're not doing anything illegal. This is just fun we're having."

"Huh!" Ludwig snorted.

Ben moved over next to the kid now, having decided to take the friendly approach. "Ludwig," he smiled, putting his hand on the boy's shoulder. "Can you keep a secret?"

"Maybe," Ludwig replied grudgingly.

"Well," Ben said, "the secret is this is a real spaceship, and we're really going out tonight on a flight, and nobody's supposed to know. Because if they did, they'd try to stop us."

Ludwig glanced from one earnest face to the next. No guile was apparent.

"I'm not so sure," he said finally. "How dumb do you think I am? You guys are in trouble."

The three looked at each other. They were at a complete loss as to how to deal with the little guy. It would be easy to bully him, scare him away, but all of them wanted to mollify him in some way so that trouble would be averted. Wolfgang knew he wasn't an evil spirit, just a mischievous one who wanted to be a part of something. But time was running out as far as deliberate negotiations were concerned. Suddenly there was the sound of a car engine, the squeak of brakes and a beam of headlights shining down into the creek bed from the overpass. The hump on the roof of the car indicated that it was a police cruiser, causing all three boys to panic.

Darren moved first. Taking a quick step toward Ludwig, he raised a threatening index finger in his direction.

"Listen," he grated. "You get out of here now and don't tell anyone about this, or I'm going to kick your butt so hard it's going to collapse your spine and you'll crawl around like a slug for the rest of your life. Got it?"

Something seemed to have made an impression on Ludwig. "Uh . . . yeah." He nodded, retreating quickly up the side of the bank.

As he did so, Wolfgang and Ben made for the spaceship. Darren took a step toward Ludwig to make sure his homeward impetus continued, then turned and crawled into the *Thunder Road* behind his partners.

"I guess I kicked *his* butt," they heard him grumble as he closed the hatch.

"You ready?" Ben asked, looking nervously at Wolfgang.

"Of course."

"Then let's get out of here without all those checklists and stuff."

Spotting the silhouette moving toward them, Wolfgang complied with all dispatch. The *Thunder Road*, wrapped in her force field, rose quickly and silently through the trees until the tiny figure below blended into the dark shadows of the forest and was seen no more.

"Good work," Ben said.

Darren nodded, smiling. He already had his Walkman headphones on and was listening to loud rock 'n' roll music as they ascended.

"Now let's really get going," he said.

"Here goes nothing," Wolfgang replied, typing data into the computer.

The lights of the city fell away beneath them as the *Thunder Road* gained accelerative force. The velocity figures on the screen confirmed their rapid rate of climb, increasing geometrically every second. It was mind-boggling, even to the adventurous Ben. Feeling his heart do a flip-flop, he reached out to test the amount of air blowing from the power pack and was relieved to find that it worked. A solid flow of air was strong enough to straighten up the hairs on the back of his arm. This was certainly a lot more comfortable than breathing through a mouthpiece, he thought.

Wolfgang interrupted Ben's private thoughts.

"Don't look directly at the sun," he ordered, once again assuming the captain's mien. "We should have thought to bring protective glasses."

Darren nodded. "You know it takes the light from the sun eight seconds to reach Earth?" he said.

"Try eight minutes," Wolfgang corrected.

"That's what I meant."

Darren looked out the window, feeling stupid once again after his brief attempt to instruct. He should have known better than to try impressing Wolfgang with science trivia.

Ben also cast his eyes toward the faraway lights. Now they were so high it was impossible to tell where their hometown was, much less the creek bed from which they had risen. It all looked so still and peaceful. Yet he knew that like any natural organism, the scene below was actually a mass of battles and skirmishes, births and deaths, hunger and anguish and pain. Somewhere in that black carpet decorated with pinpoints of light, he knew that his mother and father still lived, perhaps were still talking in the same positions in which he had last seen them. Or they may have called out to him and gotten no reply.

He spoke almost to himself, the words softer than a whisper.

"I wonder if they've missed us yet . . ."

Chapter Nine

As she did nearly every night, Ben's mother gently opened the door of his room and peeked inside. Coming from a very poor family, she disliked the habit of leaving a radio or television on and wasting energy. But that wasn't the most important reason for the bed check. Mostly, she just rested more comfortably, knowing that Ben was safe and secure in his bed. Lately his long periods of moodiness and silence had bothered her, but she assumed it was a phase he was going through. It bothered her that he apparently would not confide in her, yet there was no way she could force him to do so.

"Probably a girl," she whispered, recalling that he had gone to Lori's birthday party in such bright spirits and had returned in a mood that could only be described as morose.

The form beneath the blanket did not move so she decided not to wake Ben with a good-night kiss. But as her hand reached for the lamp switch on the desk, she noticed something that interested her—a flash of color. Tiptoeing to the desk, she picked up a slip of paper that seemed to be a list of Ben's possessions. Casting it aside quickly, she found what had attracted her eye—a smooth thigh, then the rest of the nude centerfold figure of a *Playboy* magazine, cleverly hidden among the debris of his desk.

Casting a dark look at the bed, she turned to walk out of the room, whispering a threat as she did so.

"Mister," she said, "you're that close to being grounded . . ."

In fact, her son was the *opposite* of grounded nearly 20,000 miles away, as the *Thunder Road* started to pass the moon, which grew steadily bigger in front of the spaceship's occupants.

"Incredible," Darren exclaimed.

"We could go there if we wanted to," Ben said. "Except that it's already been done."

"What do you think?" Darren asked. "We got time for a while on the moon, Wolfgang?"

"Sure, we could land there," Wolfgang replied. "NASA has to plot precise trajectories to hit the moon in its orbit, but we're going so fast I could just sort of aim for it."

"Yeah," Ben said. "But let's not."

"Why not?" Darren countered. "I've never been to the moon, have you?"

"No. But if anything happened, that would be the end of our mission. It's one thing to break down after getting to a new spot, but this would be a disgrace. It's as if Magellan set out to sail around the world but made it only to Florida. A few years before, Florida would have been great, but now he has to do better, right? So we have to go farther than any man has gone before."

As Ben spoke, Wolfgang began humming the *Star Trek* theme.

"Okay," Darren said with a shrug. "I get the point. The moon's kid stuff."

The giant satellite of Earth was very prominent in

their view now, its scarred surface in crystal-clear focus. For an instant it seemed to blot out the sky; then it began falling away rapidly as the *Thunder Road* zoomed onward in its flight to the depths of the universe.

The moment of passage impressed Ben, causing a slight tremor of nervousness.

"What happens now?" he asked.

"We keep on going," Wolfgang said. "And hope that the chart of the solar system we have is accurate."

As he spoke, the computer started making the same trilling noise it had surprised them with during their first flight. Now the sound was not unexpected, but it caused all three to tremble.

"Oh, boy, look at this," Wolfgang muttered.

Figures and numbers were flashing across the screen at a bewildering rate. And once again, as it had in the past, the *Thunder Road* began to move by itself.

"Here we go again!" Wolfgang cried. His voice was high-pitched and a bit tremulous, betraying his bone-deep terror.

"We're being called," Ben said softly.

"And I still don't like it," Darren said. "Why can't we just drive this thing by ourselves? I'd feel a lot better if we could do that . . ."

As if to respond to his plea with defiance, the *Thunder Road* began to pick up even more speed, an eerie hum building in pitch and volume as the force field seemed to vibrate around them.

Darren reached out and put his hand on the hull. The same bolt that he had tightened on the first trip had worked its way loose. As he tightened it with his fingers, he was gratified to notice that the vibrating sounds decreased. The hum did not lessen, however, continuing toward a crescendo.

Wolfgang was silent, his mouth open as he watched a

column of numbers on the video screen, numbers which were rapidly counting down to zero.

"What is it?" Ben demanded. "What's happening?"

"Don't look at me!" Wolfgang replied, his eyes wide with excitement.

"What do those numbers mean? It looks like they're counting down!"

"Brilliant!"

The hum in the ship reached a deafening roar as the numbers raced toward zero and the climax they knew must be coming. Darren threw his hands over his ears; Ben closed his eyes tightly; Wolfgang continued to stare at the screen as if mesmerized.

When the figures reached zero, a sharp blast of light filled the ship, followed by a rush of sound that caused all three to curl into the fetal position. From the outside, the *Thunder Road* appeared as a comet speeding away from Earth, a bullet of light with a tail many miles long, moving at an enormous rate of speed.

Seconds later, the occupants realized they were still alive, and Wolfgang, Ben and Darren opened their eyes to look around them. The moon was already a tiny spot in the distance and though they felt no sensation of movement, they knew they were plunging through the solar system at a fantastic speed.

A glance at the numbers in the power column on the TV screen caused Wolfgang to gasp.

"What?" Ben asked.

"We may have a power drain. That battery wasn't prepared to take a surge like this."

"What if we want to go back?" Darren asked, his brow sopping with sweat.

"Oh, great!" Wolfgang exploded. *"Now* he thinks of going back!"

"Will you guys shut up?" Ben shouted. He looked out the porthole, his eyes glistening, a peaceful calm softening his features. Despite the danger, he gave every symptom of actually enjoying the experience.

"Don't spoil it," he whispered.

Darren and Wolfgang looked at each other. What they suspected was true. Ben wasn't all there. No one who reacted this way, in the face of such peril, could possibly have both oars in the water.

"He's crazy," Darren said. "We may be stranded out here and he's taking in the view."

"Why not?" Wolfgang asked. The words were out of his mouth before he realized it. Playing them back in his mind, he realized that he too had resigned himself to the possibility of being marooned in space. Yet, despite the horror of it all, there was a strange beauty and fascination in being where no other living soul had been before.

"God, where are we?" Darren whispered. "I don't recognize anything."

"What do you expect, a McDonald's sign?" Wolfgang asked softly.

"But is this still our universe or what?" Darren continued. "How far from Earth have we come?"

"Ask Ben. He's got all the answers."

Wolfgang and Darren looked at Ben, who was still staring, transfixed, out the porthole. Slowly his lips formed a word but it refused to come out. His eyes, incredibly, grew even wider as he continued to look at the new world which had engulfed them and the *Thunder Road*.

"Oh, my God . . ." he breathed.

The edge of terror in his voice caused both boys to look to the right, where Ben was staring.

It seemed to take up half the sky and, though they had never seen it or anything quite like it before, they knew immediately what it was. Its general shape was rectangular, but there were curved surfaces and spikes and dark interstices along the length of its body. Because it was impossible to say how much distance separated the *Thunder Road* from the object, it was impossible to estimate its dimensions, but all three boys knew it was enormous. It seemed to hang, unmoving, in space, something odd and unbalanced about its presence, like a dinosaur about to attack.

"It's . . . an . . . alien ship," Ben muttered, the first to clear his frozen throat.

"I told you!" Wolfgang gasped, a sound that was somewhere between a whine and a shriek. "I told you we shouldn't have come, but oh no—"

"Will you shut up!" Darren interrupted. "How do we get out of here?"

Wolfgang, almost thankful for something to do, turned his back on the porthole and pounded the keys of the computer, frantically entering every exit or reverse code he could possibly think of. The *Thunder Road* continued to move inexorably toward the huge vessel.

"We don't," Wolfgang said finally.

"Maybe they just want to observe us," Ben remarked hopefully, not quite believing it himself.

"They want to eat us," Darren said.

"Don't be silly," Wolfgang returned. "It's not an animal. It's obviously a spaceship constructed by intelligent creatures. They won't chew us up."

"But they might disintegrate us."

As Darren spoke, a valve on the underside of the dark vessel spiraled open. Inside was nothing but blackness. It was like looking down the garbage disposal of his mother's sink, Ben thought as they drew closer to the maw. The blackness was made even more consuming by the stars' being blocked by their descent.

"Eaten alive," Wolfgang murmured, apparently having accepted Darren's analysis of the situation after all.

"I wish my dad was here," Darren said quietly.

They watched as the last star was cut from their field of vision and they began to float through a tubelike chamber. As they passed into the tunnel, the energy field around the *Thunder Road* flickered and died, but the ship remained on course, obviously guided by some external power.

Turning to the computer, Wolfgang tried one more time to program their escape, but the machine refused to acknowledge his commands.

"The thing's had it," he said.

"It's moving by itself," Ben added.

Darren's expression was cadaverous, his eyes seemingly focused on a spot just below the *Thunder Road* porthole.

They seemed to be moving through a light mist, the only sound being their breathing and the grinding of distant machinery. Ben thought of an old movie he had seen once in which the hero was trapped inside a giant robot, the climax coming when the hero approached a series of crushing gears that formed the entrance to the mechanical monster's stomach. He did not recall how the hero had escaped; nor did he imagine that it was in any way applicable to his present situation. Perhaps his mind was merely giving him something to think about instead of going crazy.

His mind also presented him with a thought that was almost positive, something so obvious and yet subtle that only Ben had noticed. They were breathing.

"There must be oxygen in here," he said. "Otherwise we couldn't breathe."

Wolfgang nodded. "We're up the creek if this is just the remains of what was in the ship."

"I don't think so," Ben replied. "The force field went off pretty far back there."

Wolfgang nodded. He found little consolation in

realizing they would be able to breathe freely until they died some horrible death.

Suddenly, as they reflected on their dilemma, the *Thunder Road* passed into a new area, largely gray now instead of black. The sides of their ship seemed to be boiling, sprays of steamlike vapor attacking it from all directions.

The change of atmosphere shocked Darren from his trance. Looking from one side to the other, his eyes came to life.

"What is this, a car wash?" he demanded.

Or, Wolfgang thought darkly, the first function of a mechanical digestive tract . . .

The spray lasted only a minute, after which the *Thunder Road* drifted into a flat, larger area that resembled a giant subterranean cavern. When the small irregularities in the cave walls failed to move any more, the boys realized they had come to a halt. All three sets of eyes peered out into the foggy chamber. Ben shone the flashlight outside but its dim beam could not penetrate the gloom.

"Ride's over, I guess," Darren muttered.

For a long while the three boys sat, looking out and waiting for something to happen. As the silence grew more and more oppressive, Ben began to fidget.

"Maybe we should get out," he suggested.

"Are you crazy?" Wolfgang said.

"You think we should just sit here?"

"What other choice do we have?"

"To get out."

"That's no choice."

"It's another thing to do that's different."

"If somebody gives you a hand grenade, you can keep on holding it or you can pull the pin," Wolfgang said. "Pulling the pin's different."

"What do you suggest?"

"I say, sit. Maybe it'll send us out just the way it pulled us in. Maybe it doesn't know we're alive. If it thinks we're just a piece of space junk, it'll spit us out."

The words sounded hollow even to Wolfgang, but he had absolutely no inclination to explore the innards of some object from outer space.

"Well, there's no use sitting here," Ben continued. "They *must* be expecting us."

"Exactly!" Wolfgang retorted. "That's why I say, play dead."

Darren suddenly shook his head like a dog drying itself after coming in from the rain. "No," he said firmly. "I say, let's go out. And if they give us any trouble, we'll kick their butts!"

"Terrific!" Wolfgang shouted. "Leave it to you to come up with a foolproof plan! We'll kick their butts! Like the flea beating up on the elephant."

"C'mon," Darren urged.

"I'm not moving."

"He wants us to just stay here until we starve," Ben said wearily.

"No," Wolfgang replied. "Flimsy as it is, this ship's our only protection. Maybe they can't get inside it. Why should we play into their hands by—"

A sudden burst of noise from above caused Wolfgang to pause in mid-sentence. The boys looked out the porthole, craning their necks to spot the source of the commotion above them.

All of them spotted the object at the same time—a huge, shining maul descending toward them with gradually increasing speed. It seemed to have but a single object in mind—to crush the *Thunder Road* into either a million pieces or one huge flat saucer of debris.

Wolfgang changed his mind, grabbing for the door. In an instant all three boys were outside the ship, moving through heavy fog that clung to the surface beneath them like mist.

A moment later, the object approached to within several feet of the *Thunder Road* and suddenly stopped. Sparks of power began to leap from the object to the ship, the inside of which was bathed with an eerie, green light. The surge of energy continued for less than a minute, leaving the *Thunder Road* glowing as if it had just emerged from a radioactive bombardment.

"Maybe it's sterilized," Wolfgang said.

"I'm glad we weren't inside," Ben smiled grimly.

Darren's reaction was spawned by the long hours of working on the ship, wondering how he could make it more aesthetically appealing. The power surge's afterglow seemed to have solved all that, at least as far as he was concerned.

"Great!" he shouted. "It looks radioactive now, like a real spaceship."

"Well, what now?" Ben asked. "Does anybody want to get back in the ship?"

"Not me," Wolfgang said.

"Not me," Darren echoed.

"So it looks like there's nothing to do but explore," Ben concluded. "That's what we're here for, anyway, isn't it? To find new things. Just think. This is how Columbus must have felt when he discovered the New World and saw all those strange natives on shore."

"Except for one thing," Wolfgang said. "He could see that the natives had spears to his guns. So Columbus knew he was stronger. We just got swallowed by a very sophisticated-looking whale. I'm not so sure we aren't the natives in this particular case."

"So what difference does it make? Like Darren says, if they give us trouble, we'll kick their butts."

As one, they looked up at the roof of the large, circular chamber in which they now found themselves. The beams of their flashlights revealed a cathedral-like arch of gray material that seemed metallic, rather than stony. The arch sloped away toward sides that were lost in the heavy layer of fog that rose to shoulder level.

"Think we'll enjoy living here?" Darren asked. His tone indicated that it would not be a pleasant experience.

"I wonder why they're waiting," Ben murmured. "I mean, they must have been preparing for this for thousands of years, just waiting for this moment to contact Earth. And we're the ones they chose!"

"Let's not flatter ourselves," Wolfgang said. "We just happened to drop in. If they'd had a choice, they'd have selected some great scientists, heads of state, a bunch of important people from each country."

"Low self-image," Darren said with a smile.

"Maybe they're just not hungry yet," Wolfgang continued nervously.

They were walking very tentatively through the fog, sliding their feet in front of them rather then taking steps, but after a minute or so of growing confidence, they began to move faster. Darren led the way, his gaze alternating between the end of the cavern ahead and the *Thunder Road,* which was becoming lost in the fog to their rear.

"Ben's right," Darren called back over his shoulder. "We're here to explore so let's do it. We'll walk down the end of this hall and see what—"

Suddenly he disappeared.

Ben and Wolfgang stared with gaping mouths at the spot where Darren had been.

"Where's Darren?" Wolfgang cried.

"He's gone!"

For a moment, they spun like a couple of tops, the

mist swirling up above their heads as they looked in every direction for their friend. But he was gone, just as if a hole had opened beneath him and swallowed him.

"Let's get out of—" Wolfgang began.

The rest of the words were choked off by the sudden shock of being hurled downward, both boys plunging into a foggy abyss opening beneath their feet. Tumbling head over heels and sideways, they whirled down a funhouse slide without sides, a terrifying, barreling, vertiginous drop that seemed never to end. Only after what seemed an eternity did the two wild-eyed boys fall out into a long misty corridor. Darren was nowhere in sight.

They lay for a moment on their backs, staring up at the vague ceiling.

"Darren," Wolfgang mumbled after a while, then repeated the name in a loud voice. There was no reaction or sound. "Where is he?" he said.

"Where are *we*?" Ben demanded. "We shouldn't be getting this sort of treatment. This must be a mistake."

"I don't get you," Wolfgang whispered.

"We're ambassadors from another planet. You're not supposed to treat ambassadors this way. You're supposed to show them respect—"

"Ambassadors my foot!" Wolfgang returned. "Mistake my foot, too! They're testing us like mice in a maze! They're seeing how we react to shock and torture and then when they've gotten all the fun they want out of us, they're probably going to eat us!"

"No," Ben said. "I can't believe we came all this way just to be eaten."

"Stranger things have happened."

As they debated the situation, a low rumbling, as of something approaching, filled their ears.

"God, what now?" Wolfgang muttered.

Sitting upright, he grabbed Ben and helped him to his feet.

"Look!" he yelled.

He pointed into the mist where a huge machine filling the corridor from top to bottom and side to side was slowly rumbling toward them on tracks set into the walls. Its appearance was slightly spiderlike, a grotesque, metallic creature with various implements projecting from its front. They rose and fell with mechanical deliberation, resembling arms or antennae with the capability of hacking objects apart or dissecting anything from a car to a quonset hut.

"Let's get the hell out of here!" Ben gasped, turning to run.

A moment later, Ben felt his body strike a solid object where no solid object had been before. Inexplicably, the tunnel behind them had turned into a wall, giving them barely five feet in which to maneuver.

"We're trapped," Wolfgang said.

With nowhere to go, the boys watched with morbid fascination as the huge, rumbling behemoth approached to within a few feet of them. A fine, acrid spray was rolling off its surface, reminding Wolfgang of an enormous sweating beast. He imagined this was what it felt like to be attacked by Tyrannosaurus Rex.

Poised as if to strike, the object waited for what seemed an eternity. They could hear faint dripping sounds, tiny mechanical chinks mixed with computer noises. Why was it toying with them? Or were they giving it credit for having too much intelligence? Did it even know they were there? Barely breathing, Ben and Wolfgang watched, stupefied.

After an eerie moment of silence, the spiderlike device suddenly reached out and pinned the boys against the wall. Working with frightening efficiency, it sent forth a myriad of hands and hooks which patted down their clothes, reached into their pockets, scanned them with beams of light, and seemed to *sniff* at them. As one wiry finger plucked Lori's picture from Ben's pocket, he shouted angrily at it.

"Don't!" Wolfgang yelled. "Let it have it! If you make it angry—"

Ben closed his mouth, realizing the truth of what his friend had said. An instant later, both boys were engulfed by a spray directed at them from the machine.

"I guess it doesn't like our smell," Ben muttered.

Wolfgang nodded, his nose crinkling.

Then, as suddenly as it had appeared, the huge machine disappeared down the long corridor, its retreat as stately as a visiting dignitary backing away from his king.

Wolfgang collapsed against the wall in relief. As soon as he touched the partition, however, it rotated quickly, whisking him out of the room before he could utter a protest or move out of its orbit.

"Wolfgang!" Ben yelled, suddenly realizing that his friend was no longer in the chamber. But no voice answered, and Ben felt himself quivering with horror and anticipation. The plan of these creatures, creature, or machine seemed to be to separate the visitors . . . and do what?

He did not have a long time in which to consider the problem. Once again the ground beneath his feet simply melted away and he began his second descent into the void.

Darren arrived at the bottom of the chute after what seemed an interminable roll, his body striking the bars of a cage that looked as if it had been constructed to catch runaway objects, a category into which he fitted. Waiting cautiously, he slowly got to his feet and looked up the tunnel through which he had just passed. Its pitch was much too steep for him to climb, so he turned back to the cage, his mind working feverishly. Was this the beginning of a lifetime sentence in some sort of space prison? Pulling on the bars of the cage, he discovered that they were somewhat flexible. If he could only get some leverage . . .

Looking around, he noted that the walls of the chute were constructed of metal sections or strips, one of which was loose. Pulling with all his strength, he tore the strip free and put it between the bars of the cage. Slowly they began to spread apart, just far enough so that he could thrust his chest through and wiggle out.

He was free, he thought, but to what advantage? Shrugging, he stumbled across another strange, alien room, weird sounds echoing through the gloomy void. Trying to keep up his courage, he talked to himself as he moved in the direction of the new sounds.

"These people never heard of furniture," he muttered darkly. "If this is the way they live, maybe it's better if we don't make contact with them."

The distant noises began to take on vaguely familiar intonations. They sounded a little like computer telephone operators, not quite human, more like machines impersonating speech. Realizing that he had no choice, Darren walked toward the sounds, his steps taking him to the entrance of another room.

He stopped and looked inside.

The new room was empty except for a single, huge object. It was a humming, glowing machine with a chair in the center of it, rather like a throne. The chair was considerably oversized, however, and Darren estimated that a person fifteen feet tall could fit in it. The realization caused him to shiver. If this was the sort of individual they were up against, kicking their butts would not be so easy a matter.

As he neared the machine, he saw that it contained a readout, with drawings of three figures in the center. One of the figures had rims around its eyes, like a child's rendition of glasses.

"That must be Wolfgang," Darren whispered.

Near the chair was a connector, an object that seemed designed to fit on the head of a huge human. Darren touched it gently. As soon as he did so, five energy globes, simliar to the boys' force field, formed in the air around him and began to spin. Not particularly enthusiastic about breaking through their orbit, Darren allowed himself to be moved toward the chair until suddenly, a spark leaped from one of the globes to his finger.

Its effect was instantaneous and dramatic. The room in which he stood simply disappeared. Replacing it was the eerie landscape circuit board he had floated over during the dream. The same background music accompanied the scene, but Wolfgang and Ben were not visible. Then, a moment later, as he floated in and out of the dark green cloud formations, he heard his name called.

"Who is it?" he shouted.

The clouds and circuit-board dreamscape disappeared and he was back in the same room. There was one important addition, however: Ben.

"Are you okay?" he asked. "You must have been in a trance or something."

Darren blinked and rubbed his eyes.

"That was weird," he mumbled. He was sure he had been out of it for only a few seconds, but he felt amazingly refreshed.

"Where's Wolfgang?" he said.

"I don't know. I lost him."

"I guess we fell through trap doors or something."

"Yeah. This place is like a wacko amusement park."

"Well," Darren said, "let's find Wolfgang and get out of here."

Ben was tempted to ask precisely how they were to start the *Thunder Road* back to Earth without power or air, but thought better of it. No use infecting them with despair at this stage of the game. Looking for Wolfgang would give them something to do instead of yielding to panic.

As they made their way out of the room and along a dark corridor, Darren continued to talk about the experience he had just enjoyed.

"I don't know how it works," he said. "But it makes you see pictures in your head. I saw the dream we had just before we came here."

"It must be a dream-making machine," Ben mused. "Can they do that?"

"They must be able to. You just went through it, didn't you?"

Darren nodded.

"I wish we could see what they look like," he said.

"Maybe they're just machines," Ben offered.

"No. There was a chair in that room."

"That's right. A *huge* chair. You're right, Darren. There must be living creatures and they must be really big."

Their silent exploration came to an end a moment later as sounds drifted toward them out of another cavernous room dead ahead of them. The first discernible noise was a sort of ping-blip, an electronic burst similar to the ray gun blasts of the martian invaders in the movie *War of the Worlds*.

"Now wait a minute," Ben muttered. "That *can't* be. What's going on here?"

They paused to listen.

"Where's it coming from?" Daren asked.

"You tell me and we'll both know," Ben replied.

A split-second later, they were both startled to hear Ben's response come back to them.

"You tell me and we'll both know."

Darren jumped, then relaxed as he realized the sound had been created by Ben.

"It's okay," his friend reassured him. "It's only an echo."

"It's okay. It's only an echo."

"Yeah," Darren whispered. "I guess we're getting kind of jumpy."

Both boys paused, instinctively wondering and waiting to see if the softest of sounds would be picked up and returned to them.

"You tell me and we'll both know," the echo responded.

Ben and Darren looked at each other quizzically. An echo that stored sounds and replayed them at random? It was no more outlandish than the dream-sending machine, but it nevertheless boggled their minds.

Despite the atmosphere of escalating terror, the boys had no thoughts of turning back. To try to run or simply stand still would avail them nothing; only by moving ahead could they solve the puzzle or at least end the anxiety about their safety. Aiming his flashlight into the gloom, Ben advanced at a cautious pace. Darren followed, several steps to his rear.

"I hate to say it," Ben whispered over his shoulder, "but this isn't how I thought it would be. I figured that meeting people from another planet would be a lot more fun, that they'd treat us as equals instead of playing games."

"I guess we're getting kind of jumpy."

"You just said that," Ben said.

Darren reached forward to touch Ben's shoulder.

"Not that time," he whispered.

"What are you talkin—" Ben began, turning to look for his friend.

Shining his flashlight behind him, he gasped and stumbled backwards.

Darren was gone. In his place was the strangest face Ben had ever seen.

Chapter Ten

IT WAS NEARLY A MINUTE BEFORE WOLFGANG REALIZED he was not alone.

He'd barely had time to curse himself for leaning against the wall that had turned into a sliding panel when he saw the tall form. The new room into which he had been hurled was rather foggier than the one in which he and Ben had been approached by the gigantic machine. At first, Wolfgang thought the object was another mechanical device.

Then it started to talk.

Its words were in perfect English and consisted of grammatical sentences that were all familiar to Wolfgang. Yet its conversation did not make one iota of sense.

"Chief Dan Matthews of the highway patrol," it said first in a voice that was very gruff, almost scratchy.

"Wolfgang Muller."

"I just want you to remember that you're not driving a car, mister. You're pointing it. Ten-four! Ten-four!"

"I beg your pardon," Wolfgang murmured.

"All we want is the facts, ma'am," the object returned. It did not move out of the mist and Wolfgang was not inclined to go toward it.

A long pause followed. Then the form spoke again, this time singing.

The huge machine warbled, as best it could, snatches of what sounded like theme songs. Wolfgang recognized some of them, but the device trilled them out so quickly, one after the other, that it sounded like it was playing a "TV's Greatest Hits" record at triple speed. Finally, the din stopped, and Wolfgang took a deep breath.

"That's terrific," Wolfgang said, even though the voice was quite awful and mechanical sounding. "Where did you pick that up?"

"And now here's a lovely number by the Lennon Sisters," the form continued.

"Who are they?"

"I refuse to answer on the grounds that it may tend to incriminate me. Have you no sense of decency, sir? At long last have you left no sense of decency?"

Wolfgang did not reply. He had no idea what he had done to offend the being, so he thought it best to remain silent.

"Kids say the darndest things," the form said after a long pause.

"Yes," Wolfgang muttered. "That's true."

"I have here a certified cashier's check for one million dollars, tax-exempt, made out in your name from a benefactor who wishes to remain anonymous. Should you reveal where you got this check to anyone but your wife, if you are married, you must return the unused portion."

To this, Wolfgang had no idea what to say. Finally his dry lips parted long enough to begin the speech he had been thinking about for just such an occasion.

"I'm from planet Earth," he began.

"Same to you, fella," the form interrupted. "Cross my heart and hope to spit."

"I'm sorry," Wolfgang said. "I hear what you're saying but I don't know how to answer—"

"Oh, Cisco! Oh, Pancho!"

"That's what I mean. There's nothing much I can say in response to that."

The form issued a strange whirring sound and then spoke. "There is nothing wrong with your television set," it said. "Do not attempt to adjust the picture. We are controlling transmission. We will control the horizontal. We will control the vertical. For the next hour, sit quietly and we will control all you see and hear. You are about to experience the awe and mystery that leads you from the inner mind to the outer limits."

A very long pause followed.

"God," Wolfgang whispered. "I'm trapped. I guess it thinks it can communicate by recycling old television phrases. Maybe I better suck up my courage and do something."

He slowly moved forward. The form did not retreat, obviously content to let Wolfgang close the gap between them. Gradually, as he did so, Wolfgang began to distinguish colors and texture, until he had the complete picture of the first alien creature ever viewed by man.

To his eyes, it was incredibly ugly. It stood on two legs, had a pair of arms and a single head, which put it in the same general category as man. But there the resemblance ended, the creature resembling more an upright spider or sea animal than Homo sapiens. It had a bulbous stomach and a long projection from the rear of its torso, rather like the body of a bumblebee. Its face was pink with freckles and large red lips, but the green eyes rose above each side of the head like twin periscopes. A pair of antennae hung out over the top of its head. It seemed to be dressed in a clothlike outfit of magenta and tan.

Wolfgang pointed to himself, tapping his chest slowly but firmly several times.

"Wolfgang," he said.

The creature seemed to get it. Turning its long green fingers toward itself, it said, "Neek."

"Neek," Wolfgang repeated. "I'm pleased to meet you."

He declined to shake hands.

Thirty seconds passed. Then, slowly, the creature reached out to touch him.

"Oh, my God!" Ben yelled.

The creature which had so suddenly risen in front of them opened its lips. Its mouth moved, but the words and voice that emerged were Ben's.

"Oh, my God!" it repeated.

Still in a state of shock, Ben stumbled backwards into Darren. They fell to the ground in a tangle of arms and legs.

"What was that thing?" Darren gasped.

As one, they looked in the direction of the creature, but it was gone. Or at least it was gone momentarily. As they continued to stare, Ben and Darren saw first one eye stalk and then the other emerge from around a corner of the room. Finally, the entire bizarre face was visible.

Ben got to his feet, realizing that this was history in the making. It was mankind's first contact with alien life and he wanted to make it both dignified and memorable.

"I've waited my whole life to say this," he whispered to Darren.

Then, turning toward the alien and taking a single step forward, he raised his hand in a gentle gesture.

"We come in peace," he said.

The creature merely stared at him.

"Great," Darren said. "So much for mankind. Now try 'how do we get back to our ship?'"

"Give it a minute," Ben replied. "He's probably translating it in his head."

Finally the creature moved. Its lips parted and from them emerged an oddly amplified approximation of earthly sounds.

"Ehhh . . . What's up, Doc?" it said.

Ben was stunned. Darren blinked and had to clap his hand over his own mouth to keep from breaking into hysterical laughter.

"It's Bugs Bunny," he gasped. "We came a trillion miles to speak with Bugs Bunny."

"No," Ben said. "Maybe it's just saying that to make us feel at home.

The creature spoke again, this time in a voice sounding strangely like that of comedian Jackie Gleason. "You wanna go to the moon?" it asked. "Do you wanna go to the moon?"

"Uh . . . no," Ben replied. "We were there just a couple of hours ago."

"What's going on here?" Darren suddenly demanded. "What'd you do with our friend?"

"Shh," Ben warned. "Don't take that tone of voice. It may think we're threatening it."

"I don't care," Darren replied, then repeated his questions to the alien.

Responding, the creature spoke in a weird Cuban accent, exactly like Ricky Ricardo. "Now, look, honey," it said. "Let's not have a scene. C'mon, honey, relax, will you?"

It followed the speech with a burst of canned laughter.

"This is too weird," Darren muttered. "It doesn't make sense. I hate this."

The creature took a step toward Darren. The expression on its face seemed almost kindly as it directed the words at the angry and frustrated young man.

"With his faithful Indian companion, Tonto," it said, "the masked rider of the plains led the fight for law and order in the early western United States. Nowhere in the pages of history can one find a greater champion of justice. Return with us now to those thrilling days of yesteryear. From out of the past come the thundering hoofbeats of the great horse Silver. The Lone Ranger rides again!"

If followed with a perfect, if somewhat metallic, version of the *William Tell* overture.

A pause followed. The alien seemed somewhat disappointed, as if expecting the boys to react in a certain way. *War of The Worlds* noises emerged from its mouth.

"What does he want us to do?" Darren asked.

"I don't know," Ben replied.

"I guess we offended him."

"Not necessarily. There's got to be a reason for all this. He mimics what we say, but how . . . ?"

The alien slowly began to move away.

"I guess we're supposed to follow him," Darren suggested.

"Yeah . . ."

Shrugging, Ben moved ahead of Darren, directly behind the creature, which emitted a tune as it walked, snapping its long, pointed fingers in time.

"What's that music?" Darren asked. "I think I heard it once."

"It's the theme from the old TV show, *Mister Ed*," Ben answered. He was glad that he had an especially good memory for such trivia, although he was not sure he could put it to any use under the circumstances.

As the creature seemed disinclined to make conversation, Ben kept up a running line of chatter as they moved from one gloomy room to another.

"Uh, sir," he said. "I just want you to know how great I think this is. I mean, our civilizations are meeting right here for the first time! This has never happened to anybody on Earth before! Are you gonna take us to your planet now, for a tour, or what?"

"I know where we're headed," Darren said darkly. "To the zoo."

Ben decided to ignore the remark. If the creature could understand English, why put ideas in its head? He threw an angry look at Darren, then quickly returned his attention to their alien guide.

"Let me ask you this, sir," he continued. "What are you at home? An emissary or a diplomat? I know! You're a top scientist! Or maybe a translator."

The creature looked back over its shoulder long enough to say, "And that's the way it is," in a near-perfect imitation of Walter Cronkite.

"I guess we're all diplomats in a way," Ben said genially. "I guess we'll have to go back to Earth now and convince everyone you're here in peace. Right?"

"Tell you what," the alien replied, its voice exactly like that of Monty Hall. "Show me a hard-boiled egg and I'll give you a hundred dollars. You don't have a hard-boiled egg? That's too bad! And what do we have behind door number three?"

"I'm sorry," Ben muttered. "I don't understand."

"You're crazy if you do," Darren whispered. "This guy's nutty as a fruitcake."

As they walked toward a huge arch in the distance, Ben heard the familiar twang of Wolfgang's voice. Or, he asked himself, was it another creature repeating what their friend had said earlier? It was possible, although he didn't like to even consider it, that Wolfgang was dead or dying, even as the aliens continued to project his voice.

Soon, as they continued to walk, the words became distinct.

"Okay, but let's face it," Wolfgang seemed to be saying in that cranky tone of his. "This energy field of yours still needs a lot of work! Talk about bumpy rides! You'd think a technology this advanced could stabilize a simple computer. And those readouts! What kind of science is that? All I ask for is a little clarity."

A moment later, Ben and Darren, preceded by their guide, entered a gigantic control room. Against one wall was a huge console, the height of the dials and switches indicating that its user was at least fifteen feet tall. Seated in an oversized chair was Wolfgang, in the flesh, talking to a creature that was hidden from view by the edge of another large chair. Stars twinkled through the clear dome which dominated the room.

"Good," Ben whispered. "At least he's alive and well."

As they neared their friend, they saw a huge, weird hand reach out to take his. In the background, they could hear chewing sounds.

"Wolfgang," Ben said.

His friend turned and smiled. Now they could see the second creature, which was similar to theirs but differently colored and dressed.

"This is Neek," Wolfgang explained. "She's very intelligent."

As he spoke, Neek took a battery from the top of

Wolfgang's flashlight, popped it into her mouth and continued chewing.

"That must be Wak, her brother," Wolfgang continued. "If that's the word."

Wak and Neek looked at each other.

"George Stevens," Neek said in a whiny voice, "I done made up my mind that I'm gonna have a husband that dresses good, knows nice people, and is got a steady job."

"Sapphire," Wak replied. "You mean to say that you is gonna leave me?"

Both followed with bursts of canned laughter.

The three boys looked at each other and shrugged.

"I guess they call it Earthspeak," Wolfgang said.

"Holy inferno, Batman!" Neek continued. "Is this the end?"

"If it is, Robin," Wak replied, "Let us not lose our dignity."

"Why don't you introduce yourself to them?" Wolfgang said, smiling. Pointing to himself, he said to Wak, "Wolfgang."

Wak seemed to take a deep breath and did likewise. "Wak," he said.

"Ben," Ben said and then pointed to Darren. "Darren," he continued.

"I can do it myself," Darren said querulously. Touching his chest, he said, "Darren."

The aliens looked at each other.

"Well, I'll be a dirty bird," Neek said.

Wolfgang pointed to a control panel near the console. "They know all about us," he said. "From seeing television."

He touched a button, causing pictures to appear in the air near them. They were chiefly wavy, snowy, unstable video images of various Earth TV broadcasts.

A giant Lucy said something indistinct to Ricky. Neek promptly opened her mouth and provided the proper dialogue.

"I don't get it," Darren said. "How could she know what Lucy was gonna say? I couldn't make out the words."

"I guess they saw this episode before," Wolfgang replied. "They have reruns even in outer space."

"It's incredible," Ben said. "They get TV up here?"

"They're crazy about it," Wolfgang nodded.

"Crazy about it! Crazy about it!" Neek repeated in Wolfgang's voice.

"You can see for yourself," Wolfgang said. "Somehow the TV signals get through and that's how they've learned to communicate."

As he spoke, Wak lifted a microphonelike object from a nearby table and launched into a bizarre litany of overlapping, hyperbolic commercial pitches, jingles, and promises. "Incredible values!" he ranted. "Rush delivery. Here's Cal Worthington and his dog Spot. And it won't upset your stomach. Double your money back! No money down! Hmm! I can breathe freely again. Why settle for less! Don't you wish everybody did? Rids you of unwanted facial hair forever! Astounding horsepower! We do it all for you-ou-ou! Your baby's comfort begins with Luvs . . . Luvs . . . Luvs . . . Four out of five doctors smoke Camels! Kills germs on contact by millions! Trident for those who chew gum . . . Brush your breath! Brush your breath! This is a nasograph! Double your pleasure, double your fun! Gives you go on ice or snow! Oh, what a feeling! We are driven!"

The nonstop commercial segments tested even the minds of the three boys, who were used to Earth culture at its most overbearing. Laughing and covering their ears, they waited patiently for Wak to finish, then applauded his effort.

"You must be proud to be from such a wonderful place," Neek said, in a foreign accent.

"You mean, Earth?" Ben asked.

With her wig-wagging antennae, it was impossible to see whether Neek nodded or not. "Hey, you should see where we live," she continued in perfect "valley" talk. "It's *sooo* boring. You could gag me with a spoon."

"You seem to know so much about us," Ben said. "I guess your people must have been visiting our planet all along, huh? Right from ancient times on. And now you're coming back to check on us. Right? And as a sort of grand climax, you're going to explain everything."

Hearing the hope in Ben's voice caused Wolfgang to sigh.

"Actually," he said, 'they've never gone down there in person. There are too many germs."

"Those pesky germs and bacteria that can lead to tooth decay, diarrhea, and other troubling ailments," Wak said in TV announcer tones.

"Have gun, will travel," Neek added, just as if it made sense. "Wire Paladin, Hotel Carlton, San Francisco."

"They had to disinfect us when we got here," Wolfgang continued. "Just to get this close. That's what that spraying was all about."

"You mean they've just been sitting out here for millions of years, watching?" Ben asked.

"Sure."

"Well, Jack," Neek said, reaching out to touch her brother, "I heard about your having dinner with Edgar Bergen. You even picked up the check."

"Yes, and that's the last time I'll ever eat with a ventriloquist," Wak replied.

The two aliens laughed together.

"Besides, we know what they do to people like us there," Neek added.

As she spoke, the images around them changed to violent movie clips of people attacking and destroying aliens. One sequence showed the military attempting to nuke an extraterrestrial vessel into submission.

"You see," Neek said. "That's what you do to others who visit your planet."

"But those are just old movies," Ben stammered. "That's not the way we really are. Don't worry. We don't feel like that. We know how important this meeting is to both our planets, our civilizations. We're not going to blow it."

"See what happens when man's inhumanity to man goes haywire," Wak said, his voice similar to an announcer promoting a movie.

"Wait a minute," Ben pleaded. "Don't you know we're really okay? If you think we're bad, why did you go to all this trouble . . ."

"Don't you know we're really okay?" Neek repeated in Ben's voice.

"We wanted to talk to you so much. So you could explain," Wak said.

"We suspected you weren't so bad all along," Neek said, smiling. "But we wanted to be sure."

"Thanks," Wolfgang said.

"Think nothing of it," Wak replied, his antennae wagging. Then his mouth opened wider and a song, complete with band accompaniment, poured forth.

The song was beautiful, a mixture of melodies snatched from Earth broadcasts and oddly harmonious alien squeaks and squeals. Wak performed for all of them, belting out his homemade composition. His antennae swayed back and forth to the rhythm, as Neek, off to one side, accompanied him with her own bobbing head.

The boys smiled and joined in as best they could with what they assumed was the chorus.

"He sings all the time!" Neek shouted over the din.

Suddenly, the song turned to a strangled shriek in Wak's throat as a blinding light poured into the room.

Neek did a perfect imitation of the *Star Trek* battle stations alarm, following it with an ear-piercing fire engine wail.

"Holy spaceship, Batman!" Wak cried, looking up.

The three boys followed suit, each gasping as they spotted a huge spacecraft looming above them. A section of the new ship began to open, as if intent on swallowing the vessel which they now occupied.

"Let's get out of here!" Ben yelled.

Everyone, including the aliens, seemed to understand. As one, five bodies hurled themselves toward the door and raced down a long corridor. Ben, Wolfgang, and Darren moved very quickly, soon opening a sizable gap between themselves and the two aliens, who obviously were not built for speed. As they trundled along, Neek and Wak pumped out bits and pieces of Earth dialogue that sounded as if they were from an old movie trailer—but highly appropriate.

"Can your heart stand the shock of grave robbers from outer space?" Wak shouted. "Space pirate! Scourge of the universe!"

"Merciless!" Neek added. "They mustn't find you here!"

Ben waited until the aliens caught up, then cried out to them. "But what about you?" he said. "Do you need any help? You can land on Earth if you want. I'll explain everything to my parents, and we'll find a germ-free atmosphere for you at some hospital."

"Mother of mercy," Neek gasped in a gutteral voice. "Is this the end of Rico?"

The group came to a small door and Wolfgang threw it open. Through the portal they could see the *Thunder Road* in the landing bay. Wak started through the opening first, his finger raised to his lips.

"Be vewwy vewwy qwiet," he said in an Elmer Fudd voice.

The boys and the aliens slipped through the door to the end of the ramp, where the *Thunder Road* sat. They had tiptoed nearly across the open area when they heard a threatening growl. It came from above.

Looking up, they saw only a form, but it was huge. Light from the ship above them fell on its head and shoulders, outlining its form, but obscuring the features. A blood-curdling roar followed. Wolfgang was sure their time to be eaten had come at last.

"What is it?" Ben yelled.

The words were barely out of his mouth when the monstrous creature made another sound. This was less threatening; in fact, it was almost pathetic, something between a cough and a gasp. Darren recognized it immediately. To him it was the universal sound of a domineering parent who has yelled so loudly he was forced to fight for air. He looked up at the alien above, suddenly no longer afraid.

"It's their father," he said.

"What?" Ben shouted.

"Yeah," Darren persisted. "It's their father."

"No way!"

"I'm telling you. I've heard that sound a million times before."

Ben looked at Neek and Wak. They were so large,

compared to Darren, Wolfgang, and himself. Was it possible they were mere children?

Darren sensed his thought process.

"They're kids," he said. Then, pointing a finger at the two alien creatures, he demanded, "Come on, admit it. You're kids, aren't you?"

Neek and Wak exchanged glances. The expression in their eyes and body language signified pure guilt.

"He's right," Neek finally admitted. "We're not supposed to be doing this."

Wak rolled his eyes at the huge alien towering above them.

"He's pissed," he said, then added in a Beaver Cleaver voice, "Gee, I sure got myself in a mess, didn't I?"

The alien father growled something in a strange language. Wak and Neek obeyed, stepping out toward him. Wak began to make a low-pitched whining noise, but another roar from the parent silenced him.

"I guess we got them in trouble," Ben whispered. "But it wasn't our fault. They were the ones playing the tricks."

"Just like kids," Darren muttered scornfully.

"Gggreckteooow!"

The father was looking directly at the boys now, its arm and icepicklike fingers pointed at the *Thunder Road*. Wolfgang broke into a trot and the others followed at a more leisurely, grudging pace.

"Keep your pants on," Darren muttered in his best kick-their-butts tone.

"He says go, let's go." Ben nodded. He still couldn't get over it, despite the evidence and sheer logic of the situation. They had been taken in by children, probably younger than themselves. Perhaps they were just toddlers, the equivalent of four-year-olds on Earth.

He looked balefully at Neek and Wak, who sulked in the shadow of their hulking father.

"Kids . . ." he said, shaking his head.

"And I'll tell you something else," Darren added smiling. "They're not only kids, this is their dad's car."

Hearing them, Neek took a half step in their direction.

"We're not even supposed to touch it," she said.

"See?" Darren gloated, proud of himself. "I was right. No wonder their dad's mad. If I'd taken *my* dad's car out for a spin, you can imagine what he'd have done to me."

Ben was experiencing a great letdown. They had traveled beyond the limit of the astronauts, farther than any unmanned space probe, and achieved the ages-old ambition of actually communicating with creatures from another world. But the creatures were children, pranksters, beings with no desire to spread peace and good will from one solar system to another; they were only kids joyriding. What Ben had envisioned as a noble mission was the equivalent of a scavenger hunt or trick-or-treat outing.

"But what about the meeting of the civilizations?" he demanded, unable to hide his disappointment. "This is supposed to be a historical moment."

Wak summarized it quite well. "You were great," he said, the voice that of Bob Hope. "You were a million laughs."

"What a line for the history books," Ben said, shaking his head. "Suppose some Indian had said to Columbus, 'You were a million laughs'?"

"I wouldn't have minded," Darren replied.

Wak quickly darted away from his father's shadow, holding out a small object. Darren took it. It was a sphere with a button on it.

"Here," Wak said. "This'll kill you."

"For me?" Darren smiled.

"Who else?" Wak replied, the voice now that of TV's Molly Goldberg.

Darren looked at the sphere, his finger poised above the button.

"No," Wak said quickly. "Save it for sometime when you're with a lot of friends."

"Why?"

"You'll be the hero of the party."

"Just what I need," Darren said.

He held out the Walkman radio-cassette player. "This is Bruce Springsteen," he said, pointing to the headphones. "He's from New Jersey."

Wak took the Walkman and nodded gratefully.

"I'm sorry you can't come with us," Neek said to Wolfgang. "He wouldn't understand. Especially about us, Wolfgang."

"Call me Wolf." Wolfgang smiled, taking off his glasses.

Darren smiled wickedly at the exchange, but refrained from commenting.

Ben stepped first into the *Thunder Road*. Still feeling left out and frustrated, he mumbled over and over, "Just a bunch of kids . . ."

He was surprised a moment later when the two alien children walked slowly toward him, their hands extended.

"Ben," Neek said softly. "This *was* a historical moment, for *us*." She gestured to Wak. "We've never met anybody from another planet before, either."

"Really?" Ben asked. It seemed incredible to him that with all their technology, these strange people had not been able to contact other societies.

"Yes," Neek said. "That's why we started playing

our little game, why we sent you the force field and the dream. I see now that most other Earth people would have forgotten the dream by the next day, but you really understood that we were out here, calling." She untied a small crystal from her neck and handed it to him. "This is for you, because you were the one who understood."

"What is it?" Ben asked.

"The stuff that dreams are made of," Neek replied, her voice emulating that of Humphrey Bogart.

Ben was temporarily embarrassed at not having a present to give his new friends. Then he remembered the harmonica and fished it out of his pocket.

"Here," he said. "I want you to have this."

"Thank you."

Bowing slightly, Neek took the harmonica, popped it into her mouth, and swallowed it in one discordant gulp. "We'll always have Paris," she said, the voice still that of Bogart.

Wolfgang edged close to Neek, took her hand and laid it on his shoulder. Instantly an irascible roar came from the father.

"Cool it, Wolf," Darren whispered. "It looks like she's jail bait."

"Let's scram," Ben suggested.

A minute later, the boys and the *Thunder Road* were expelled from the alien ship as if shot from a cannon, their friends, their friends' father and the experience of a lifetime disappearing from their sight at a dizzying rate.

—— *Chapter Eleven* ——

As they craned their necks to get one final view of the father ship, the three boys dealt with their experience in different ways. Wolfgang was silent, Ben smiled softly, and Darren was ebullient.

"Wow!" he said. "I'm sure glad I came on this thing. And I thought *my* dad was tough!"

Ben was trying to look on the brighter side of the situation. "Well, at least they did send us the dreams, right?" he said. "They brought us here and everything, so that makes us special."

"Actually," Wolfgang said, "Neek was a little confused. They didn't send the dreams. They were all yours. All they did was tune in on them. I guess they liked what they saw, but no wonder. They've obviously watched every TV program, good or rotten, since Earth started broadcasting."

"Couch potatoes from outer space," Darren interjected acidly.

"Then they sent the diagram to see what would happen," Wolfgang continued. "And *we* figured it out."

"Which means that *we* were the ones they

wanted to meet," Ben said, ". . . out of everyone on Earth!"

"Well, let's put it this way." Wolfgang smiled. "*We* were the ones who earned it."

"I guess you had a lot of time to talk with this space chick, huh, Wolfie?" Darren cracked.

"Yeah."

"So what else did she say?"

"She said they're also really into dolphin dreams. But let's see *them* build a space ship. No thumbs!"

"And no water," Ben added.

They moved silently through space for a while, until a potentially unpleasant thought struck Ben.

"What about power?" he asked. "Did they shoot us full of juice?"

Wolfgang shook his head. "We're moving primarily on the boost they gave us," he said. "Basically the battery's still low. It'll be touch and go as soon as we enter the Earth's gravitational field and need the power to guide us in."

"Great," Ben muttered.

"Don't worry," Darren said. "That truck battery of my dad refuses to die."

Somehow they managed not to think of the consequences of being powerless—and therefore breathless—in outer space. Entering the network of stars called the Milky Way, they plunged deeper into the system, finally recognizing the rings of Saturn as they moved toward the faraway sun.

"Only three planets to Earth," Wolfgang said. "Too bad they're not all lined up the way you see them in books so we could have a look at each one."

Darren looked disappointed. "You know, that's the way I always thought they were," he mumbled.

Soon the curvature of the Earth hung blue and

beautiful in space. Only a few clouds obscured the land masses, which stood out as clearly as those on a classroom globe.

"It's eleven o'clock, Mrs. Muller," Darren quipped. "Do you know where your son is?"

"Ten thousand miles in space," Wolfgang said with a smile. "Who would have thought it?"

As they pursued the familiar land mass of North America, the ground beneath them grew darker and lights blinked on, the area switching from day to night in a matter of seconds.

"Fortunately," Wolfgang said, "I don't have to steer this thing. Otherwise I'd be lucky to land three states from home."

The computer seemed to be working well, an orderly line of figures indicating that they were nearing their point of origin with mathematical precision.

"How far are we now?" Ben asked.

"Less than a mile."

"Come on, baby," Darren said. "Don't let us down now." Now they could make out the beltway of roads surrounding the town and one or two landmarks became recognizable. Dropping faster, they could soon make out writing in neon, cars, and road signs.

"There's Safeway!" Ben shouted.

"And there's my house!" Darren added. "I can see that Dad's up late."

Wolfgang checked the readouts again. Everything seemed normal.

"It's returning to its point of origin," he announced. "So we'll—"

Murphy's Law promptly went into effect, the power failing and the ship beginning to wobble. Instead of being guided to a coordinate near the Earth's surface, it was falling, developing a spin all its own.

"What's going on?" Darren yelled.

"No power!" Wolfgang shouted back. As he spoke, he continued to flip the power switch back and forth.

"Are we gonna crash?" Darren gasped, his face deathly white.

"What usually happens to a falling object?"

"The battery can't be dead!"

"You're right! It's not!"

Just at that moment, while Wolfgang flipped the switch, the power blinked back on. The *Thunder Road* seemed to throw on a set of invisible brakes as it tore through the atmosphere, the sound and effect rather like that of a jetliner lowering its landing gear.

Ben, who had been staring straight ahead, clapped his hands together gleefully.

"It's not over yet," Wolfgang warned. "We're almost out of power. It'll cut out again. We gotta hope and pray it doesn't go again, because I have a feeling that'll be it."

"Let's land then," Darren shouted. "Get us down— right away."

"We're going as fast as we can safely."

"There's the river!" Ben yelled. "Aim for that instead of home. Then if the power goes at least we'll have a chance for a soft landing."

"Good idea," Wolfgang said.

Pushing buttons wildly, he punched in new coordinates, getting the last one in before the power died again. As it did, the *Thunder Road* veered off in a new trajectory.

"That was it!" Wolfgang said. "here we go!"

Shuddering terribly, the ship began to spin like a top, completely without guidance now. One moment, ground was visible through the porthole; the next, water. Flashes of light created a strobe effect and air began to whistle in through tiny openings in the ship's skin which had formerly been protected by the force field. Darren, feeling the terrible pressure on his eardrums, opened his mouth and emitted a long rebel yell that continued until the ship struck the surface of the river with an impact that threw the boys against each other, then back against the shell of the *Thunder Road.*

For a long moment, they simply lay there in shock. Then, as they realized they were still alive, the boys sat up and began to dig themselves out of the ship's debris. It seemed they were lying under everything they had brought and, even worse, water from the river was beginning to pour in through cracks, soaking everything and threatening to trap them in their own vessel. Wolfgang shook his head, and looked down at his hand, which still held a broken component from the controls.

"The computer's gone," he muttered.

"Never mind," Darren replied. "We've got to get out of here."

He pushed open the hatch and looked outside.

The *Thunder Road* had made the river only by a few yards, landing in comparatively shallow water that housed a graveyard of ancient, rusting cars. The water itself was oily and foul-smelling, heavy with mud and industrial runoff, not the kind of liquid to swim or even wade in.

"Come on," Darren said, pulling himself outside and thrusting a helping hand back for the others. In a few seconds, he had assisted Ben and Wolfgang out of the battered wreck that was once their glorious *Thunder Road.* Hopping from hulk to hulk, they made it to shore, a trio of tough-bitten, thoroughly exhausted individuals.

"Well, we made it," Darren said.

"The explorers are home," Ben added.

Reaching for the reminder of their trip, he found that the crystal given him by Neek was now nothing but a mess of finely crushed powder. He sighed.

For a minute the three stood on the bank, watching solemnly as the *Thunder Road* slipped deeper and deeper into the river.

"So long, guys," Ben said, the instant it was no longer visible.

He turned away and was closely followed by the others. As they walked, no one spoke at first. The letdown was simply too great. Mixed with it was the disappointment of being anonymous despite having accomplished what no one else had done in the history of the world. No cheering crowds greeted them; no television or newspaper reporters were on hand to question them; there were no smiling friends and jealous enemies. There wasn't even proof that they had traveled so many million miles. Ben wondered if they would begin to think it was all a dream when they grew old.

"You know," he said, "back when this all started, I thought that—"

"Let's not talk about it," Wolfgang snapped.

"But, Wolfgang, we—"

"And that's another thing. I've had it with that name. From now on, I'm going to be known by another name entirely. No matter what my parents say."

"What's it going to be?" Darren asked.

"Wolf."

As he pronounced the new name, Wolfgang whipped off his glasses. He seemed to be a couple of inches taller already.

Almost before they knew it, they were back in school. This was the final indignity, ultimate proof that the incredible mission so filled with adventures was nothing more than a shared hallucination. Despite their new status with each other, the three boys returned as ordinary drones of life—take clothes off, put clothes on, brush teeth, watch television, and go to school.

One thing was different. They were a team now, virtually inseparable. If they could not enjoy the honor of being esteemed explorers and ambassadors to outer space, at least they had each other's admiration and strength. And so they met each morning for the walk to school (Darren eschewing the convenience of his motorcycle for the privilege of keeping the club intact), met for lunch, and walked home again, all the while discussing their next mission. Within the space of a few weeks, they had changed from boys to elderly men, veterans of a pennant-winning team many decades ago who could be understood only by other team members. Did they really enjoy each other's company that much? Or was it, as Ben suspected during his more realistic moments, that they needed constant refueling in order to keep believing it had really happened?

Whatever the motivation, they became known as the tightest clique in school, a fact that irritated Steve Jackson more than anyone. One of his pleasures had been harassing Wolfgang Muller, the simple, dreamy kid who never fought back. Now, with the three together all the time, this source of fun was denied him. He didn't care much to tangle with Darren, whom he considered a tough dude, so he bided his time until one day when the odds were overwhelmingly in his favor.

Jackson and his five friends watched as the three boys turned the corner of the school wing into a deserted section of the playground.

"Now's our chance, guys," Jackson said with a smile.

A minute later, they swooped down on the trio, three

against Ben and Wolfgang and three against Darren, a situation that allowed the bullies to back their victims against a brick wall.

"Now," Jackson said, "I think we're going to beat up all three of you this time."

"Why?" Ben asked. "What do you have against us? We've been minding our own business."

"Yeah. That's part of the trouble. You're too good to even talk to anybody else."

Ben shrugged. No use denying that he hadn't sought out Steve Jackson for conversation during the past few weeks.

Before ordering his pals to attack, Jackson looked at the ground, where Wolfgang's knapsack had fallen. Next to it lay a curious object, a small sphere with a button. He picked it up and examined it.

"What's this thing?" he demanded, his gaze fixed on Wolfgang. "A science project?"

"Give it back!" Wolfgang shouted. "It needs to be tested in a controlled environment."

Jackson offered it to Wolfgang, then yanked it back at the last second.

"Tell me what it is, punk," he said.

"I don't know."

"Bull."

"I'm telling you—"

"Shut up!"

"That's right, Wolf," Darren interjected. "Shut up and let him have it."

"No," Wolfgang shot back, nearly cryng. "That was a gift from Wak. I'm not gonna let this scumbag—"

Steve Jackson glowered, flipped the sphere in the air and grabbed it tightly when it came down. The action compressed the button, immediately creating a curtain of green gas, which completely enveloped him. For a moment the green mist hung suspended in the air as

Steve coughed and choked. Then it dissolved, leaving the young man looking confused and angry.

"What the hell was that?" he stammered.

He took a step toward Wolfgang.

Rrrriiiiip!

The small crowd which had gathered to see the confrontation suddenly burst into gales of laughter, Steve Jackson's pants had ripped right up the seat, exposing his underwear. In fact, all of his clothes had started to shrink at an alarming rate. Buttons on his shirt began to pop, falling to the ground; ripping and tearing sounds came from every seam as the size sixteen shirt shrank in ten seconds to baby-size. And as the outer garments fell away in shredded fragments, the crowd saw his underwear retreat to bikini size and smaller. Mortified, Steve curled into the fetal position, trying vainly to cover his bare parts with his hands and elbows. But there was no help. Even his buddies were collapsed on the ground with laughter.

"Shut up!" Jackson yelled. "Get me some clothes!"

His friends were too helpless with laughter to lift a finger in his behalf.

Desperate, Steve turned to the trio he had been about to attack.

"Help!" he gasped.

"Not a chance." Darren smiled. "You better watch out, or we'll do something even worse."

His clothes shrunk to almost nothing. Steve Jackson turned and ran around a corner of the building toward a bathroom. Throwing open a door, he was confronted by an entire class on its way out of the building.

Cursing as he raced past their laughing faces, he staggered into the bathroom and locked the door.

Ben, Wolfgang, and Darren stared after him, the reality of the situation hitting them at the same time.

"That was meant for us, you know," Ben said.

Darren nodded. "I had an idea Wak was up to no good. That's why I told you to let him have it."

"Great sense of humor," Wolfgang said, his eyes looking skyward.

They turned to go and Ben suddenly looked into the familiar, beautiful eyes of Lori Swenson. She had seen the entire Steve Jackson fiasco, along with several dozen other kids. But her eyes seemed to be filled with more than just amusement. There seemed to be a measure of growing comprehension in them. Or was it Ben's imagination?

"Hi, Ben." Lori smiled. "Did you have a nice trip?"

"Huh?" he replied. "Oh, sure."

So it was not his imagination. She knew more than the others.

"Why'd she say that?" Darren asked.

"I don't know."

"You didn't tell her, did you?"

"No. I swear it."

"Then what did she mean about the trip?"

"It's a mystery," Ben muttered. "Maybe our minds are closer than I thought."

As they went their separate ways, Ben glanced back over his shoulder at the departing Lori. She was smiling slyly at him.

What Ben could not have known was that Lori had been the sole witness to their historic return to planet Earth. She had been lying on the bed, unable to sleep, when her eye caught a flash of light outside the window. At first she thought it was a falling star, but it was moving too slowly for that. And then, when she saw it swerve in mid-flight completely unlike a falling object or even an airplane, she gasped, pulled on a coat and shoes, climbed out the window and slid down the tree next to her house. She arrived at the river too late to see the *Thunder Road* hit the surface, but it was still afloat when she got there. Crouching in the bushes on the bank, she was close enough to recognize Ben, Wolfgang and Darren as they waded ashore.

She wasn't sure why she remained silent after that. Perhaps she wanted Ben to confide in her; she may have been unwilling to admit that she had spied on him. And she wasn't positively sure the falling object was the vessel in the river, although she had lost sight of it for only a few seconds. She therefore adopted a tentative attitude toward Ben, hoping he would pick up her hint and tell her what was going on. From the surprised and guilty look in his eyes, she was certain it would only be a matter of time.

As the weeks passed, Ben remained true to his promise, keeping the mission a secret. Indeed, it was pointless to tell anyone, since the trip was impossible to prove and divulging it would only get them in trouble.

One afternoon the three boys found themselves on the top of the hill where they had carried out their first outdoor experiment with the force field. The leaves were beginning to fall from the trees and the boys wore warmer clothes than they had before. Ben and Wolfgang talked as they explored the area, reliving the excitement they'd felt weeks ago. Darren sat at the base of a tree reading a paperback version of H.G. Wells's *War of the Worlds.*

"It's weird," Ben said, looking down at the town beneath them. "I feel sad."

"You too?"

"Yeah."

"It's like it never happened," Wolfgang mused. "We were almost killed a couple, three times and nobody even knows. It's like we took the risks for nothing. It's like it never happened at all."

Ben looked up at the sky. "We don't have anything. No proof."

"It's frustrating, too! I mean, is that it? Nothing in my life will ever top that?"

"Well, we're not dead yet, Wolf."

"Sometimes I think we might as well be. When we crashed in the river, we lost everything. I guess we could reconstruct it somehow, but I'm not sure I have the energy."

"Columbus made four voyages," Ben said. "It took a lot of energy to do that."

"Yeah, but all he's remembered for is the first one," Wolfgang countered.

Later, as the boys reminisced about their adventures, Darren sighed. "I kind of miss them," he said.

"Yeah, you wonder what they're doing right now, what new trouble they're causing their father."

"Whatever it is, it's more exciting than what we're doing now," Wolfgang muttered.

They sat on the hill until it began to grow dark, then silently got to their feet and went to their separate homes. As Ben walked into the kitchen, his brother was just leaving.

"Hey, Ben," he said. "Need a ride anywhere?"

"You mean on this planet?"

"Smart guy."

Jingling his car keys noisily, Bill walked to his car, a confused expression on his face.

Ben's parents were in the kitchen, just chatting as they so often did.

"Hi, Mom," he said, giving her a hug as he entered.

"Well, hello. What's all the excitement about?"

"Nothing."

Ben started to go to his room, but his mother held up her hand gently. He paused, his eyes moving from one parent to the other. It was obvious they wanted to talk to him about something. Had they somehow found out what he and the others had done?

"Ben, we had a talk," his father began. "Sometimes I lose track of how important things can be to you. What seems frivolous to me isn't necessarily that to you. In fact, it can be very educational and beneficial. That's why I've given a lot of thought to your suggestion about that camp . . . Your mother had a lot to do with my thinking, I should add. Anyway, if you promise to earn half the money, I think we can help you go to that space camp."

For a moment, Ben had no idea what he was talking about. His parents looked at him expectantly, his mother smiling as if awaiting a whoop of happiness. When it occurred to Ben what they meant, he did his best, but his heart wasn't in it. After all, who could get excited about a week in Alabama cavorting in simulated space capsules after being to the moon and beyond in the real thing?

"Oh, *that*," Ben smiled, trying to look grateful but knowing he wasn't very convincing. "I don't need to go *there*. I mean, it's okay. Never mind."

His parents, perplexed, could only stare at each other.

"But you were so crazy to go," his mother said. Ben suddenly realized how much lobbying she must have done for him in the past few weeks.

"I . . . I really appreciate it," he said. "It's just that I . . . thanks!"

"What does that mean?" his father asked.

Ben hesitated. It was a good question and he wasn't sure how to respond.

"Does that mean you'll go or not?"

"Uhh . . . I guess so."

"You don't have to go if you don't want to," his mother said defensively. "It's just that we thought you wanted to go, so . . ."

"I'd like to," Ben lied.

"Then you'd better start thinking about how to earn some money," his father said.

"Sure. I will."

He smiled tightly, turned and walked out of the kitchen, leaving them a bit happier but still considerably puzzled.

——— Chapter Twelve ———

IT ALSO ENDED WITH A DREAM.

Or was it reality? The line between fact and fantasy was becoming so blurred Ben simply wasn't sure what the truth was. At the same time, he wasn't certain it mattered that much to be sure. A world in which he felt exhilarated and fulfilled was what mattered most to him. If that world happened to be his hometown, that was fine. If it was a million light years away, either in fact or his mind, that was all right, too.

He was watching television in his room when the final episode began. *Kronos,* an old sci-fi movie, was on and he was watching out of habit, despite its seeming silly and old-fashioned. As a segment ended, a slide came up and the announcer said, "Don't go away, Ben. There's someone here who wants to speak to you."

Ben shook his head, not quite sure he had heard the announcer correctly. Then a familiar face appeared on the set—the police officer who had found his jacket and accused him of being up in the UFO. His expression was less severe now as he stared directly out of the set. Still somewhat stunned, Ben was prepared for a public service announcement as the officer began to speak.

"Ben," he said in a friendly voice, "go look in the living room."

"What?" Ben could not help saying.

"I said, go look in the living room," the image of Charlie Drake repeated.

The officer then proceeded to stare silently out of the set like a parent who has just ordered its child to do something. As he leaped off the bed and started toward the stairs, Ben heard Drake call a cheery "thanks" after him.

He raced past the kitchen, noting that his parents were out on the back lawn, chatting with neighbors. He had no idea what to expect in the living room and was consequently quite shocked when he saw the *Thunder Road*, as good as new, sitting in one corner. It looked very large and out of place next to the conventional lamps and chairs.

"What?" he yelled.

Running over to the ship, he threw open the hatch and saw two smiling faces looking up at him.

"Hi," Darren said nonchalantly.

"Nice to see you again," Wolfgang added.

"What . . . ?" Ben repeated, amazed.

"We're dreaming," Wolfgang explained. "He's sending again."

"Oh."

"So get in," Darren urged.

"My parents—" Ben stammered.

"Don't worry. We'll be gone before they get here. If you get off a dime," Wolfgang chided.

Ben scrambled up the side of the ship. Wolfgang and Darren pulled him inside and slammed the hatch.

"What happens now?" Ben asked.

Wolfgang shrugged, looking skyward, toward where the aliens lived.

"Now it's up to him. Or them," he replied.

Ben noticed that the computer and power pack were also miraculously intact and ready to go.

Wolfgang pushed a button. Numbers flashed on the screen and a whirring sound began, growing more and more intense by the second. Just when he felt he couldn't stand it another instant, Ben was blinded by an incredible flash of white light and heard a deafening rush of noise. He thought he heard himself scream but wasn't sure, so traumatic was the experience. Then, bit by bit, the aural and visual bombardment lifted. Different colored smoke drifted by, through which he slowly realized that the shell of the *Thunder Road* was gone. Also missing was the living room, which had been replaced by the clouds of his dream, dark green and rolling. Above was a sky filled with stars. As they had done in the dream, Ben and Wolfgang and Darren floated above a diagrammatic landscape resembling a circuit board.

With a yell, Darren pushed himself forward through the void, Wolfgang following quickly. Ben remained behind, attracted by a faraway object.

"Come on, Ben!" Darren shouted.

"Wait a minute, you guys," he yelled back.

Squinting, he was now able to make out what it was—a window approaching through the air. Lori was standing at it, unsupported except by her arms and hands, which rested on the sill.

"Lori!" Ben shouted. "Come on! Jump! It's a dream! You have to jump!"

"I . . . I'm afraid . . ." she called back.

Ben continued to urge her to jump. The window drifted by, Lori staying inside, unsure of herself. As it disappeared into a cloud, Ben turned himself to a vertical position, sighing with disappointment.

"Lori!" he shouted one final time.

No sooner was the name out of his mouth than Lori

suddenly flew out of the cloud bank, smiling at him. She swooped past him, did a loop-the-loop in the air, and continued after Darren and Wolfgang. Ben followed, grinning broadly.

A moment later, the group of four met above the heavy cloud bank.

"All right!" Darren said, seeing Lori.

Wolfgang's reaction was less enthusiastic. "What's she doing here?" he asked Ben.

"Well, excuse *me*!" Lori shot back.

"She's my guest," Ben replied. "It's my dream so I can invite whoever I want."

Wolfgang shrugged, realizing he would have to get used to the idea.

The four flew along, Ben and Lori smiling at each other. Then Darren suddenly pointed above them.

"Look!" he shouted.

As one, they spotted a new diagram in the night sky, one that was much more complicated and beautiful than the first. Staring as they flew, they moved toward it.

"Look," Lori said to Ben.

She held out her hand, on the third finger of which she was wearing the martian rock ring he had given her at her birthday party. Ben smiled, reaching out to touch her hand with his. Their faces moved gently but inexorably toward each other and finally joined in a soft, lingering kiss. Then, smiling, they shot up toward the schematic and the promise of exciting adventures in a world they had not yet seen.